CHILD SOLDIER

CHILD SOLDIER

A Novel

by

Herman F. Bosman

Paperback ISBN - 978-0-620-68468-2
eBook ISBN - 978-0-620-68469-9

Website: www.hermanfbosman.blogspot.com

For Helga, Lili and Alison

with all my affection

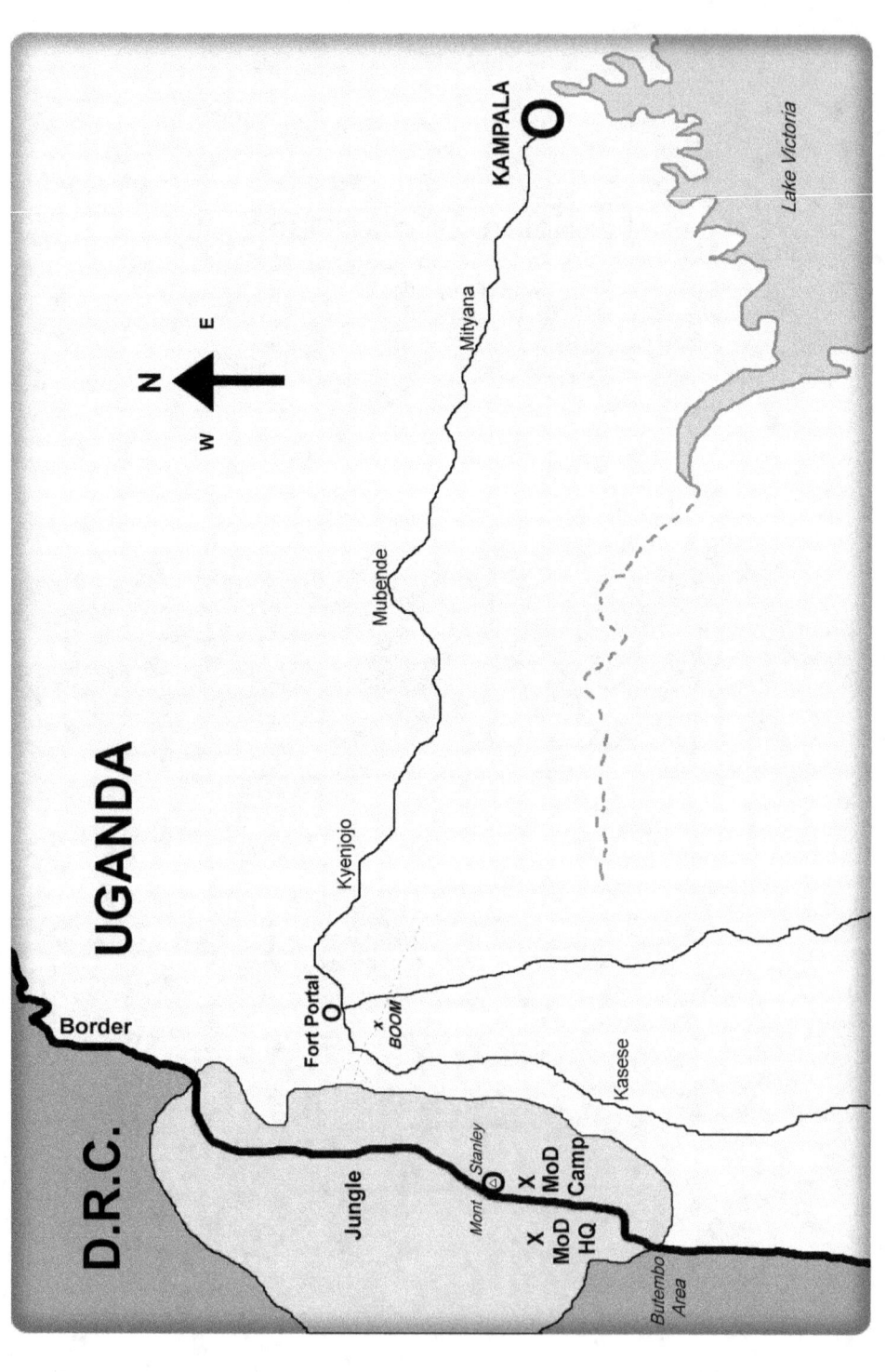

PROLOGUE

The AK-47 which was slung over the boy's right shoulder ran along almost the entire length of his lean body. The child was barely twelve years old.

When following the contours of the rifle down from where the muzzle was protruding behind his ear, to where the wooden stock touched a calve below the knee, it was as if the *Avtomat Kalashnikova model 47* was mapping the entire miserable story of the child's life.

As the boy turned his face to peer intently into the pitch black of the night, the muzzle of the rifle kissed his dark features and caressed a long scar running diagonally across a swollen cheek. Where the barrel touched the exposed skin behind his upper arm, a circular scar of hardened, pinkish-white tissue was clearly visible. Possibly the result of a bullet wound which had healed poorly.

The barrel's route continued along his ribs where a tear in his grubby T-shirt exposed a burn mark of which the exact origin was uncertain. The trigger guard and stock of the rifle rubbed against a multitude of small scars covering his right thigh and calve - the remnants of shrapnel.

The boy's bare elbows and knees were calloused. The skin there thick and hard. Months of crawling through rough terrain, over stones and through thorns, had toughened them.

Jamba was alert. His eyes were piercing the darkness. His ears focused like radar antennas attempting to register the faintest noise which may seem out of place. Even his nose was poised to catch a whiff of cigarette smoke or maybe the sweet odor of somebody's aftershave, the scent of the toothpaste or soap they use.

The boy's skin was the color of the darkest, blackest oil, as dark as that moonless African night. If he stood perfectly still, the eyes of a nocturnal animal on the hunt would have struggled to detect him. His own natural scent was that of the jungle which for months had been his true home.

His dark green shirt was torn in numerous places and his black shorts so dirty that the word 'filthy' could not even begin to describe them. The child was barefoot and had never owned a pair of shoes in his entire, short and miserable life.

Behind him two other boys of around his age were busy digging the earth furiously, gravel and clay flying recklessly through the air in all directions. Except for the constant digging and scraping there were no other audible sounds. The boys were fully concentrated on the task at hand. Nobody was speaking. They barely bothered to breathe.

"Hurry up, *putas!*"

Jamba was becoming irate. He did not feel like running into the wrong people that night. Confrontation had to be avoided at all cost. Tonight was not the time for killing anybody who just happened to be in the wrong place at the wrong time. All the killing had to wait for the coming day.

The boys were digging in their search for DaD.

They had it on good information that this was the exact spot where the government forces had dumped DaD's body into a shallow grave. An old man living in a nearby dilapidated shack had told them so. The man had no choice when it came to giving the boys the correct information first time around.

According to him, a Jeep had arrived in the early morning hours. Its occupants were soldiers who then hurriedly dug a hole and had dumped something which resembled a human body into it. They then covered the shallow grave even more hurriedly and had left in a puff of dust.

The boys had known exactly where to start their search for information regarding the whereabouts of DaD's remains, because this area was notorious. Set against a hill on the outskirts of the city, it was no secret that it was a place where the enemies of the state would often find their final resting place.

A garbage dump for human flesh. The locals named it *Nafasi ya Chuki*, in Swahili meaning 'the Place of Hatred'. But those words were almost never spoken out loud because of the loathing and fear which came with their utterance, like vile vomit constantly pushing up in one's throat.

DaD...

He had been a father to these boys. A leader, a mentor, a master. He used to be their tormentor, their punisher, their god. But above all he was their provider, their savior and the hand of fate which ultimately mapped the road their lives were to travel.

The boys simply *had* to find his body. At that very moment and no later. There was still a necessary and crucial ceremony to be performed that same night. Perhaps DaD was even still alive. It would not have come as a surprise if indeed he was, for that was the awesome power of the man.

And early tomorrow, after the ceremony had been concluded, the boys will again become instruments of death, that which they were born to and have chosen to forever be.

They were the wrath of God or the Devil - call it what you may. The wrath of DaD. His mighty fist, obliterating and crushing his enemies before him and beneath him. The boys will cast death, destruction, pain and untold misery upon the worst of their enemies. Upon DaD's enemies. Upon his murderers.

These child soldiers will both sow and reap tomorrow. They will sow instant death while wielding their weapons - and with their bullets they will reap the worthless lives and souls of those who stand in their way.

It had always been their only purpose in *life*... to trade in and bestow *death* upon their enemies.

These were the children of the Merchants of Death.

DaD... They had to find DaD.

CHAPTER 1

Jamba was only around twelve years old when DaD discovered him.

The boy had been wandering aimlessly and alone through the poorest part of the city of Kampala, the capital of Uganda. Constantly in search of food, constantly trying to find something to steal or sell, permanently fighting simply to survive. And survival was no simple matter.

There were many street children in that area. Fights often broke out over territory or food. The residents of the neighborhood were themselves the poorest of the poor living in their shanty shacks built from anything which could provide cover against the torrential rain, the incessant insects or against bad people.

The shanty town was a living hell. Its occupants were fighting their own battles for survival and simply did not care about the pathetic existences of the street children. Their presence was considered a nuisance and their petty crimes a constant irritation. The adults would chase the boys with sticks as if they were stray dogs. They threw stones or bottles at them and shook their fists violently in anger and disgust.

Plastic bags and other garbage littered the tracks between the corrugated tinplate shacks. Water from the constant rain formed dirty mud puddles everywhere, attracting multitudes of disease-carrying mosquitoes. People and animals alike urinated all over. Children and even adults were openly defecating in the mud or in the bushes next to shacks attracting flies in their millions.

A nearby stream was completely unusable due to the filth, garbage and human feces which had been washed down into its waters by the rain. Cholera was rampant. A nearby open field was often used as the neighborhood toilet, but the rain kept returning their waste to the town and when the wind changed direction the stench became unbearable.

During the early mornings and late evenings the reflection of the sun off the tin shacks was so blinding that people could barely see where they were going. Some of the 'cooler' inhabitants constantly wore sunglasses they had either stolen or bought on the black market for a bargain.

This was Jamba's world, his own personal hell.

The boy had never joined any of the numerous gangs which consisted solely of street kids. He was never accepted by the other boys because he was different. His skin was much blacker than theirs and he was taller and leaner. The bone structure of his face was more defined and his hair was straighter. Jamba knew from a very early age that being different, being one of the minority, meant being treated differently. Acceptance came slowly or never came at all.

He realized that for some unknown reason he barely ever noticed any girls among the street children. Maybe girls were loved more by their parents and not discarded so readily. Maybe they were sold to human traffickers or warlords. Jamba simply did not know.

His real name wasn't Jamba. In fact, he could not recall his actual name or even his age. It was DaD who later named him 'Jamba' on the day of his discovery.

All the boy could remember was that his family was of an ethnic group of nomads called the Luo peoples. They were nomads, warriors and cattle herders. Their cattle had been their lifeblood and the Luo constantly traveled across borders in search of better grazing for their animals. Areas ranging from parts of the South Sudan, Uganda, the Democratic Republic of the Congo and as far away as the Central African Republic.

Their cattle were possessions so priceless that raids and even small wars broke out between the different nomadic groups on regular occasions. Jamba's biological father had always carried an AK-47 wherever he went. The rifle was as if an extension of his body, an inseparable part of him. He never left it unattended, not even when washing or sleeping.

His father had always only called the boy, 'Filho da Puta.' It was a Portuguese phrase which the constantly-angry man had picked up from some Angolan weapons traders who traveled the continent. The same men he purchased his AK-47 and ammunition from as a means of protecting his valuable cattle.

The civil war in Angola was long over, leaving thousands of weapon caches buried and hidden all over that country. And these men had traded or sold their instruments of death and destruction to anybody who was willing to buy. War-torn countries such as Sierra Leone, Sudan, the Democratic Republic of the Congo, Uganda and the Central African Republic were their favorite hunting grounds.

Whenever Jamba's father had spoken to him, or shouted at him, or beat him or slapped him around, it was always accompanied by that phrase - 'Filho da Puta' - Son of a Bitch.

The word 'bitch' was apparently in reference to his mother. Jamba remembered her as always looking tired, indifferent and listless probably due to the abuse she herself had to suffer on a daily basis. All she used to do was to cook and clean, collect wood for the fire and then again just cook and clean and sometimes gathering bananas or crushing some maize into a powder for their porridge. Then again, just cook and clean. Whenever she had bothered to speak to him she simply called him, 'Boy'.

Then one horrific and utterly terrifying night their camp had been raided by other nomads. Most of their fellow Luo were brutally murdered where they lay sleeping. It was the first time Jamba had ever seen a dead person, or at least what remained of one. It was a man who had been hacked into several pieces with a machete. The boy had frozen and kept staring at the gruesome sight when his father had scooped him up and they wildly fled that scene of utter chaos, death and devastation. The slaughter had shown mankind at its worst.

All their cattle were lost to the raiders. All their possessions were left behind and gone forever. Everything they had ever owned was lost, even though it never was much.

The family had walked across borders for weeks, talked their way past soldiers and eventually arrived in Kampala. Here the native people spoke both English and Swahili. English was widely used as a middle-ground between the multitude of local languages and dialects. As a young child Jamba had picked up the English language quickly by simply listening to those around him.

His father was a broken man and had started drinking heavily. He barely ever returned to the shanty shack they had built among the many other makeshift shacks on the outskirts of that big city.

Then one day his father never returned. Maybe he was dead, maybe he had just decided to run away. Perhaps it was better that way because he always returned intoxicated and attempted to do things to his mother in his drunken stupor, while Jamba tried to close his eyes and ears tight against the shouts, objections and grunts which always followed.

His mother had quite suddenly become seriously ill and died soon after in a nearby clinic, coughing up blood. She at least died in a relatively clean bed with some sheets and a real mattress.

Jamba had only stood there and looked on as she coughed her last breath. All that time his mother never uttered a word. The doctor had said that he was sorry and that his mother died of something called TB. But the doctor also mentioned that she could not fight the disease because of something else called Aids. The young child didn't know what any of those words meant.

Then the doctor had walked away and Jamba was left standing there, all alone and utterly lost, staring at the corpse of what used to be his mother. He was only ten years old and not knowing what to do or where to go.

He cannot remember whether he had cried or not. Eventually he had wandered out of the clinic in a daze and fell asleep in the lonely and empty shack. A single blanket was the only remaining object and it still carried his mother's scent. When he had walked out of the clinic earlier that day, nobody bothered to stop him and ask him who he was, what he was doing there or where he was going.

That was his past. He could remember nothing other than that. Trauma had blocked out everything else.

So the boy managed as best a child of ten years could under such cruel and sometimes nightmarish circumstances. He abandoned the shack and at night slept under the banana trees which were growing on the outskirts of the shanty town. It felt safer there. He would cover himself with the large banana leaves when the night became chilly or when the rain started to pour down. It was mostly warm and humid here right on the equator.

The insects were his biggest irritation. He would sometimes rub mud all over himself in a dismal effort to keep the constant stinging and biting critters off his face and body. At night mosquitoes and more mosquitoes were the bane of his life. It was a slow torture he eventually became used to, just another part of his miserable life.

Jamba's drinking water came from a leaking communal tap. He already understood that water meant life. He could go days without food, but not a day without that clear liquid. Simply attempting to use the dripping tap often resulted in full-blown confrontation or running battles between the children.

The boy sometimes had to sit for hours watching it from the nearby bushes and wait for a time when there were fewer or no people nearby. Then he would rush to that dripping vein of life as if in full military assault and lap up the water like a wild animal. If he had enough time he would hurriedly fill a bottle he may have found among all the rubbish which littered the streets.

The boy further managed to survive by digging for food through the garbage and sometimes stealing a chicken, but the raw poultry made him ill because he had no way of cooking it. Somehow the blood at least seemed to nourish him. He once heard a rumor that some locals believed the blood from a chicken pleased the spirits of their ancestors and that the feet of a chicken could ward off evil spirits. Jamba did not care for and did not understand such talk. The raw chickens made him vomit.

When the bananas were in season there was plenty to go around. Banana trees littered the city and its surrounds. Yet, eating too much of the fruit gave Jamba painful stomach cramps and often caused diarrhea which lasted for days and made him immensely thirsty. So, the bananas themselves were never enough and had to be substituted often.

This is how the small boy struggled and survived for close to two years after his mother's death. That he survived at all was a miracle.

His favorite meal came from a very specific shack which doubled as an illegal bar - or a 'shebeen' as it was sometimes known - and which was also a kind of restaurant where men came to drink beer and eat a thick porridge covered in a meaty stew. The leftovers were unceremoniously dumped behind the shack, thrown out right there onto the dirty ground. This spot was highly contested by the street kids.

Fistfights and knife fights often broke out between the drunken patrons inside the shebeen for whatever reasons while the street children fought over the discarded scraps behind the shack. Sometimes the place represented a war zone.

And this was where DaD found him.

CHAPTER 2

The owner of the shebeen had just tossed an especially large lump of solidified porridge onto the ground and then disappeared back into his shack. Jamba's mouth was literally watering and he pounced like a famished leopard towards his future meal with no regard for any danger.

At that very moment another boy came rushing out from behind a shack to claim the same prize. The two boys collided with a loud thump and immediately continued to brutally punch and claw at each other. Jamba scratched at the other boy's eyes with his long filthy nails and the boy yelped like an injured dog.

Temporarily blinding him, Jamba quickly picked up a rock and repeatedly brought it down on the boy's head.

"*Puta!*" Jamba screamed at him as another blow struck the boy in the throat. The child went down instantly and his body convulsed into spasms as he desperately clutched at his throat and gasped for air.

Within moments his body went limp whilst a gurgling sound came out of his mouth and his eyes rolled over. Jamba could only see the whites of his eyes and how hideously they bulged from their sockets.

He stood there and stared at the boy's lifeless body, the food completely forgotten. He had just killed another human being. And he felt almost... nothing. All he felt was a kind of awe. Then some elation. Then a primordial sense of victory.

In a mad fit he raised his eyes towards the sky and pumped his small fists into the air. His entire body was shaking. Like a feral animal he spontaneously howled with complete abandon.

"Owoooooah!"

Just as suddenly the boy was hungry again. The adrenaline was slowly fading and his stomach was cramping up. He needed his food, craved the prize he had just killed for.

There was a black boot standing in it. Porridge had splattered all over under its weight. Jamba's eyes slowly traveled upwards as he traced the leg which belonged to that massive boot standing in his food.

The boy was awestruck. Never before had he seen such an enormous man. The black boots led to camouflage pants and the pants connected with a pristine white vest. The muscles of the man's arms were bulging under thick veins and were flexing as if though they were constantly being electrified.

His skin was as dark as Jamba's. His head shaved bald. There was a small leathery bag hanging from a string around his neck and on his face a grin from here to the South Sudan. Large white teeth were showing. The man was still fairly young - and he was absolutely monstrous.

Jamba felt no fear. He rarely ever experienced that emotion. He only felt awe and amazement. Maybe the boy had eaten too many bananas or it may have been due to the excitement of the fight, but at that moment he suddenly and loudly farted...

The man roared with laughter, slapped his thigh and roared some more. Then he spent some time scrutinizing the filthy child standing before him. The boy was covered in mud and dust and was unashamedly picking his nose with a dirty index finger whilst eyeing the obliterated porridge on the ground.

"So, tell me," the man said in a deep voice. "What's your name, boy?"

The boy didn't reply. He could not reply because he did not know his own name. He never knew.

"Are you scared of me? Is that why you don't answer me?" The smile had vanished. Instead the man was now staring him straight in the eye as if searching his soul.

"Nah. I'm not scared. Just don't know my name," the boy replied honestly.

"Ah. Okay then. I will call you... Jamba."

The giant roared again and Jamba just blinked. The child knew that word well - *Jamba*. It meant 'breaking wind' in Swahili. He didn't like it at all. Yet, this monster of a man had just given him a real name, an identity. Nobody had ever done that before. And somehow it seemed more like an order than a request as to whether he approved of it or not.

He simply accepted it and that was the end of that. With the baptism over, the colossus again stood scrutinizing the child.

"You've just killed another boy, but you don't run. You're not scared and you don't care. What are you then, Jamba? Are you stupid?"

The boy had been looking down and was busy drawing circles in the sand with his big toe. When he heard the word 'stupid' he spat on the ground in contempt.

"I'm not stupid!" he shouted at the man.

Immediately he went flying through the air and his head hurt as though it had been hit by a brick. For a moment the boy only saw very bright flickering lights. He dragged himself to his feet and stood scowling at the man while rubbing one side of his head. Jamba was used to being slapped around but had to admit that he had never been hit that hard before.

"You show me some respect boy. When I talk to you, you don't spit on me or even on the ground near me." The man was shaking a long index finger almost in his face. "You only speak when I tell you to and you do as you're told. Never shout at me. Never question me. People who disrespect me just so happen to die for no apparent reason."

He looked the boy straight in the eye again. The man's own black eyes were suddenly burning with anger and there was something buried there behind the lenses which could have been defined as pure evil.

Jamba knew all about hell and evil. This shanty town he lived in was hell and his personal little world was saturated with evil people. People out to hurt him whenever they had an opportunity. That was his life.

But Jamba wasn't that sure regarding what he saw in this man's eyes. The boy was still dazed and so he just nodded sheepishly.

As quickly as that anger raised its ugly head it disappeared and the man was grinning from ear to ear again.

"My men call me DaD. It stands for 'Death and Destruction.' Get it? D and D." The giant waited for some reaction but none was forthcoming. He sighed and continued. "Because that's my life and my vocation. My gift to my enemies. They are plenty, but they become fewer with every passing day. They present me with problems and I present them with Death and Destruction." DaD had slowly been walking towards the child as he spoke and then bent over to a point where their noses almost touched.

"You are not my enemy now are you, Jamba, boy?"

Jamba did not quite understand the whole 'D and D' thing. He had no idea of how to either spell or read. But his reply came instantly, almost instinctively.

"No, DaD. I'm not your enemy."

And for the first time in many months the boy now did experience a very real twinge of fear. A voice at the back of his skull told him that he had to respect this DaD, this enormous beast of a man whose sheer presence was oozing power and demanding respect - or he might not live to see another day.

His young mind struggled to make sense of all the emotions and their various implications which were now flooding him like a wild river.

He was still only a child, barely out of infancy. The definitions and meanings of certain emotions were still alien to him. Concepts such as 'respect' or 'hatred' and 'evil'. Words yet to be clearly grasped and understood. His full personality which would one day define the man he would become, was still in the process of being molded. At his age he was impressionable and lacked guidance of any kind.

"Where are your parents?"

The boy just shrugged his shoulders and DaD nodded his head in understanding. Jamba watched the man closely as he paused for a moment seemingly trying to make up his mind about something. With hands in his camo pockets he looked up at the sky at nothing in particular. Finally he turned to the boy again.

"I'm going to give you food. It's very good food. But first we have to make a deal." DaD frowned to emphasize just how serious he was. "You're going to work for me. Not for money. Just for food, shelter and protection. I give you food and I give you orders which you will obey without question. In return you will never go hungry again. How does that sound? Do we have a deal?"

Jamba nodded. He did not have to think it over at all especially since he was so hungry at that very moment that he could consume an entire ox.

DaD offered his hand to shake on their deal. Jamba placed his own hand into that giant lion's paw and shook. Or rather it was DaD who was doing all the shaking, because Jamba's small hand simply vanished between the man's clasped fingers.

And so it all begun. A pact with the Devil was sealed. The contract which would decide his fate and his future was signed.

The boy Jamba had traded his soul for food.

Chapter 3

As they walked toward the front of the shebeen, they left the body of the dead boy lying there. Neither DaD nor Jamba gave it a second glance or thought.

Men outside the shebeen bowed their heads respectfully and many looked down whilst others briefly saluted as DaD walked passed them. Some of the men hastily grabbed a few belongings and fell in behind the colossus and his new companion. Nobody said a word and that silence was the way things were to be in the future more often than not.

The group reached a green 4x4 pick-up truck. One man leaped into the driver's seat and DaD got in next to him. Everybody else jumped onto the back. Jamba did not know where to go. He had never been in a vehicle before. Through the open window DaD shoved his thumb towards the back.

The boy hastily jumped on as the 4x4 came to life and started rolling. Nobody offered the boy a hand, but he managed to grab hold of something and pulled himself over the side of the pick-up and onto the back.

There were AK-47's lying on the floor within easy reach of the men. In one corner were several stacked ammunition boxes on-top of which some of them were sitting. There were also a couple of diesel drums and some crates containing unknown contents. The boy saw a military radio and some cell phones lying in another corner. It was a tight fit with all the supplies. Occasionally some of the men would glance at Jamba, but showed little interest in him and still nobody said a word.

He noticed that all the men had beards. One had a beard so long that it was touching his chest. Another man was much younger than the rest and only had a few fluffy patches of hair on his face but it was obvious that nobody bothered to shave. Except DaD that is. His face was clean-shaven.

These men were clearly hardened fighters and for the first time the boy found himself wondering just what exactly he had gotten himself into. He was also wondering where they were going. His first time traveling in any kind of vehicle was exciting and an adventure already but his stomach was rumbling by now and he was terribly thirsty. He noticed a water bottle clipped to a man's belt and stared at it for a very long time as if hypnotized. The owner caught his eye and after some hesitation offered the water to him. Jamba gulped the warm fluid down eagerly, but the man plucked the bottle from him again almost immediately.

"You be careful with that water, boy. You need to count everything carefully where we're going. You must count your water. You must count your bullets. You must count your grenades." He looked at the other men and added, "And you must count your bodies..." They all burst out laughing.

Jamba did not know how to count past five yet, but he smiled with them. The talk of bullets and bodies scratched him a bit. Then the boy spent some time taking in his surroundings. The vehicle was heading towards the west. As soon as they left the outskirts of the city there were hills which were almost entirely deforested and covered in banana trees or other plantations of what looked like coffee, sweet potatoes or cotton growing on terraces against the hills. There were some villages scattered in-between. The villages mostly comprised of mud adobes or brick houses and often contained kraals made of thorny branches to keep goats or cattle in and the wild animals out.

When he looked back in a south-easterly direction towards the disappearing city, he could see an enormous expanse of water so big that it covered the entire horizon. His mother once told him about a lake, called Lake Victoria, but she didn't know anything about who this Victoria was and mumbled something about white people and colonialism. Jamba had never seen a white man and had no idea what 'colonialism' meant.

For some time they were driving on asphalt littered with potholes. After endless hours the banana trees gradually gave way to islands of tall, lush trees which were growing ever-denser by the minute.

They passed through towns with names such as Kibwa, Mityana and Mubende. Government soldiers and police were spotted walking or driving through almost every major town. It did not seem to bother the men in the back of the pick-up too much, although they appeared much more alert whenever soldiers were seen very nearby.

Jamba noticed a large mountain range in the distance towards the same direction that they were driving. One peak was so high that he could see something white glistening on its summit. Near a place called Fort Portal the men clearly grew much tenser and more alert. Just before the large town they turned off the main road and onto a dirt road leading towards the south. The vehicle evaded the town until they came across a small guard post with a boom spanning the road. The men briefly checked their weapons and then lay them back on the floor of the pick-up.

Jamba felt a shiver of excitement and expectation run through his body. Since there was nothing he could do he just observed the actions of the men. There was a small square building which served as a guard room. Behind it a tall antenna pierced the sky. A concrete watchtower was overlooking a nearby river and the road.

The pick-up stopped at the boom and two government soldiers with rifles hanging from their shoulders casually strolled out towards the driver's side of the vehicle. They hardly glanced at the men sitting in the back.

After a brief exchange of words one of the soldiers took a wad of money from the driver and the other soldier lifted the boom. They continued through and everybody relaxed visibly.

The vehicle crossed a wide stretch of river running under a low bridge. Just a mile further down the track there was another bridge spanning a deep ravine. The gash in the earth was not very wide but incredibly deep. While they crossed it, the boy peered over the edge of the pick-up and could barely make out the bottom where trees and shadows were hiding its floor.

After rejoining the asphalt a few miles down the gravel road, they soon again turned off the main road and headed in the direction of the mountains in the west. Large trees, aloes and shrubs were closing in on them and growing thicker and denser with every passing mile. The boy noticed fewer and fewer settlements.

The road turned into a track and the track eventually all but disappeared. By now the dense jungle was almost swallowing them whole. Nearby mountain peaks were sometimes visible through the trees.

It grew dark very quickly and the sounds of wild animals and unseen birds occasionally pierced the air. Jamba could hear monkeys and owls and many other sounds he was not sure of. It was truly turning into an adventure.

At one stage they stopped to refuel the pick-up from one of the diesel containers. Then they continued to drive at almost a walking-pace through the foliage. Jamba had no idea how the driver knew where he was going in the darkness. No stars or moon reached down here either. He certainly also could not see a track of any kind even with the headlights of the pick-up on full beam.

The boy was now so tired and hungry that he eventually fell asleep exhausted. He only woke up when he realized that they were not moving any more. They had stopped in a semi-clearing and he could see the glow of the sun's first rays through the canopy of the jungle, already painting the bits of visible sky a bloody red.

The clearing was just big enough to let in some light from above, yet leaving enough foliage to cover most of the make-shift huts, vehicles and equipment which the boy started noticing around him through still-sleepy eyes.

The small group of huts was built from bamboo and banana leaves. There were some men and a few boys standing in a huddle and sharing cigarettes. All of them were armed with AK-47 assault rifles.

Jamba caught a glimpse of some women also moving between the huts. There were a couple of adults among these women but most of them were young girls. He thought to himself that they must be the wives and children of the soldiers.

On the edge of the encampment he could make out a pair of soldiers seemingly patrolling the perimeter. Nearby a long copper wire ran from one hut up the entire length of a tree. The crackle of radio static emerged from within. A few chickens were picking at the ground around the area and some of them were perched on top of several other vehicles parked beneath the densest of trees.

One pick-up had an enormous machine gun mounted on the back. The massive gun fascinated Jamba and as he jumped from the vehicle he slowly wandered over in that direction.

"Jamba!" a firm voice called before he could reach the gun.

DaD was standing at the entrance of a hut and with him were three boys of various ages but all still very young. Just like Jamba, they wore only T-shirts and shorts. The boys seemed very muscular for their years.

"These guys are Yoweri, Okot and Tito." He pointed at each in turn as he named them. "They'll show you what to do. Listen to them and learn. Do what they say."

And with that DaD walked off briskly, not to be spotted again for many days. He became like a ghost from then on, only to be seen again when the soldiers left for battle or when the men gathered to get drunk and high on some mysterious drug.

The boys did not utter a word. The one called Tito at least nodded towards him in recognition. He was around the same age as Jamba but smaller and almost brown in skin color. What struck him most about Tito was his large eyes which bulged slightly, almost like that of the boy he had killed the previous day. It was a bit unnerving in a sense.

Jamba briefly wondered whether from then on Tito's eyes would constantly remind him of the boy he had killed in Kampala.

Chapter 4

The boys led Jamba to a hut where they gave him a battered tin plate. As they entered the hut a woman and two girls made their exit without so much as a glance towards the boys. One girl had a swollen cheek which covered almost her entire eye.

The one DaD called Yoweri passed him a slice of bread and pointed towards a large black cast iron pot hanging above a small fire in the center of the hut.

"Soup," he said. "Eat. We've got lotsa work to do."

Jamba almost tripped over his own feet in his haste to get to the soup. He was so hungry that the smell made his mouth drool. Tito offered him some bananas which Jamba refused quite vehemently. There were large chunks of all kinds of vegetables floating in the soup. Jamba could not remember when last he ate vegetables, let alone fresh ones. He unconsciously licked his lips in anticipation.

Yoweri was the oldest and biggest of the boys. Jamba was unsure of his own age, but guessed that the boy must be at least two years older than himself. He was also the only one with an AK-47. The rifle was slung over his right shoulder and the stock almost touched his feet.

He scowled at Jamba and then said, "Fart. We've got rules here. We're soldiers. If we break the rules we die or our comrades die. If the enemy doesn't kill us, DaD will have us killed for breaking the rules. Or you will end up working in his diamond mines." Yoweri paused to see what effect his words had on the new boy. Jamba was slurping at his soup with a spoon. Not even a glance. "There you'll dig in the dirt every day for the rest of your life and be flogged with a whip until you've become vulture food... Fart."

Jamba continued eating, eagerly dipping his bread into the delicious soup. Then he replied slowly and deliberately.

"My name is Jamba. That's what DaD named me. That's what you will call me." He took a few bites from his bread and then added calmly, "Yesterday I killed a boy in the city. He was just as big and old as you are."

There was silence, except for the sound of Jamba now greedily slurping up the remainder of his soup, using the tin plate as if it was a cup of some sorts.

After a period of utter quiet, Yoweri spoke again. "I'm Yoweri. Next week I'm joining the veterans in my first battle. I will bring you the little finger of the first man I kill." As if to drive home his point he tapped the barrel of his AK with a pinkie.

Tito and Okot just sat there with very little expression on their faces, but it was clear that they were quite enjoying this war of words between the new boy of probably only twelve years and the older Yoweri.

Jamba again replied without looking up from his bread and soup. "I will be happy to eat that man's finger. Now, do you have some more bread?"

Tito grinned, his big white eyes sparkling and Okot decided to say something to defuse the situation.

"There are many more rules, Jamba. Our soldiers are not allowed to fight with each other. The penalty is death or working in the diamond mines." Okot was scrawny and smaller than the other boys but he looked intelligent. He was gesturing with his hands as he talked and his words were well-articulated.

The boy continued his lesson. "We also speak as little as possible. It keeps us all alert. Speak only when necessary. When battle comes, we must be quiet so the enemy can't hear us and the only men who speak then are the sergeants and captains. We use English here because we're many from many different places."

Jamba nodded at Okot. He preferred silence in any case. Then he was struck by a thought and asked, "What's a diamond?"

"Come. I will show you," Tito replied this time with yet another grin on his face.

After Jamba had washed his plate in a plastic container filled with oily water, the boys walked over to the hut from which the radio antenna was crawling up the tall tree. In one corner a military two-way radio was perched on top of an empty plastic beer crate.

There was a heavily bearded guard lying back in a rickety wooden chair, his legs stretched out in front of him and busy carving away at a stick with a small knife. The man looked bored beyond rescue and barely glanced at them when the boys entered.

In another corner was a collection of plastic Tupperware, neatly stacked one on top of the other. Tito flipped a blue lid off the topmost container to expose a pile of dirty white stones inside. Some were as small as a grain of sand and others as big as the eggs of a dove. The guard now kept one eye on them while not interrupting his monotonous carving.

To Jamba the stones meant little. The were just that - a pile of rough, dirty, white stones. Then Tito reached into the pocket of his dingy shorts and produced a folded piece of paper. He carefully unfolded it and smoothed it out. As if dealing with a matter of enormous importance he presented it to Jamba.

On the paper was printed a picture of the most beautiful stone Jamba had ever seen. It was glistening both blue and white like the sun reflecting off clear glass. The stone had a multitude of fine ridges and edges shaped into incredible patterns. It was set in a golden ring and sparkled in some unseen light.

"Diamond," Tito simply said. "White people's women want it and DaD sells it to their husbands and lovers for money or weapons. DaD's the richest man in the world".

Jamba did not know how big the world was, but thinking of what he had recently seen of the camp, he was quite certain that DaD must be incredibly rich. This whole village with its many vehicles and weapons all belonged to DaD. He could clearly even afford to feed an entire army.

Okot told Jamba that some of the diamonds just recently arrived from the mines across the border in the Democratic Republic of the Congo. Flashing a sidelong glance at the guard, he added that nobody would ever dare steal the contents of those containers.

"Nobody steals from DaD. He will hunt down anybody who takes from him or cheats him or stabs him in the back, even if it means searching the entire Africa." Here Okot spread his arms to indicate something of immense size. "He will torture the thief, keep him alive for a long time just so he would suffer and think about what he'd done. DaD will kill his entire family. To steal from DaD is to weaken the cause of the MoD. It's like stealing from everybody in our army."

Jamba nodded slowly in understanding and then asked, "What's the MoD?"

"The Merchants of Death," Tito replied with obvious pride. "That's the name of our army. We trade in death." To emphasize his statement, Tito slowly traced his index finger across his Adam's apple, imitating slitting his own throat with a knife.

"The diamonds may be pretty," reminded Yoweri, who was up to now quietly observing the others, "but the mines where they come from are a hell you don't want to end up in."

Jamba already knew the meaning of the word 'hell' but those mines sure didn't sound like a nice place to be. He decided to just follow the rules and see where his new life leads him. And maybe one day he will even possess a shining diamond of his own.

CHAPTER 5

Their conversation was interrupted by the sound of a shrill whistle. The other boys started running and Jamba followed, a bit confused by the sudden activity. They reached the center of the clearing and the children gathered there immediately stood at attention, stiff as poles and in a straight line abreast of each other. Jamba just mimicked them and hoped he was doing whatever was expected of him.

It suddenly dawned on him that he was now a real soldier, so he thrust his small chin a bit higher and pushed out his chest in pride. A soldier!

Other boys appeared from nowhere and joined the parade. There were many of them, as many as all of Jamba's fingers and toes in total. He tried to look at some of them from the corners of his eyes. Only a few of them had rifles on them.

He noticed that the boy next to him had an eye missing. Jamba turned and stared. His wandering mind was instantly interrupted by a man shouting very loudly.

"Eyes in front!" the man almost screamed. Jamba was not sure whether it was directed at him for openly staring or whether directed at all of the boys on parade.

A short, stocky man with a very bushy beard was marching up and down before them, more like wobbling, because he was clearly missing a piece of leg from somewhere below the left knee. His camouflage pants there were rolled half-way up and a smoothly carved chunk of wood was visible where it had replaced the missing limb. People around here seemed to be missing an awful lot of body parts, Jamba noted to himself. The man was probably around the same age as Jamba's father was before he had disappeared.

"For those who don't know yet, I'm Sergeant Wambuzi. Some of you are new here and some of you are already veterans but a few reminders never did any harm. Around my arm I'm wearing a blue ribbon. This means that I'm a sergeant and I'm in charge of you little shits."

He paused for his words to fully sink in. "We have nine sergeants in this glorious MoD army of ours and we give the orders in battle. If you have anything to say, you come to us. Above us are three captains. They instruct us sergeants what to do and we again tell you little shits what to do. You're nothing but wannabe soldiers who obey orders."

Again he paused, eyeing the ragtag group of boys with what resembled intense dislike. "Captains wear red ribbons around their arms. Nobody will speak to a captain except when addressed by one. Ever. If you speak to a captain out of turn, you'll be digging toilet pits forever and be swimming in whatever is contained in those pits... forever."

Jamba did not know how to count yet. He had no idea how much 'nine' was, but it certainly sounded like a lot. The boy had only learned how to count up to five, the exact number of cattle his father had owned so many years ago. There was no need to learn how to count past that. Cattle was everything back then and they had lost everything of value soon after.

Sergeant Wambuzi stopped wobbling and scowled at the boys. "Our Supreme Commander in Chief is DaD. If you ever speak to DaD without being summoned personally, it will be the last words you ever utter in your miserable lives. DaD does not need a ribbon. You all know who DaD is. He is the big mother of a guy with the scrotum sack of an enemy hanging around his neck."

The one-legged man spread his arms wide, tilted his head back and looked up into the sky. "He's the agent of Death and Destruction! He's our savior. He's the reason you maggots have any life or future whatsoever. He's the reason you have food and shelter. Be grateful. You all owe DaD in a very big way. Never forget that!" With the theatrical performance complete, he dropped his arms to his sides to again scowl at the boys.

As Sergeant Wambuzi spoke, Jamba developed an itch. The tropical heat here right on the equator was sometimes ruthless - wet, sticky and suffocating. He did not know what to do. A single drop of sweat was running down the back of his spine and itching like crazy. He had to scratch and he did so.

In an instant Wambuzi slapped him behind the head. Jamba had no idea that a man with only one leg could move that fast. Being slapped around the head seemed to be Jamba's past and future. Maybe DaD should have rather named him 'Slappy' or something similar, he thought to himself.

"You will be digging toilet pits as from today, son. You will even wipe the butts of those who use them," the sergeant spat at him.

A voice to Jamba's right spoke up. "Permission to speak, sir?"

"What is it, Tito?" Sergeant Wambuzi snapped irately.

"The boy is new, sir. Arrived just a few hours ago with DaD from Kampala. We're teaching him the rules," said Tito in a confident voice.

Sergeant Wambuzi seemed to be in deep thought for some seconds.

"What's your name boy?"

"Jamba, mister."

The entire parade burst into laughter and then just as suddenly fell back into perfect silence under Wambuzi's deadly stare. The foul look he gave them was command enough for them to shut up immediately.

"Okay... *Jamba*. Listen to me you little Fart. Learn quickly. And call me sergeant. I'm not your mister and I'm not your sister. At this rate you'll be digging toilets for the entire population of Kampala by the end of this day. Wake up, boy. I see you already made a friend here. Good ol' Tito seems to be your guardian angel. Do you have many friends, son?"

Jamba mulled this over for a moment and then said, "No, sergeant. I've never had any friends... sir," he added as an afterthought. That last part seemed to please Wambuzi somewhat.

"Good. And keep it that way. Having friends will distract you in battle. When a friend dies beside you, you will forget that you're busy fighting to kill the enemy. You might forget that you're not in battle to be killed or have your head blown off. Full concentration is needed. Friends distract you from your duty to kill the enemy. So don't get too cozy, boy." The sergeant's face was now so close to Jamba's own that the boy could smell his breath. "Emotions are the biggest killer of all."

Wambuzi hobbled back to where he was previously standing just before he had slapped Jamba behind the ear.

"Let me remind you. We are the Merchants of Death. The glorious MoD army. We fight for freedom from any government and oppressor. We fight the government pigs who've taken everything from you and condemned you to eternal poverty and misery. Some of us will die so that we may one day prosper and be rich beyond our wildest dreams. We fight so that DaD may lead us to victory and wealth. The goals are simple." He held up a single finger. "Freedom..." He held up a second finger. "And prosperity. Anybody who stands in the way of these goals is the enemy."

His speech delivered, Sergeant Wambuzi then spelled out the daily orders. Jamba's group will continue digging underground tunnels which are used for hiding in the event of a surprise discovery of their position. They could also be used in case of a possible aerial assaults or helicopter reconnaissance.

At lunch time the boys were to help gather firewood for the kitchen. Fires were made inside the huts to minimize the smoke trail from giving away their position. Only very dry wood was to be used.

In the late afternoon they were to assemble for what Sergeant Wambuzi termed 'combat readiness exercises'. That part sounded really fun to Jamba and he wished that it was afternoon already. Digging tunnels and gathering wood did not sound like any fun at all.

CHAPTER 6

Yoweri explained the workings and design of the tunnels to Jamba while drawing lines on the damp ground with a stick. It was in fact very simple but also ingenious at the same time.

First there was a vertical shaft of almost six feet deep. Then the tunnel, just wide enough for a man to crawl in, was dug horizontally in a straight line for roughly another thirty feet or so. Here an elbow or dog-leg was then dug and the tunnel continued for only a few more yards from there to open into a small chamber.

From this chamber a second shaft was dug upwards towards the surface, but not all the way up as to break it.

When all was done, the metal lid of an oil drum was left at the dog-leg bend in the tunnel to be used as a kind of door and shield. In the small chamber at the back of the tunnel were deposited any implement suitable for future digging and a piece of rubber or metal piping. There were also a bucket with water and two pieces of cloth left there.

Yoweri explained that whenever they had more anti-personnel mines in stock, that one would be left near the entrance of the tunnel to later be planted by its occupants should the use of the tunnels become necessary during a ground assault.

When the orders came to hide in the tunnels, two or three soldiers would share the space. A shrub, bush or large leaves are pulled over the entrance to hide its location. The first thing the enemy or government troops would usually do once a tunnel is discovered is to bring in a flame-thrower or drop a grenade inside.

However, the first vertical shaft makes the angle difficult for a flame-thrower to be used very effectively since it cannot reach the back of the tunnel. A grenade can also only really be thrown a few paces down the tunnel. The dog-leg is the primary defense against the blast, a resulting cave-in and the shrapnel. The metal lid from the oil drum is the secondary defense when used to literally plug the hole at the bend.

The enemy might also try to smoke them out, but since there is only one exit, the smoke often simply keeps escaping the most direct route towards open air. This is where the bucket of water and cloth come in. Those hiding inside can dip the cloth in the water and hold it over their noses and mouths for easier breathing should any smoke reach the back. The water can also be used for drinking should they have to stay hidden in the tunnel for extended periods of time.

The biggest threat comes from 'tunnel rats' though. Yoweri explained that tunnel rats were men who are paid a lot of money and trained specifically to crawl down tunnels and flush out its occupants. These guys are apparently very bad news. They know how to look for tripwires and diffuse mines also.

But you can usually hear them coming and some of them even use torches which give away their positions. When hiding beyond the dog-leg, it is a simple question of firing your weapon around the bend and down the tunnel to neutralize a rat. They dare not use a grenade in the tunnel themselves.

A very real danger for everybody is loss of hearing. Because the deafening sound of gunfire or exploding grenades cannot escape anywhere and just keeps bouncing off the tunnel walls, it is well-known that some men had permanently lost their hearing. Plugging your ears with cloth or rags first is therefore highly advisable.

Jamba found this absolutely fascinating and wondered if he would ever find it necessary to hide in one of these tunnels.

Yoweri was not done yet. What the enemy then usually ends up doing is to simply fill in the entrance to the tunnel and bury its occupants alive and that is the reason for the second vertical shaft at the back chamber, the digging tools and the pipes. When the air begins to become unbreathable after a couple of days or possibly only hours, the shaft can be extended by simply digging upwards until the surface is slightly broken.

A small hole should be dug towards the surface which is just big enough for the pipe to fit through. This should ventilate the bad air and is also used for listening for activity on the outside. If the tunnel was well-planned, there should be bushes or shrubs hiding the location of the pipe.

Jamba could not help but imagine what it must be like to be buried underground for a day, or even two, without any light or clean air to breathe. It must be quite unnerving. He decided that he was surely capable of doing this.

As if reading his mind, Okot told him that as part of their training each soldier was expected to stay in a tunnel for at least one entire day and night.

Jamba was suddenly not quite that excited any more and concluded that since that was the case, they had better do a bloody good job of digging these tunnels.

The boys spent the rest of the morning digging, scraping and shoveling dirt and mud. They took turns rotating their duties since the digging was suffocating work. One boy would dig at the front and a second boy would scrape the dirt into a bucket connected to a rope. The third boy would haul the bucket to the surface and scatter the dirt far away from the tunnel entrance. The damp clay made the roof and walls of the narrow tunnels quite solid and they did not need any reinforcing.

In these mountainous regions it also meant that they quite often hit rock. Then they either had to unearth the rock or change the direction of the tunnel sooner. Some tunnels had to be completely abandoned where the rock proved a major obstacle, meaning many hours of toiling blood, sweat and tears had gone to waste for their diggers. Fortunately for them this had not yet happened so far.

The sound of a whistle indicated lunch and they gladly left for the huts, utterly filthy and covered in sweat, mud and dust. Completing just a single tunnel was going to take for ever.

CHAPTER 7

Before the boys could eat they first had to gather some firewood. Finding wood was not a problem at all, but finding completely dry wood which would minimize smoke seemed more challenging though.

After about twenty minutes the wood was gathered and dumped next to the kitchen hut. Jamba expected some kind of queue but there was barely anybody there. It seemed the whistle only indicated that the food was ready. People could collect it any time once they had finished their individual duties or changed shifts for guard duty.

The boys were really dirty from all the digging, Jamba being the exception in a sense because it was not possible for him to get much filthier than he already was when he had arrived that morning. It had been many weeks since he had last hurriedly cleaned himself at the contested communal tap in Kampala's shanty town.

Yoweri lead the way to a communal washing area under a tall wild African rubber tree. Plastic containers hung from a horizontal rod and a flexible pipe was connected to the bottom of each container. A tap set in the dangling pipe completed a primitive but effective shower. It could be used to simply wash your hands or take the full treatment.

The containers could be filled from the top and even catch the rainwater.

Jamba's eyes sparkled and he immediately ripped off his shirt and shorts. Without bothering to ask permission he opened a tap and guided the water all over his body. The shower was exhilarating. He had never had a real shower in his entire life and for once the boy knew the meaning of happiness. It was a new and strange emotion, alien to his understanding of the world, yet somehow he now understood part of it.

It was only interrupted by Yoweri scolding him for apparently wasting water and them not having all day. The other boys tolerated it for some time because it was pretty clear that Jamba was in serious need of some cleaning and when they were working in the tunnels his stench became unbearable to them at times.

Jamba's features looked completely different after the shower and his companions were surprised at how deep black his skin was. The thought never occurred to them that he may not be native to the area. Nobody asked. Their soldiers joined from all over the region and every person had a history which was their own personal business.

The level-headed Okot saw this as a timely opportunity to give Jamba a few more survival tips.

"We never use anything smelly. During an ambush or patrols the enemy can smell soap or toothpaste a mile away. We must always smell like the jungle we live in."

Now the beards, sported by all the men Jamba had encountered, suddenly also made perfect sense to the boy.

"When on patrol or guard duty, no cigarettes are allowed either. The enemy can smell them or see their tips glowing in the dark," Okot continued while picking at his nose.

Jamba did not care much for this. He didn't smoke anyway but the information was still valuable and he filed it to the back of his memory.

While he put his clothes back on he found himself wondering when he could give the rags a good wash. Tito told him that there was a stream nearby which was used for drinking water and refilling the shower tanks. They sometimes washed clothes and other things such as dishes further down the stream.

The notorious latrine pits were on the opposite side of the stream and located far away from the camp and drinking water. These were simply pits dug into the ground. A plank with a hole in it spanned the pit and was where you sat and did your business. Leaves were used for wiping your behind except when supplies happened to include toilet paper which was considered a luxury.

The boys went to collect their lunch. It was a fantastic stew with sweet potatoes on the side. They moved outside to sit under a tree eating their food in silence. According to Tito the stew was made of monkey meat. Jamba did not care because it was the best meat he had ever tasted or could remember tasting. The sweet potatoes were excellent too.

After finishing his meal, Jamba lazily leaned back against the tree and asked some questions which had been nagging him for some time.

"Where exactly are we? Do we stay here forever?"

Although Yoweri was apparently the boy in charge, it was Okot who was as always the one overflowing with knowledge on just about everything and anything.

"We're in the mountains near the border with the Democratic Republic of the Congo, the DRC. That's where the real war is. That's where DaD protects his diamond mines and where the heavy weapons are. Many groups fight over the resources there. And they are all our enemy. Without the diamond mines we have no money and without the money we can't fight the war or be rich and free one day."

Okot continued as the other boys lay on the ground or sat propped against the tree. Tito seemed to be taking a nap and Yoweri clasped his *Kalashnikov* to his chest. Jamba just listened.

"This camp has been here for a long time without any need to move. Its been quite safe and had been the headquarters for maybe two years now. DaD uses it for recruitment and training. This area is actually a nature reserve and DaD paid the head ranger lots of money to keep quiet and keep his rangers or tourists away. If the man fails or gives away our position, he will lose his job, his life and his family. So far it's been working out just fine."

Okot was in deep thought for a moment as if wondering what else he could add and then nodded when he did think of something. "These jungles are almost impenetrable. From here we can reach the towns here in Uganda by vehicle for supplies or raids. To get to the DRC we have to travel by foot through the jungles and across the mountains." The boy was pointing in all the directions of the compass as he explained the topography.

"There's another camp on that side where we have more vehicles and weapons. The main army. We have radios and cellphones to communicate with them. DaD does not like using the radios too often though. We usually use cellphones and change them every month or so before the government can trace their signals. During our last meeting DaD told us about a new phone he bought from some white people which hides the signal. He called it 'encryption' or something like that."

Jamba had absolutely no idea about all this technology. He had only ever seen a cellphone or two in Kampala. The military radios also intrigued him but he was certain that they were different from the usual AM/FM radios he knew fairly well and which delivered some good music sometimes.

Okot explained that the radios were used for communications and simply transmit or receive between two parties at a certain wavelength. But these channels are not always secure so the enemy can quite easily overhear their conversations. For added safety all communication takes place in a code language as often as possible, even when they use the cellphones. Only the officers and those on guard duty had phones.

Jamba's head was spinning with all the information but he was quite proud of himself when he considered how much he had already learned in less than a single day of arriving at his new home.

CHAPTER 8

The boys went to wash their plates in the kitchen hut. The dish water was by now the color of a soup. A woman almost the size of the hut itself pointed at the water and made a fuss with her hands. This apparently meant that the water needed changing. Jamba had to agree with that.

It took two of them to carry the container with its oily contents. Of course Yoweri just looked on while Tito and Okot settled who would help to carry it by playing a quick game of rock-paper-scissors. Tito lost while Jamba had no choice in the matter.

They crossed the stream and the dish water was dumped in a toilet pit. The stench was unbearable. Even Jamba found it quite overwhelming, especially since he was actually clean for once in his life.

The boys then ambled towards the stream which was meandering through the thick jungle only a few feet from the camp. It was a peaceful setting and Jamba saw plants he had never noticed before. Some had thick stems with a single flower growing at the top. There were ferns everywhere. Other plants even grew high up in the tallest of the trees where they gripped onto branches with their roots spread like the fingers of a hand.

The stream was flowing steadily and the water seemed crystal-clear. Never had he seen such clear and clean water. Washing the container was left up to him without an order needed and after he refilled it, Tito and Okot played another round of rock-paper-scissors. Tito lost again and pulled a face.

When they reached the kitchen the shrill sound of the whistle pierced the air again. And again they lined up at the parade area. However, this time only three other boys joined them and Jamba wondered how the soldiers knew who had to do what when the whistle blew.

He was actually looking forward to this briefing. Sergeant Wambuzi mentioned 'combat readiness exercises' earlier on and Jamba wanted to become a real soldier. He just hoped it didn't mean spending an entire day and night cooped up in a tunnel already. Or digging toilet pits.

It was not Sergeant Wambuzi who took charge but another bearded man with a blue ribbon tied around his arm. The man was stocky with well-developed muscles and legs the size of tree trunks. He also had very thick, very red lips.

He simply said, " I'm Sergeant Oboto. Today you'll continue your training with the *Kalashnikov* assault rifle. Some already know the basics, but you will improve on what you know so that you can kill your enemies before they kill you."

This all sounded very impressive to Jamba and he certainly wanted to kill the enemy before they killed him. He also badly wanted a weapon of his own. The AK-47's seemed big and heavy to him though. He vaguely remembered a time when his father allowed him to pull the trigger just once. But his father was holding the rifle as he squeezed the trigger and the resulting noise almost deafened him.

Sergeant Oboto held his AK up in the air with one arm and said, "This is the *Avtomat Kalashnikova* model 47. It was designed by a clever Russian named Mikhail Kalashnikov. It's the most successful assault rifle ever made and is used in every major conflict on the planet. Unlike the fancy Western rifles, you can bury it in the ground for more than a year, then dig it up and it will immediately fire. This is your instrument of *death* so that you may *live*."

He lowered the rifle and continued, "This rifle will be your girlfriend. Look after her and she'll be nice to you. This rifle will become a part of you like that small sausage between your legs. You'll carry it with you at all times and it will be the last thing you say goodbye to when you die one day."

Sergeant Oboto paced up and down in front of the six boys. "This is not a gun. It's a *rifle*."

He pointed at the AK-47 and then said as if reading a nursery rhyme. "This is my rifle..."

Then he grabbed his crotch with a hand. "And this my gun..."

Pointing at the AK again he continued. "This is for fighting..." and once again grabbing his crotch he finished his rhyme, "and this is for fun."

The young Jamba enjoyed this.

"This is my rifle.

This is my gun.

This is for fighting.

And this is for fun," he whispered to himself.

How his crotch is made for fun he did not yet fully understand, but he guessed it had something to do with what his father did to his mother in their shack whenever the angry man had arrived back in a drunken stupor late at night.

Sergeant Oboto then continued for some length of time to explain in thorough detail the workings of the assault rifle. How to slide the sharp bullets into the curved magazine, how to clip the magazine into the rifle, how to load a round into the chamber with the sliding bolt and how the safety works.

When not in combat or on patrol, there should never be a round in the chamber and the rifle must always be on safety. The reasons for that were pretty obvious. You did not want to shoot yourself or a fellow-soldier by accident. If this happened and you were not dead already, you will dig toilets or join the diamond mines for the rest of eternity - as Jamba already fully understood by now.

Then Oboto gestured towards him. "Come here, boy."

Jamba immediately walked over to the sergeant and stood there waiting expectantly. Oboto pointed to a small lever on one side of the *Kalashnikov*. There were three settings. The safety, fully automatic and rapid fire or semi-automatic.

"You will never – and I repeat – *never* fire your rifle on full automatic. This is not the movies. The only possible exception is *maybe* if you are the absolute last man standing and have twenty enemies advancing on you. In all other cases you will *only* use the semi-automatic setting. You will aim and squeeze the trigger twice in short succession. Always like that. Aim and squeeze twice. It is more accurate and saves valuable ammunition. And if accurate, it kills the enemy just as dead as ten bullets."

Sergeant Oboto slotted a round into the chamber, flipped the lever and then pulled Jamba quite roughly towards him. He shoved the rifle into his hands and said, "Here's another reason why you do not use the full automatic setting. Now aim at that oil drum over there boy and squeeze the trigger. Don't hold your breath. Just exhale slowly and squeeze."

Jamba's heart was racing and it felt as though it might jump out his mouth at any moment. He was excited and unsure all at the same time. It was the first time he had ever held a rifle all by himself in his small hands. The AK-47 was heavier than he had expected and his arms quivered slightly under the strain.

The sergeant waited patiently as Jamba aimed at the black drum which stood quite some distance away at the edge of the jungle. It was already pitted with several bullet holes. Before he could pull the trigger Sergeant Oboto corrected his stance and the way he was holding the rifle. Once he was satisfied he nodded.

Jamba lined up the sites again, slowly exhaled and squeezed. The Lord of Chaos arrived instantly. The noise was ear-shattering. Puffs of dust and lumps of clay jumped up far behind the drum while leaves tore to shreds as if made of the flimsiest paper. Chickens went fleeing in all directions, overcome by panic.

The muzzle of the rifle went straight up into the air with a life of its own, whilst the boy was thrown off his feet. He dropped the weapon which was a moment ago kicking like a wild mule in his hands. There was simply no way of holding on to it no matter how strong his grasp.

It was as if the *Avtomat Kalashnikova* model 47 had a life of its own and simply refused to stop spitting deadly bullets in all directions until Jamba let go. Not a single projectile came even close to finding its intended target.

Within moments soldiers came running from all directions, rifles at the ready, but they immediately returned to their duties after quickly assessing the situation. Some were swearing under their breaths whilst others were shaking their heads. The boys on parade were all frozen in the act of either ducking or defending their faces from an unseen assault.

Jamba lay on his back and then sat up slowly. The boy was slightly in shock while simultaneously feeling like a complete idiot. He looked up at Oboto sheepishly, expecting a slap at any moment.

The sergeant picked up the rifle and simply said, "And that, ladies, is why small boys will never fire their rifles set on fully automatic."

Oboto turned and walked away. The lesson was over.

As he slowly dragged himself back onto his feet, Jamba caught a brief glimpse of DaD's huge bulk disappearing back into a hut. He hoped that he did not somehow disappoint his new master.

The moment night fell over the camp, the boys retired to a hut. Darkness here came almost instantly. One minute it would be perfectly light and the next minute the sun would suddenly disappear behind a high mountain peak to the west. The trees snuffed out whatever rays still struggled to hang on to the very last.

Almost all the boys who were present at both parades were gathered in the hut. None of them bothered to introduce themselves and in a way that suited Jamba just fine.

He did not quite feel ready as yet to willingly flaunt the new name which DaD had bestowed upon him. Most boys already knew anyway after the events of the day involving Sergeant Wambuzi. Jamba thought about maybe inventing a new name for himself, but something at the back of his young mind told him that their Supreme Commander in Chief will not be too pleased about that. He dismissed the idea quickly.

Yoweri threw an immaculately clean blanket at him and pointed towards a spot in the center of the bare floor, Jamba's new bed. It was still very hot and humid, so he folded the blanket double and put it down to serve as both a mattress and pillow.

Utterly exhausted after a long and eventful day, the young boy fell asleep as soon as his head touched the ground. For a very brief moment he considered his habitual ritual of covering himself with mud against the biting insects, but realized there was no need for that anymore and there were almost no insects in the hut anyway. For the first time since he could remember he almost felt at peace.

That night he dreamed of bearded AK-47's chasing him through tunnels and through toilet pits filled to the brim. Yet, to him it wasn't a nightmare. It was an adventure.

CHAPTER 9

Jamba spent the next few weeks learning his new trade as a soldier. He never went to school or had a trade before and found all the new training stimulating. He developed a thirst for knowledge. Slowly he became part of what seemed to be a crude and primitive, yet well-oiled machine. The boy even managed not to be slapped around the head even once during this period and thought unto himself that he must be doing something right.

Finally, at the late age of twelve years, the boy learned how to count properly, to thirty at least. Thirty was the number of cartridges needed to fully reload the standard AK-47 magazine. Later he would learn how to count to forty for the interchangeable box-magazines and then to seventy-five for the larger round-drum magazines.

Knowing how to count opened up a new universe to him. The boy started to understand and make sense of simple concepts such as distances. He now knew exactly how long a tunnel should be before the direction was changed for the dog-leg. He could now also better understand the concept of time and how timing was an essential component of a successful assault. Okot showed him how to read time on a cheap digital watch which used to belong to some soldier long since dead and forgotten.

Jamba could now also make more sense of age. Many of the men were in their twenties and thirties. One captain was even in his forties but the majority of soldiers were mere boys between the ages of twelve and sixteen. And so were most of the females in the camp, just young girls without any parents. Jamba thought to himself that this may be the reason why there were so few girls among the street kids of Kampala.

He did not know when his birthday was. After some thought he decided it will be the day when DaD had discovered him behind the shebeen. The day of his rebirth - and the day he killed his first enemy. He asked Okot to remind him what date he had arrived on at the camp and after much more mulling, he picked the number twelve as his age.

Most mornings the boys would wake up just before dawn and was then made to run around the camp in circles for almost an hour before breakfast, constantly being shouted at and encouraged by a man wearing a blue ribbon to push harder and go faster. They would do push-ups and sit-ups and carry heavy objects such as logs or rocks.

As a result of the nutritious meals he was receiving and the constant digging or fitness exercises, Jamba was quickly starting to develop strong and lean muscles. During their shooting practices, the rifle became much lighter in his hands by the day. But still he was not awarded a weapon of his own yet. Jamba badly wanted that day to arrive. He could barely wait for it.

That day would arrive out of the blue.

One evening orders were given for all but those on guard duty to gather in a clearing deep inside the jungle. He left for the area together with Tito who showed him the way. It was a twenty minute walk along a small footpath which they could barely see. But even so, Jamba's night vision had improved dramatically.

There was the shimmering of a large fire as they approached the clearing and the sound of men becoming quite rowdy. Once the boys arrived they stayed well clear of the adults sitting around the fire. The men already gathered there were drinking what smelled like beer and were becoming louder by the minute. The women and the girls from the camp were also present. They all looked rather solemn and never smiled or said a word. Some of the men had pulled girls onto their laps and were groping and fondling them all over. The females offered no resistance as if performing a duty and just resigned themselves to their fate.

Jamba could not remember ever hearing the soldiers making such a racket. It went against everything he had learned over the past weeks. He and Tito joined a group of boys on the outer edge of the circle. Suddenly a horrifying scream cut through the night air, resembling something like a pig being butchered. Everybody fell silent at once.

A man rushed into the firelight, jumping up and down whilst circling his head in wild motions. He was completely naked. White mud covered his face and beard. A necklace consisting of small bones hung from his neck. Jamba was not sure whether the bones were human or animal.

The man fell to the ground and rolled around on the leaf-covered carpet. Then his entire body started shaking violently and spasms ripped through him as though he was being shot repeatedly. All eyes were fixed on him almost in hypnotic trance.

The man stopped shaking and he lay deathly still with his eyes closed and his mouth foaming. Suddenly his eyes opened wide and he just stared towards the sky. Then he threw a white powder into the air and started licking the bones around his neck while still lying prone on his back.

Jamba looked at Tito, puzzled. The boy dared to answer, "It's Mganga, the witch doctor. DaD's spiritual adviser."

Jamba could barely hear what Tito was whispering. The boy was clearly very cautious, even nervous.

Suddenly the witch doctor leaped into the air and left the circle with a wild howl. Almost immediately he returned, triumphantly leading DaD into the light.

DaD was cradling an enormous machine gun under his right arm as if it weighed no more than a standard AK-47. Jamba recognized it as the same gun which was usually mounted on the back of one of the vehicles. It was a Russian 7.62mm PKMS heavy machine gun and must have weighed at least twenty-five pounds. The gun was of such a high caliber that it was sometimes even used as an anti-air weapon against targets such as helicopters.

DaD entered the circle and stood almost frozen in the light of the fire. Then his muscles grew taut and rippled as he raised the gun above his head with both hands. The men cheered and roared as one. Jamba was caught up in the excitement and roared his own approval as he jumped up in the air and punched his small fist.

Some of the soldiers moved away to clear an opening on a large log for DaD to sit on. He laid the mighty PKMS across his knees and was joined by his captains. Two took up positions at his sides and one stood behind him.

"Tomorrow we leave for the border," DaD said in a firm voice impregnated with authority. "I've received some intelligence regarding a group of South African soldiers who are training the government dogs in the DRC. They're said to have many new modern weaponry at their base... including the latest model sniper rifles."

The men roared their approval and again punched the air. The Democratic Republic of the Congo was an enormous country in central Africa with much of it completely inhospitable and inaccessible due to its vast jungles. The 'DRC' as it was commonly referred to was ideal for waging guerrilla warfare. It was also where DaD had his mines.

DaD raised an enormous hand and the men fell silent again. "All combat-ready troops will join in the operation. We'll be walking through the mountains and jungle for at least two days. Carry only your weapons, grenades, water and med-kits. The main reinforcements, ammunition and food will be supplied at our HQ on the other side."

The men listened intently as DaD continued. "This also means our camp here will be vulnerable. Sergeant Wambuzi will take over command and organize shifts and guard duties for those troops who are staying behind. Most of the tunnels are operational and equipped in the event of discovery. New cellphone communications have been established should reinforcements be needed. If the Lord of Chaos looks upon us favorably, we should return within a week." With this he paused and then added, "As always victorious and richer than ever!"

The soldiers jumped up and shouted wildly. Some started chanting, "M... o... D... M... o... D!" and soon others followed. Jamba found himself joining in and being swept away by the wild frenzy of the drunken mob.

Almost at once he could feel a pair of eyes on him. Eyes following his every move like a beast in the night. He looked around him and caught DaD's gaze. The Commander in Chief was staring right at him. Then he motioned Jamba towards him with a flick of his head. The boy started sprinting over to his leader and nearly tripped over a log in his excitement, but remained on his feet and stayed focused on DaD's steady gaze.

Jamba stood at attention. Even when standing up straight he still had to look up at the enormous man sitting in front of him. It was the first time since his arrival at the camp, now so many weeks ago, that he had a face-to-face encounter with DaD. The soldiers realized something was about to happen and fell silent again.

"Jamba," DaD said. Nobody dared to laugh this time. There wasn't even an attempt at a snicker. "I can see that you're fed well. I can see that you've grown stronger. I hear you're learning fast. I've seen the tunnels you've been digging... and I approve."

Jamba felt proud at receiving such open praise from his commander and thrust his chin upward. Without his gaze leaving the boy's eyes, DaD extended his right arm to his side and a captain immediately lay a glistening AK-47 with a reddish wooden rifle butt into his open palm. Its sling consisted of what was once somebody's belt.

DaD presented Jamba with the rifle and the boy accepted it with some hesitation. He very slowly reached out and took the weapon with both hands. Suddenly DaD slapped him hard on the head, but this time it was a blow of approval rather than one in anger.

"Go!" ordered DaD and the boy spun around sharply. He looked around the circle of men staring at him. Instead of immediately leaving, a triumphant smile broke across his face. Emulating his leader's actions earlier on, he instinctively raised the assault rifle above his head with both hands and shouted at the top of his boyish voice, "M... o... D!"

There was a moment of complete silence as the child's spontaneous reaction caught everybody by surprise. Then the men all leaped up as one and cheered.

And with that simple gesture the boy truly became one of them. He was now a full-blooded Merchant of Death. All which remained now was for him to one day trade that Death in battle - either for victory... or his own life.

Jamba was burning to return to the group of boys and show Tito his new prize. He was sure the other boys would be jealous since many of them had been at the camp long before Jamba and still did not carry a rifle. He also badly needed to talk to Yoweri, because he was unsure whether this meant he would be joining the boy in the assault group leaving for the DRC the next day.

Before he was halfway across the clearing, DaD's voice boomed, "Boy!"

Jamba froze. Then he spun around on his heals to face his master.

"Tunnels. Now."

CHAPTER 10

DaD's command needed no explaining. Jamba just nodded and was off like a tracer bullet speeding through the night. Holding on to his rifle tightly and taking great care not to stumble, he followed the faint path back to the camp.

Before heading to the tunnels he had an idea and quickly made for the kitchen. There he grabbed a bunch of bananas and sped off again. He considered taking a box of matches with him also but thought better of it for that might be looked upon as theft and the penalty for stealing was death. At least the bananas were in abundance and certain food rations were often allowed.

He decided on the first tunnel he had dug with Yoweri, Okot and Tito. Somehow it seemed significant and fitting the occasion, ceremonial in a way. When he reached the spot, he uncovered the entrance by moving some dead fern leaves they had placed there. Then he slung the AK-47 across his shoulders and onto his back and without hesitation went diving head-first into the pitch-black hole.

The distances and layout were well-known to him. After all, he was both architect and engineer of this realm. He quickly crawled down the entire length of the primary tunnel, trying to measure the distance. When he thought he was near the bend, he stuck a hand out to the side and traced the wall until he felt it curve away. There were tree roots growing from the sides and the top, some brushing against his face as he continued. He was sure he felt some insects crawl over his hands. It could have been anything from an innocent ant to a poisonous spider. There was no way of telling in the darkness and for the first time the boy felt a twang of discomfort.

As the ghosts started to play tricks on his mind, he entered the final chamber. And that is when his hair literally stood up on the back of his neck. His body went instantly cold and goose bumps covered his arms and legs. From just in front of him came an unmistakable hiss.

The identity of his unwelcome guest was pretty clear. The only question which now remained was whether the snake was poisonous or not. Most were not, but then again many found in this habitat were - and some of them were of the most poisonous on earth.

Visions of all kinds of snakes passed through his mind's eye. There were numerous types of cobras and spitting cobras. This was a possibility. If only he could see whether the snake was standing upright and had a hood. Oh, what difference does it make? he thought to himself.

The most fearsome were the black mambas and green mambas but they were often extremely aggressive and Jamba decided he would already have been bitten by now if that was the case.

The puffadders or gaboon vipers were the cause of most snakebites in the area, because they did not flee like most other snakes tend to do when humans approach, so people step on them more readily. But would they have warned him with a hiss? Jamba had heard terrible stories about gaboon vipers and how much venom was concentrated in their bites.

The boy was frozen to the spot. He dared not move, barely breathed but he had to make a decision and soon. No sudden movements. Should he just remain still like this or risk reversing away slowly? He even considered using his rifle to shoot at the intruder but the weapon was now useless where it rested on his back. He didn't even know whether the magazine was loaded or not.

Sweat started running down his forehead and into his eyes. It was burning like acid. A droplet crawled its way to the tip of his nose and started to itch.

Jamba briefly thought about the irony of his situation. Imagine a soldier dying of a snakebite instead of being killed in battle. It seemed absurd and a waste of purpose.

He usually prided himself on being fearless but the boy was now thoroughly scared. In fact, he was terrified.

In a panic he decided to bolt. It was not really a conscious decision but rather a primitive survival instinct which took hold of him and forced him to flee from danger. He simply could not stand confronting the unknown any more - not being able to see through that utter and complete darkness what was there in front of him, what was threatening his very existence. He needed to face and see his enemy, not this uncertainty of the unknown which was squeezing him around the throat.

At the very same moment that he bolted, he felt a sudden breeze cooling the sweat on his face and the unmistakable texture of scales grazing his cheek. The snake had struck, but by some incalculable odds the attempted bite had missed the boy's face by a fraction. Jamba retreated towards the entrance as fast as his hands and knees could possibly carry him.

He emerged from the hole like the boulders spat from an erupting volcano. After running a few paces he finally stopped and gasped for air. Then he sat down to calm himself and catch his breath. It was all a bit much for the boy and he felt the tears coming.

Tears? This was an emotion alien to him. It is a sign of weakness, he thought and vehemently scolded himself. For a fleeting second he even considered running away from this new life, but the heavy rifle on his back reminded him of his purpose and the elation he had felt earlier when DaD presented him with this symbol of acceptance. Not to mention that desertion and death by execution were synonymous.

Jamba calmed his nerves and collected his thoughts. Once the adrenaline had retreated and his body stopped shaking, he decided to use another tunnel closer to the huts. That way he might also be able to hear what was going on at the camp. He also wondered how they would actually find him or know which tunnel he was in to tell him when his ordeal would be over.

This time the boy carefully searched for a long stick. He would crawl down the new tunnel, poking and exploring the darkness in front of him. He would do so very slowly and very carefully.

After what felt like an eternity, the boy reached the chamber of his new lair where the bucket of water, cloths and pipe were located. He lay back against the cold wall of the tunnel and finally relaxed. Exhaustion overcame him and he dozed off almost immediately.

He didn't know for how long he drifted off but he woke up feeling hungry. The bananas were lost and forgotten. Most probably snake food by now. Jamba sighed and lay back again, wondering how long they would have him stay down here before he could leave. The boy had no idea of the time and regretted not eating more during supper.

With nothing else to do and no company but for himself, the boy had a lot of time to think. He recapped his life and the events which led up to him being here. He stroked his new weapon and wondered what the future had in store. The presence of the *Kalashnikov* in his grip was comforting and made him feel safe again. For as long as it was in his hands he feared nothing.

The boy found himself trying to guess at the number of people who had died after being torn apart by the death emanating from his rifle's cold inner darkness. How many Merchants of Death carried that exact same weapon into battle and how many of them had died falling with it clasped in their hands?

Fear...

He was ashamed of himself, angry. Tonight he felt fear and he almost even cried. No soldier should feel fear. No soldier should flee. What if he was in battle and he ran? The enemy might be just as invisible and just as unknown as that snake was tonight. It may be just as dark when they go into battle and into the unknown.

What if he was overcome by fear and fled the fight? He already knew the answer to that. He would be shot by an officer or another soldier right there on the spot. Right in his fleeing, cowardly back. But what he did not know the answer to was whether he would run in terror or fight bravely like a man, like a soldier, like a Merchant of Death?

Jamba needed to empty his bowels. He knew this had to be done in the tunnels, but it was early and the men would still be out in the jungle getting drunk or preparing for their march the next day. Nobody would notice him going out for a dump. Guards were patrolling deeper into the jungle.

By now it was certain that he would not be joining the team which would be leaving tomorrow or else DaD would never have sent him down into the tunnels tonight. Jamba did not know whether to feel relieved or disappointed.

Before leaving for the exit he had an idea. He hastily started digging upwards so that he could insert the pipe. Not only will it help with the bad air, but he might be able to better hear what was going on at the camp. He dug through in only a couple of minutes. Looking up through the hole, he could actually make out some light coming from faint stars or the moon maybe.

After forcing the pipe through the opening he left his chamber, prodding with his stick in front of him and then crawled out at the exit after a quick scan of his environment.

First he searched for where the pipe broke the surface and then quickly concealed it with some broken branches and leaves. He then did his business and returned to his prison. Before crawling back down he glanced back longingly at the kitchen and wished he had never left the bananas behind with the snake, no matter how much he came to dislike the fruit.

Back to his hole. Back to the loneliness. Back to his thoughts.

Fear...

CHAPTER 11

As he tried to make himself as comfortable as possible, Jamba thought about his training and the way in which the officers spoke to them. Even the way DaD addressed him or the other soldiers. Fear was never mentioned. Nor were the words 'retreat' or 'flee' ever mentioned.

Yet, there were constant reminders and the instilling of other, mostly negative emotions and doctrines. Terms such as hate, anger, kill, death, torture, hell, oppression, destruction and annihilation were constantly used and enforced. More than any other words and in almost every conversation. Other more positive terms were also mentioned though. Words such as victory, honor, respect and pride. These were used mostly in the context of either DaD or the MoD army in its entirety.

That was pretty much the extent of Jamba's encyclopedia of emotions and the only emotions whose meanings were fully understood by him. Or at least as far as any twelve-year-old child could understand them. It was the opposites to these negative emotions however which were sorely lacking from his vocabulary and understanding.

The child had little or no idea of concepts such as love, compassion, mercy, peace, serenity, sadness, joy or even friendship. Friendship was frowned upon as it may influence one's judgment in battle or affect your actions and decisions negatively when you become emotional.

Any loss of life had to be accepted as 'normal'. Thus death itself becomes a part of life. Death being merely an extension of the life they lived as if in some symbiotic relationship. Death was an unavoidable end game in this chess game which was life - and from which no person on earth can ever escape anyway.

Jamba had seen death and had understood its meaning. He had even killed somebody already. Yes, death was part of life.

He did not know what happened after death though. Never had he been exposed to any form of religion which may have indoctrinated his innocent views on it. What happens after death simply never really crossed his mind. For the time being he believed one simply switched off like killing the engine on a pick-up truck. Turn the key and the vehicle comes to life - birth. Turn the key again and the engine stops running – death.

The last time he experienced something resembling sadness was when his mother died. Yet, after that his world became a place of such eternal and constant misery that any sadness simply became fused with what he believed to be 'normality'. Just the constant battle for survival alone left no time for sadness or grief. There were more pressing matters which needed his immediate attention such as the small matter of merely staying alive.

Maybe what he was experiencing at that very moment, being alone by himself in that dark prison called a tunnel, could have been defined as a form of serenity. But the child's mind was never truly calm or tranquil. Constant uncertainty about what awaits tomorrow and even that specter called fear, too often scratched with its claws uninvited. How could it be any different when finding yourself alone in a claustrophobic tunnel, which choked you from all sides in ultimate darkness, buried under the earth as if in a premature grave?

When he accepted his *Kalashnikov* that evening, the boy finally felt some joy. But could that be defined as true joy? Legitimate joy? Is the acceptance of an assault rifle by a mere child a legitimate source of joy? Gifting a child with an instrument whose sole purpose was to snuff the life out of another human being?

These questions did not matter to the boy. For the small twelve-year-old child, Jamba, those concepts and positive emotions such as 'love' and 'compassion' carried very little weight and their meanings were as foreign to him as the existence of the rest of the world outside of their camp.

How could this child ever even begin to understand the complexities of such things as normality, ethics or conscience when he could barely distinguish between such basic principles as good and evil? Does evil not maybe start with the simple lack of conscience within a human being? Is it not that conscience which hinders a person from committing murder or stealing from another?

What Jamba felt for his rifle that night was probably the closest he would come to experiencing love. And only giving that love without receiving any in return. Even his feelings for DaD were based on fear, respect and a sense of duty not to be confused with love. Instead his love could only be projected upon an inanimate object, his *Kalashnikov*.

Thinking about how he never got to show his beloved rifle to Tito, the boy fell asleep. Before he finally drifted off into oblivion, he decided to name his rifle after DaD, his savior and baptist. It will be his secret, to remain a secret only until such time as the weapon would live up to its name for all the world to see.

Death and Destruction... DaD.

CHAPTER 12

Some time during the night he woke up with his teeth chattering uncontrollably. His entire body was shivering. The ground was freezingly cold and moist. His shorts and T-shirt offered no insulation or protection but had rather absorbed much of the moisture and was soaked through.

He curled himself into a fetal ball and tried to sleep as best he could. He was constantly itching. Unknown and unseen insects were crawling all over his body and into places he did not even know existed. The sleep came and went in bouts of nightmares. Jamba dreamed he was drowning in a lake of crawling critters, then struggling to advance against a strong wind which was pelting his body with freezing hail and rain. He would attempt to scream but could not utter a sound against the raging tempest.

The boy woke up for the umpteenth time, this time due the familiar call of the whistle. Instinctively he jumped to get ready, just to hit his head against the roof of the tunnel and immediately being reminded of where he was.

It was still pitch dark and he peered up the pipe to see whether there was any sign of daylight outside. There was none. His teeth wouldn't stop chattering and he begged the sun to please just rise. The boy pushed his ear up against the pipe to listen for any signs of what was going on outside at the camp.

Over here he heard the door of a vehicle slam shut, over there a chicken clucking frantically as if trying to get out of somebody's way. He could even make out the noise of the radio static and then realized there was a conversation taking place. It was all just a muffled jumble of words to him though.

Jamba could not stand the freezing, damp cold any more. He needed to somehow heat up or he was surely going to die in there. As if to add further insult to his already-miserable predicament, drops of water started running down the pipe and dripping onto his legs. He again listened carefully near the pipe's entrance and could make out the unmistakable sound of rain hammering against the leaves outside.

He needed to move. Almost forgetting about his rifle he slung it onto his back as an afterthought. The cold had numbed his senses and slowed his thinking. Even the chilly metal of the AK was biting him and felt as if though it might freeze stuck solid against his skin.

Again using his long stick to prod the darkness, he crawled to the entrance. There he stood upright in the vertical shaft with only his head poking out. Although it was pouring with rain, the warm, humid air instantly hugged his body. The rains came and went unpredictably in these areas. It never really got cold, even when it rained and even that early in the morning it was pretty warm already.

The camp was a hive of activity. He could make out the silhouettes of men and boys standing in huddles and smoking cigarettes. The headlamps of a vehicle was used to cast light on the proceedings, raindrops slanting across its beams. Some of the men had small backpacks strapped to their backs whilst others had only belts with several ammunition pouches tied around their waists. The older men all wore boots, camouflage pants and black vests. The boys were barefoot and just like Jamba, wore only shorts and dirty T-shirts.

Maybe the boots and camo pants don't come in small sizes yet, Jamba thought to himself.

He saw the large figure of DaD moving among the group, his massive PKMS machine gun casually resting on his shoulders with his arms hooked around it. Somebody switched off the lights of the vehicle and with that the small army started to march.

Jamba practiced his counting and thought he counted about thirty people. One by one they disappeared into a thicket and they were gone within seconds, silent as cats, barely breaking a branch.

Suddenly he was grabbed by the hair and his head violently snapped backwards. The cold blade of a knife was at his throat and he was certain he could feel a trickle of blood crawling down his neck.

A face appeared above him, ugly, bearded and belonging to a mouth without any teeth. The foul stench of rotten breath hit Jamba in the face with its full force. "Don't move", the toothless mouth spat at him.

He didn't want to move. The knife which pressed against his throat felt awfully sharp. There were definitely drops of blood running down onto his T-shirt already - warm and sticky blood.

"You a spy, huh? Looks like a spy to me heh, Castro?" The ugly face turned his head to address a man standing next to him, a man so dark that he was almost not visible.

"Yes, a spy," the Castro person mumbled in a voice which sounded terribly bored and tired of life.

"No! No! I'm Jamba. DaD sent me to the tunnels and gave me my *Kalashnikov* at the fire last night!" the boy rambled anxiously, panic now only nanoseconds away.

These were not the street kids of Kampala's shanty towns. These guys were hardened veterans who had probably killed more people than Jamba had meals in his life.

What if they were the enemy? The thought choked him just as ferociously as the awkward position of his tilted neck and the blade scraping against his Adam's apple.

The man almost predictably laughed at hearing the boy's name which was a very bad thing, since it made that salient object in his hand quiver and grate up and down Jamba's neck almost uncontrollably.

"We weren't at no fire. We're doing patrolling," the ugly face replied. "How can we be sure you didn't just spy on the fire also?" he demanded from the boy.

Jamba had to convince them. He had to think and answer carefully. His thoughts tripped up and stumbled over themselves within his brain.

"Sergeant Wambuzi. Sergeant Oboto. Yoweri. Tito. Okot," he rambled on. "DaD named me Jamba. I gather the firewood. I built these tunnels!"

The knife disappeared from his throat and a hand plucked him from the hole as if he was a mere sack of feathers. Nails bit into his scalp and he was certain that he had lost half his hair. The boy was stripped of his rifle and then shoved towards the camp. Jamba was feeling sorry for himself and sulking. He knew that only bad things could come from this.

They stopped near the parade area and Castro sauntered off somewhere. No-tooth stared at Jamba with something resembling disgust on his face. He permanently grinned that ugly toothless smirk of his.

Sergeant Wambuzi appeared out of nowhere and careened over to them. He took Jamba's AK-47 from the man and after a short conversation dismissed him with a, "Piss off, Bubba".

Jamba knew this was not good. He knew he was in serious trouble this time. Or as Wambuzi often stated, in deep shit.

The sergeant started with a list of allegations, ticking them each off on his fingertips as he recited. "Let me see if I've got this straight. Firstly, against direct orders, you left your tunnel. Secondly, you were disarmed and your rifle was taken from you. Thirdly, you spilled the names of the entire army to men you don't know and which names included mine and that of DaD. Am I correct?" Wambuzi's eyes were wide in expectation of some explanation.

The boy was in a corner and had little choice. For once he was thinking straight again. "Yes, sir. But I heard sounds and went to investigate. They surprised me and put a knife to my throat. I had to convince them or they would have cut me up. I knew they were our men, sir, so I used names to convince them." Much of it were half-truths but he felt as if he was fighting for his life all over again.

Images of toiling in diamond mines, floggings, beatings and firing squads flashed before his mind's eye and he saw juicy chunks of meat in tasty stews vanishing forever. This is bad man! His day was turning out to be an utter abortion before the sun even broke the horizon.

Sergeant Wambuzi offered no verdict. Instead he only sent Jamba back to his hole. At the very least he returned the boy's rifle to him which was a small consolation.

Not knowing what was going to happen to him later on was as bad as any physical torture. The boy spent most of the morning in his underground prison battering himself psychologically with images of death, banishment and slavery. He developed diarrhea and had to go more than once. This time he simply dug a hole in the tunnel floor and filled it in again after doing his business.

The emotion he was experiencing was in stark contrast to the elation he felt the previous night at the fire. His entire world came crashing down in an instant as his pedestal was chopped from underneath him. And all because he felt cold and damp and needed some heat to survive.

There was a faint light now penetrating the tunnel, almost not noticeable, yet there. The boy could only just make out the contours of his hands and that of his rifle. He decided to unclip the magazine and to count the cartridges. He counted twelve rounds.

This puzzled him a bit. Jamba counted the cartridges again and then checked the chamber of the rifle to make sure he didn't miss something. The count remained twelve. It seemed an odd number for the bullets in a thirty-round magazine. Maybe it was pure coincidence. Just some random reload by whoever prepared the rifle for him.

The only connection he could find with the number 'twelve' was his age. But surely nobody could have known for certain. And what purpose did it serve anyway? DaD being 'nice' or even funny?

He spent the next few hours occasionally rehydrating himself with water from the bucket, feeling terribly hungry and wondering what it must be like to be shot in the head or stomach. It was a very bleak and miserable start to his day indeed.

Chapter 13

He heard the whistle again at around midday and knew that most of the other boys were having their lunch. His hunger pains were becoming quite severe but he has had worse days back in Kampala. Knowing that they were eating a nice, hot meal only yards away was torturous though.

Pins and needles ran through his legs and he crawled over to the dog-leg to get some circulation back. He peered around the corner and saw plenty of light entering the tunnel. It was a welcome sight and he spent some time just sitting there and concentrating on the rays. It even managed to make him feel a bit warmer. The walls and floor of the tunnel were still cold and damp, but at least it was slightly warmer now and his shivers had stopped.

Jamba saw a shadow move at the entrance, interrupting the flow of light. Something was up. He waited and listened intently but nobody called. The movements and noises increased. He saw some liquid being poured into the tunnel. First just a few drops and then what must have been at least a gallon started splattering onto the muddy tunnel floor.

This was not right. Was somebody taking a pee up there? The smell of gasoline suddenly hit his nose with a force. Jamba knew he had to move fast. As he was about to turn towards his chamber, he heard a 'whoosh!' and the entrance exploded into flames. The fire lapped at the roots growing from the walls and roof of the tunnel entrance. Smoke started to billow towards him. The heat blasted his body and face like an open furnace.

The boy scrambled for the lid of the oil drum and struggled to plug the entrance at the dog-leg which was leading to his chamber. The fit was a good one and well-planned.

Smoke started creeping in between the lid and the walls. Jamba grabbed a cloth and dipped it into the bucket of water. He held the cloth over his nose and mouth but something kept nagging him at the back of his mind.

There shouldn't be so much smoke. The open pipe! It created a draft and was ventilating the smoke. He hurried to plug the pipe with the other cloth. It needed a few attempts as darkness once again completely enveloped him. He had no idea whether his plan worked or not. There was no way to see.

The boy removed the cloth from his mouth and took a careful breath. There was still smoke in the chamber. Lying with his face near the ground he breathed slowly and deeply through the damp material. His eyes were stinging now. It felt as if a block of concrete was pressing down on his chest and his lungs started to burn.

Were they trying to kill him or test him?

Since last night his waking hours have been saturated by fear, even terror. The encounter with the snake, the damp cold, the knife to his throat. The uncertainty of his future punishment. Now this!

Tears were rolling down his cheeks. Jamba was not sure whether it was only because of the smoke or whether he was in fact crying. He was in denial. No, I'm not crying, he assured himself. The boy was now angry - at his situation, at his tormentors and at his own weaknesses.

"*Putas!*" he swore loudly at the world and at his unknown assailants. He actually hoped that they could hear him. Was it No-tooth and Castro? Or maybe Wambuzi? He repeated the insult for good measure and felt better.

Feeling suddenly thirsty, he scooped some water into his hands and slurped up a few drops. Then he dunked the cloth again and covered his face. The smoke seemed to have dissipated almost entirely.

He tested the air with a few careful breaths and was certain. For just a moment he unplugged the pipe and took a few deep breaths from it before shoving the cloth back inside.

Then there was a loud explosion. It felt like his eardrums had popped right out of his head and the ground shook violently. Chunks of mud and gravel fell on him. The poisonous claws of terror were tearing away at his insides again. He badly wanted to start digging upwards and break the surface. Wanted to get himself the hell out of that grave.

But once again his fear turned to anger. And this time his anger tuned into rage and hatred. Something within the child had snapped. Something had broken and shattered - perhaps even permanently. He lost all self-control and started screaming at his tormentors again and again.

"*Putas! Filhos da Putas!* You mothers! You bitches! *Putas!*"

Jamba was breathing heavily from the exertion and the release of the hate-filled poison which had been contained in his rage. He decided with some gratification that his own angry explosion had closely matched whatever shook his prison a few moments earlier.

Once again the boy curled himself up into a tight ball, but this time hugging his beloved rifle close to his chest. The cold steel was comforting. His ears were still ringing, his eyes were still burning and breathing was difficult. He was cold again, hungry and lonely. But he had DaD with him.

"*Putas...*" he whispered.

CHAPTER 14

The assault on his senses had finally ceased. His ears were still ringing faintly and his body was aching badly.

Jamba could hear the rustling of leaves outside and footstep near the pipe. He tensed himself for more attacks. The pipe might be discovered soon.

A voice called from the direction of the tunnel entrance. "Jamba! You can come out now boy!" It sounded like Sergeant Wambuzi but he wasn't certain. His head was hurting too much.

He decided that he will face them prepared this time. It may be a trap. Jamba checked the magazine of his rifle with his fingertips, clipped it back into the *Kalashnikov* and fed a round into the chamber. He was armed and ready. They can try their worst.

The boy violently kicked the lid of the oil drum out of his way, then peered around the dog-leg and observed the situation. The tunnel smelled of smoke and gasoline. Part of the entrance had collapsed and there was no immediate movement visible there. Then an upside-down head popped into the shaft and seemed to be searching the darkness within.

It was Wambuzi. The boy doubted whether the sergeant could see him. "Come on, boy. It's lunchtime." And with that the head disappeared again.

He started crawling towards the light at the end of the tunnel, shuffling on his knuckles and elbows as he gripped the loaded rifle in both hands. Black soot covered the walls all around him.

Jamba peered up the shaft, blinked as the sharp light stabbed him in the eyes and saw a sea of faces staring down at him. It almost seemed like some ceremonial welcoming committee.

Most of the boys from the camp were there waiting for him outside. The boy pulled himself from the half-collapsed hole and blinked again. He was enveloped in grime. His clothes were completely soaked and covered in soot and mud. Clots of dirt and the remains of burnt roots were stuck in his hair. He smelled of gasoline and diarrhea.

There was open admiration on the faces of some of the boys. None of them had rifles. None of them had ever run the gauntlet of the tunnels before. Jamba had and Jamba survived. The boys just stood around and stared at him.

Sergeant Wambuzi was standing to one side and simply stated, "Shower. Eat. Debrief. Sleep. You've got guard duty tonight." His face was expressionless and the boy couldn't read anything in it.

Jamba slowly unclipped his magazine and then discharged the round in the chamber. He picked up the cartridge, blew some dirt off it and slid it back into the magazine. Then he replaced the clip into the rifle and started walking in the direction of the showers.

Wambuzi and the boys watched his metamorphosis from an angry combat-ready soldier to a tired and hungry little boy dragging his aching body towards the camp.

He showered quickly but did not enjoy it because the damp cold from the tunnel was still biting at him right down to his bones. His rifle always stayed within an arm's length, well within reach. The kitchen was a welcome sight and he helped himself to leftover soup consisting of meat and mashed peas. His strength returned almost instantly as the warm food entered his system.

Jamba sat dead still for a few minutes enjoying the moment. Then he got up with a purpose and went in search of Wambuzi. No sense in prolonging the inevitable.

He found the sergeant where he was busy scratching around the back of a pick-up looking for something. The boy silently stood at attention behind him, occasionally glancing towards the man in impatient anticipation.

Wambuzi eventually turned and started his debriefing. "You did well in the tunnels today. However, shouting at the enemy isn't really encouraged. You want to keep them guessing if there is actually anybody down there or whether they're still alive. Advertising yourself defeats that purpose."

He turned back to searching the rear of the vehicle and

emerged with a hammer. Then he pulled up his pants around the wooden leg and started tapping at the wood near his knee.

While tapping away he continued. "Being disarmed is a serious offense. Two days of extra guard duty and two days of extra duty monitoring the radio." The sergeant inspected his wooden leg carefully. "And we need a new toilet pit," he added.

Jamba felt a wave of relief roll over him. It seems he had escaped the diamond mines or being shot - for now. *Extra* guard duty before he had even done one shift in his entire life was not an ideal start though.

While the sergeant continued hammering away at his home-made prosthetic limb, Jamba had a burning question.

"Why did those two men not join the assault group, sir?" he ventured. "They are veterans." The boy stated the obvious.

Wambuzi's face pulled into a grimace which resembled disgust and mumbled something about drugs and fried brains. The soldiers often used drugs during assaults to make them even more aggressive and fearless. But prolonged abuse had turned some men into a danger to themselves and a danger for the entire operation. 'High risk encumbrance' as Wambuzi called it.

He dismissed the boy and told him to get some sleep. Somebody will wake him for guard duty.

Jamba first struggled to fall asleep, but eventually boredom and the exertions – or torture – of the past hours caught up with him. For once he actually wrapped himself in his blanket, his rifle snug against him. It felt as if though he had only just closed his eyes for a moment when the tip of a boot nudged him in the ribs.

The boy looked up drowsily and slightly annoyed, then recoiled violently. In a lightning fast movement he had discarded the blanket and without even thinking about it, his AK-47 was aimed straight at the ugly, toothless face staring down at him.

"Easy boy. You might hurt somebody with dat," the man hissed at him. Again his foul breath assaulted Jamba's face, even from a distance. "Move your arse. We've got rounds to do," No-tooth said and slouched off.

This must be Wambuzi's idea of a bad joke, Jamba thought to himself. Or just piling on more punishment. The nightmares of the past day were turning into a hell. Even the threat of having to toil in the diamond mines as some form of punishment started to sound devoid of any real worry or suffering.

He rolled up his blanket and made sure to check his weapon before following Bubba out of the hut. The man was patiently waiting for him outside. Jamba purposefully made a spectacle of checking his rifle and magazine again. There was a smirk on No-tooth's face. The boy noticed Sergeant Wambuzi where he was sitting outside one of the huts cleaning parts of an AK-47 he had disassembled. Wambuzi paid no attention to them.

Bubba started walking off in the direction of the jungle and Jamba followed wearily and for the most part unwillingly. It was still light, but as they entered the undergrowth, the rays diminished quite rapidly.

Then Bubba started on his instructions. "I'll show you the route we have to patrol. We have to patrol for four hours. No talking, no smoking and no sleeping. Sleeping on guard duty is punished by death."

The boy reflected on how this new life of his seemed to be entirely ruled by and governed by death. Death was prescribing the laws of life. There was the possibility of death during conflict, death for stealing or death for disobeying orders. Death for fighting a fellow soldier. Death for deserting and death for lying. Death was everywhere and death was the norm. The Hand of Death was defining the child's perception of 'normality'.

They walked in single file following a faint path. Ignoring his own advice regarding silence, Bubba continued to make some remark every few minutes. It was as if his sole purpose was to irritate the boy rather than to give him advice or instructions.

"You've gotta stay alert," he muttered. "There are many wild animals here. A leopard will claw your back and rip out your throat before you even knew it was there." The man just kept walking while babbling on. Jamba had never seen a leopard but knew of their ferocious and infamous reputation.

Bubba spat at the ground and continued. "I've heard many stories of spirits wandering the jungles. I've seen a man foaming at the mouth, screaming and kicking after one patrol. His comrade had to knock him out because he attacked him after demons apparently instructed him to do so."

No-tooth glanced in his direction to check what impact his words had on the boy. Jamba was starting to feel uneasy but did his best not to show it. He was carrying his rifle in both hands instead of slinging it over a shoulder, gripping it tighter than necessary.

Bubba continued unabated. "Then there's the enemy. They lie in ambush to tear you apart with their bullets or slash your throat with a knife," and at this he turned towards the boy and grinned with a perverse expression of satisfaction on his face.

Jamba's eyes were involuntarily drawn towards No-tooth's side where that enormous and familiar blade was hanging from his belt, tucked into a yellowish leather sheath.

"Sometimes they plant mines in your path," he said after enjoying the uneasiness he saw in the boy's eyes. "The mines are just big enough to blow off your leg or your foot. Then you lie there and slowly die of pain while your blood and guts spill out onto the earth."

Jamba attempted to picture himself lying on the ground, gushing blood everywhere and trying to stuff his intestines back into his body - all alone and not a person nearby to help him or even willing to help him.

Almost as if reading his mind Bubba said, "We leave soldiers like that behind. They're a hindrance, an obstacle. If you want to help a man like that you will just be slowed down and be killed yourself. Heroes are only heroes once they are dead heroes. The only hero is a dead hero, boy."

The man suddenly stopped and was listening intently. Jamba could feel the tension in the air and was very alert. He was not sure whether this nasty creature was trying to play more tricks on him or were being serious.

The stories had coiled his nerves into a tight ball in the pit of his stomach. Bubba had dropped onto one knee in front of the boy. Jamba followed suit without needing instructions. He realized his rifle was shaking in his hands and becoming heavier by the second. It was so quiet that his ears were ringing and he could literally hear the blood pumping through the veins near his skull.

He saw Bubba slowly and quietly slide a round into his rifle and Jamba followed his example. It was almost completely dark by now. In the distance he could now suddenly hear leaves rustle and branches breaking. The coil in his stomach tensed even more and was ready to snap or make him vomit. There were not supposed to be any people here, not even other guards. And the enemy was supposed to be many miles away on the other side of the mountains.

The familiar feeling of having to face the unknown in complete darkness again started to crawl up Jamba's back with its sharp claws. The claws were digging in deeper and deeper at each passing moment. His rifle was feeling even more leaden and he flicked the lever to remove the safety. Then his hours of training reminded him to make sure that the lever position was set to rapid fire and not fully automatic. It was. His finger was itching to pull the trigger. His nerves seemed to be controlling that same finger wrapped around the metal trigger. He had to force himself to relax his grip before he accidentally fired a shot.

The rustling was drawing closer. Branches now kept breaking wildly and randomly. No enemy would move through the jungle in such a chaotic and careless manner. Then the boy heard snorting. Almost like a man trying to clear his throat to spit a streak of phlegm or like a man being strangled slowly.

Jamba at once had vivid images of demons chasing him and ripping his throat out. He had no idea what a demon looked like, but his mind drew clear and fantastic images in front of his eyes. He was now certain he could see leaves moving nearby and they were moving in their direction, faster and faster, gathering pace.

Then the Lord of Chaos once again took charge of his world. The rustling of the leaves turned into crashing. The breaking of twigs and branches sounded like small explosions. The chaos was avalanching towards them. The boy heard squeals which sounded as if they were emerging from the pits of hell itself. Even more chilling than the witch doctor Mganga's blood-curdling display that night at the fire. The demons were upon them.

Jamba fired his rifle. He did not bother to take proper aim. Instead he just pointed the muzzle in the general direction of the approaching mayhem. The boy did not bother counting two rounds at a time either. He just continued squeezing off round after round. Tat-tat-tat-tat-tat.

Bubba had followed his cue. But the difference in their experience was clear. The veteran was on one knee taking careful aim and squeezing off only two rounds at a time. Then he paused, aimed and squeezed again.

Jamba's own assault came to an abrupt end. His twelve cartridges were spent within moments. His eyes grew wide in horror as a dark blob came hurtling towards him, then stumbling and then sliding and skidding over the muddy jungle floor. As if arrested by some invisible hand, the blob came to an abrupt stop barely inches from where the boy was kneeling. An enormous, hairy snout spurting dark blood lay buried in a pile of leaves just in front of him. Two massive tusks, the size of curved machetes, were protruding upward from below the bleeding snout.

The boy's heart was pounding in his throat and he was breathing heavily. Sweat was pouring down his face and his arms felt paralyzed. He was utterly hypnotized by the huge head of the carcass lying in front of him.

Bubba's voice tore him from his trance. The man was talking on a cellphone almost in a whisper. "It's Bubba here. Ignore the shots, sergeant. We were attacked by a forest hog." He pushed a button and returned the phone to a trouser pocket.

For the next three hours they continued their patrol in silence. The boy struggled to concentrate and kept replaying the attack over and over in his mind. At some stage Bubba had given him five cartridges and spat some insults at him regarding firing wildly and not aiming properly. The boy did not give it any attention. Even when he became thirsty and realized he had forgotten to bring any water with him, he hardly took any notice of the other man.

All he could think of was firing his AK until it was empty and a huge head with sharp tusks staring up at him. His weapon had finally been introduced to the art of inflicting death.

Yes, that particular rifle may have done so many times before, but this time it was in Jamba's hands when it wielded that force of death.

The killing had begun.

CHAPTER 15

Early the next morning Jamba, Tito, Okot and two other boys returned to the spot where the giant forest hog was still lying. Some wild animal had taken a few bites from the carcass during the night.

The boys immediately discarded any notion of carrying the beast back to camp. The carcass was enormous. It must have measured close to seven feet from snout to tail. Eventually they tied its legs together with a rope and unceremoniously dragged the hog back to the village.

It was hard work and the distance felt like ten miles. What took them only less than an hour's hike towards the location of the carcass, turned into a three hour struggle in the opposite direction. While four boys pulled, a fifth boy did his best to cover their tracks as much as possible by sweeping a branch over the drag marks.

Once they had returned, somebody emerged with a scale which had a sharp hook attached to one end. The scale was tied to a thick overhanging branch of a tree and the hog hoisted into the air until the rope which tied its hind legs together caught on the hook.

The proper name for the animal was not 'the Giant forest hog' without good reason. This particular specimen weighed over six hundred pounds. It was a monster and as big as they get.

Some of the men whistled and a couple of boys patted Jamba on the back. Surprisingly Bubba did not try to claim the honors for himself. Instead he just wandered off and disappeared.

Sergeant Wambuzi was his usual uncomplimentary self. Why didn't he take a full cartridge with him? Why did he fire so wildly? Why didn't he count his shots? Why this and why that.

All Jamba could do was apologize and take the heat. It will not happen again, sergeant. My first patrol, sergeant. I *did* manage to kill the pig, sergeant. And so on. He was dismissed and reminded about the new toilet pit which needed digging. And it needed digging at that very moment.

The boy sulkily dragged himself away to follow orders. He had become an expert at digging. The pit had to be three feet by three feet wide and just over six feet deep. Jamba started on the job completely resigned to his fate. Even as he worked, his beloved *Kalashnikov* hung from its strap across his back.

It took him the entire morning and most of the afternoon. The heat was unforgiving and his hands were developing stinging blisters even though they were already hardened and calloused from all the tunneling he had done previously. The spade kept slipping and as he burrowed deeper it was impossible not to have lumps of dirt fall back into his eyes when he flung it from the hole.

Nearing completion and with his mind completely distracted by all the events of the past days, Jamba realized too late that he was not going to be able to get out of the pit. He jumped up and grabbed the edge of the hole, but the loose dirt around the pit was damp and muddy and he kept slipping back. All his attempts failed. Deciding it was not the end of the world, he sat down on the ground and continued to wait for anybody to pass by who happened to need the toilets. He whistled a few tunes and practiced his counting.

The boy did not have to wait very long. He heard some footsteps and called out. A head appeared over the edge.

"*Puta!*" the boy swore under his breath. He couldn't believe it. When was this nightmare ever going to end? He politely asked Bubba to give him a helping hand out of there.

The man replied by spitting down at him. Jamba first scowled and then swore loudly as he watched with disgust when No-tooth casually unzipped his fly and started urinating on him. He covered his face and tried in vain to evade the yellow liquid pouring onto him in a thick arch.

When he was done, Bubba disappeared without a word. The boy tried to dry his face with his dirty and urine-soaked T-shirt. Suddenly the light was blocked out and he saw a large plank with a circular hole cut in it being rested across the opening. A man then continued to undo his pants and sat down on it.

Jamba was now horrified. *"Puta! Filho da puta!"* he screamed up at Bubba. The first feces hit his arm and the boy squeezed himself tightly into a corner in an effort to avoid it. He managed to stay out of the way of the human waste but wherever it hit the ground it splattered all over his legs. The smell was indescribably vile and it was chocking him. He started retching and it was only worsened as the taste and smell of his own vomit mingled with that of the feces the defecating man above him was discharging into the pit.

His ordeal ended in a flurry of leaves dropping onto him from above. Then Bubba was gone. Jamba spent the next minutes plotting his revenge. For the first time in his short life he planned and premeditated in great detail a hundred different ways in which to murder another human being. No, not a human being. A savage monster.

After what felt like an eternity, somebody else arrived at the pit and Jamba noticed he was busy undoing his pants. The boy called out in a voice teetering on the brink of panic and saw a boy he hardly knew peering down at him in disbelief.

"Get me out of here," Jamba said. It was not a request. The other boy discarded the plank which was covering the toilet and reached a hand out towards the miserable creature in the hole. Then he quickly let go of the trapped boy when he realized what his arm was covered in. Jamba stepped into splotches of liquid containing human waste and vomit.

"Just get me outta here, *puta*! And if you say just one word to the others I'll kill you." There was so much anger and conviction in Jamba's voice that the boy realized he would probably act on that threat. After much slipping and sliding, the foul-smelling Jamba was eventually rescued from his hell.

Reaching the camp he did his best to avoid running into anybody and made a straight line for the showers. He tried to clean himself as thoroughly as possible but couldn't refrain himself from retching continuously. After the long shower he left for the lower part of the stream where he washed his clothes, scrubbing them with a nearby stone.

Back at the village he looked around to see whether he could spot Bubba anywhere, but the man was nowhere to be seen. It was time for him to eat something before his shift in the radio room was supposed to start, but the boy had no appetite. He lay down on his blanket plotting some more revenge.

A boy with a runny nose interrupted his vengeful thoughts and informed him that he was needed in the radio room. Jamba gathered his rifle and got up without as much as a nod.

Chapter 16

Manning the radio was uncomplicated but boring and tedious work. The orders were simple. Listen for an incoming transmission and then find Sergeant Wambuzi. The call-sign should be something along the lines of, 'This is the clinic calling doctor Umdada.'

Jamba spent a few minutes staring at the Tupperware containing the diamonds. What if he ran away with all of it? He could run to India - even though he had no idea where that was, but it sounded good. In an attempt to stifle his gnawing curiosity he looked around the hut for other distractions.

For the first time Jamba noticed an FM/AM radio on the floor next to the beer crate which was serving as a table for the military radio. It was a small instrument with two dials and a single speaker. Intriguingly there was a lever protruding from one side. The boy had never seen such a contraption before.

He fiddled with the knobs and dials but nothing happened. The radio remained silent. Then he gave the lever a few twists and it made a whining sound as he turned it in a few circles. To his amazement the radio came to life. It had to be some kind of power source, like when one winds up a watch.

He gave the lever a few more twists and listened to the music pouring from the small speaker. It was a soothing tune with bongos and a kora. The music abruptly ended and a female voice in a heavy twanging accent which he failed to recognize said, "*This is the Voice of America.*" It was followed by a short jingle and then the woman's voice continued. "*It is now six o'clock Central African Time and here follows the news...*"

Jamba had to concentrate very hard to understand every word the woman was saying. The foreign accent was so thick he could barely make out whole sentences.

"*The government of the DRC today confirmed that a group of South African soldiers were ambushed by rebel forces. The South Africans were working in their capacity of supplying logistical training for the government of the DRC. According to a statement by a military spokesperson, twelve South African* soldiers were killed in the ambush. In a phone call to VOA, the leader of one rebel group insisted that they had killed as many as fifty South African combatants. He however refused to state which rebel group is claiming responsibility for the attack."

Jamba's jaw dropped. This was the assault DaD was talking about! He wondered whether he should call Wambuzi, but was completely rooted to the spot as if magnetized. He simply *had* to know what else happened during the attack.

The voice continued in a monotonous, almost disconnected tone. "*An anonymous South African source claimed that as many as six hundred rebels had been killed in the defensive manoeuvres which followed the assault. According to the source, many rebels surrendered and a ceasefire was brokered. The rebel leader denied these claims and stated that his forces had captured an undisclosed number of soldiers and also took possession of numerous new weapons which included the latest in sniper rifle technology.*"

The boy was so excited that he could jump out of his own skin. But six hundred of their men captured? He could not even count to six hundred. Was the MoD army really that massive? And so many killed and captured in a single battle? The numbers were swimming in front of Jamba's eyes and he tried to picture wave after wave of men firing wildly at the enemy.

The radio died and Jamba frantically wound it up again. "*One South African soldier who was talking to the VOC on condition of anonymity stated that he saw numerous children taking part in the battle. According to the soldier, children as young as ten-years-old were firing at them with assault rifles. He stated that it was an horrific ordeal having to shoot at children. 'It was kill or be killed. I will never forget it for as long as I live. I will never forget their faces,' he said in the interview.*"

The boy jumped up as if he was hit by a bolt of lightning and bulldozed his way out the door in search of Sergeant Wambuzi. He found him in his hut near the kitchen where he was busy taking a nap. Jamba excitedly started blurting out what he had heard on the radio and Wambuzi had to shout at him to calm him down and then made him repeat everything slowly.

They left for the radio hut but the bulletin was over. Instead of the news bulletin there was a heated debate going on regarding whether 'logistical support' meant you are actively taking part in the war or that you are simply a consultant in a manner of speaking. This was all too complicated for Jamba to understand.

Wambuzi took the small radio with him and disappeared. He left the boy sulking and subconsciously kicking at phantom stones lying on the floor. Jamba spent most of the remaining couple of hours picking his nose and planning even crueler methods of torturing and killing Bubba. Occasionally he mimicked shooting at the enemy and telling them in some detail what *putas* they were. He stroked his AK-47 lovingly.

Outside a light drizzle started to tap on the roof of the hut. A few drops splattered on the floor near him. The rain intensified. Soon it was a torrent and the drops inside the hut turned into small cascades.

The military radio was only emitting static. It was a thoroughly boring evening. He had a quick peek at the rough diamonds lying snug in one of the plastic containers but decided to rather abandon the exercise before he just ended up in more trouble. 'Trouble' had become his middle name lately and Jamba didn't appreciate that feeling very much.

When it rains, it pours.

CHAPTER 17

Everybody in camp ate extremely well for the next couple of days. They had hog stew, hog soup, barbecued hog and hog sandwiches. The women had cured the remaining meat and hung it in the kitchen to dry. There was always some girl on duty armed with a large leaf which she constantly fanned in an attempt to keep the flies from laying eggs in the meat.

Jamba compared this to digging toilet pits and did not envy the women. They still never spoke a word and rarely even looked the boy in the eye. In a sense they reminded him of his mother. That same tired, cold and indifferent look in their eyes. Resigned to their fate and just going through the motions as if it was some unavoidable duty which needed performing and from which there will never be any escape.

He went out on patrol several more times and taking different routes. Thankfully this time he accompanied Bubba's friend Castro. The man was as quiet as a corpse. This suited Jamba just perfectly. Neither of them uttered a word, not even when they left the camp or stopped to examine a track or some broken branches.

Castro seemed very tranquil compared to Bubba, but the boy knew that looks could be deceiving and reminded himself of the reasons why the two men did not join the main army for the assault on the South Africans' position.

And then the day arrived when some of the soldiers of the mighty and victorious MoD finally returned to camp. It was to become a day and a night so filled with incredulous events that Jamba would not forget it for as long as he lived.

The previous afternoon Sergeant Wambuzi had gathered all the people in the camp with the familiar whistle and continued to explain that some of the soldiers would be returning the next day. DaD had contacted him on the cellphone and he gave very specific instructions, including for guard patrols to be extra alert - preferably out of the way - and not to accidentally engage them in combat on their route back.

That evening the boy could barely sleep in his excitement and rolled around for hours contriving fantastical stories of battle and valor

An odd feeling had woken him in the middle of the night. He immediately felt uneasy and something just seemed out of sorts. The boy listened intently at his surroundings. All he could hear was the snoring of a couple of the boys nearby. Then a steely hand clasped down on his mouth and forced his head so hard against the ground that the cartilage of his left ear almost shattered.

A familiar and foul breath whispered in his ear, "If you want to live, come with me, boy."

He searched for his rifle with a hand, but No-tooth had already taken possession of it. It needed only the sight of that enormous blade being waved in front of his eyes to shut him up and make him get up quickly but quietly.

Bubba walked behind him as stealthily as a cat and prodded the boy between the shoulder blades. He shoved him in the direction of the kitchen hut and then motioned for the boy to circle behind it. There he grunted for him to stop.

Jamba turned slowly and looked Bubba in the eyes. The orbs were all glassy and watery and fogged over. He was swaying slightly and there was a huge black hole gaping at the boy from between fat, bearded lips.

"What do you want, *Puta*?" Deep, dark hatred and disgust were seething within the boy. The flickering red of his rage almost blinded him as it tore at his vision.

"Shut up!" the savage swaying in front of him hissed. "I like little boys. But I don't like you. I wanna to teach you a little lesson. Know what I mean?" He grabbed hold of his crotch and shoved it in Jamba's direction.

The boy did not quite know what the man meant, but he knew that this can only mean very bad things. Suddenly the tip of that big blade was pushing against his throat. It nicked him and burned like the sting of a hornet. Another hand grabbed hold of the front of his shirt.

"Pull down your pants!" Bubba's voice was louder now. He was forgetting himself and had started to tremble. Jamba just stared at him. He was not scared this time. All he could feel was uncontrollable rage and perfect, blind hatred building toward boiling point. He was going to kill this demon who was pushing a knife against his throat. He was going to fight him and kill him even if it meant dying while trying.

"Your pants!"

"No!"

They were now both shouting. In one movement Jamba swung his left arm towards the hand holding the knife whilst he spread the fingers of his right hand into an open fan and stabbed at Bubba's eyes.

The knife tore through his forearm as if the flesh consisted of melted butter. Bubba winced and retreated as the boy's fingers darted at his eyes. In his retreat he tore the T-shirt from the child's body.

Jamba was now free and bounced in front of the man like a boxer, blood gushing from the gash in his arm, but not feeling a thing. He could run but his hatred and rage kept him anchored to the spot. Jamba wanted to get to his rifle which was slung over the man's back and kill the scum with it.

There was a commotion coming from all sides. Boys were carefully peering around the corner of the hut. Tito and Okot's faces also appeared and both carried a look of disbelief. Two camp guards rushed in with their weapons at the ready, but didn't draw too close. Nobody said a word. The only noises were those coming from the boy and the man who were both breathing heavily, visibly pumped-up and shaken.

Suddenly there was a strong beam of light. Jamba was completely blinded and could not see the owner behind the torch. Then he heard Wambuzi's booming voice and the authority contained in it jolted him back to reality.

"Drop the rifle and the knife Bubba, or I'll shoot you dead where you stand." The order was firm and unmistakable. Bubba took a deep breath and without taking his eyes from the boy he dropped both weapons on the ground.

Sergeant Wambuzi took in the scene which was confronting him. There was a young child, barefoot and wearing only a pair of shorts with blood pumping from his forearm in rhythmic squirts. There was a toothless and bearded man with a drugged stare still clutching a torn T-shirt in one hand and breathing like a raging bull.

Wambuzi took control. "Okot, get bandages. Hurry up man!" Then he turned his attention to the man clutching the torn shirt. "Explain yourself, Bubba."

Bubba's stare never left the boy. "The fuck attacked me! Put his fingers in my eyes," he babbled almost incoherently.

The sergeant turned to the boy. "What happened, boy?"

"Put a knife to my throat... told me to take off my pants. I'll kill him," the boy breathed. It was clear that he meant the last part of his statement with every fiber in his body.

Wambuzi did not take long to make a decision. He was an old hand who knew his men well and who was appointed as a sergeant for very good reason. He knew all too well that this kind of thing went on among the men and the girls and even between the men and some boys. But certain boys had the potential of becoming well-oiled fighting machines and were not to be corrupted or destroyed too early on. The born fighters were assets the army thrived upon and needed.

In the same breath there were veterans who threw rust into the cogs of that oiled machine and hampered the efficiency at which it operated. Those kinds of men had to be disposed of like the garbage they were.

Sergeant Wambuzi often had to make crucial decisions when it came to the molding or weeding and DaD relied on his judgment for that. Yet, ultimately the final decision always remained DaD's to make, like some god who had the powers to play either creator or destroyer of lives.

"You two guards, tie up this piece of shit and throw him in the hole." He was pointing towards Bubba. "If he tries anything, just shoot him."

Wambuzi was about to tell the boy to get his arm bandaged but Jamba had already fainted and lay on the ground in a bloody heap. Okot had returned and was frantically applying water and bandages to the boy's forearm. He shouted at Tito to help him apply pressure on the wound in an attempt to slow the profuse bleeding.

Some of the other boys helped in carrying Jamba to a hut which he had never entered before. He could feel his body being lifted by many arms supporting his back and legs as he slipped in and out of consciousness. The hut served as an infirmary. There was nobody else in the make-shift hospital, but both Tito and Okot stayed behind to keep an eye on Jamba. Tito had gathered the AK-47 where Bubba had dropped it and laid it down on the ground next to the semi-conscious boy.

Jamba could not at that very moment appreciate the bitter-sweet irony of Bubba's predicament. But he would have appreciated it fully if he had been present. The guards tied No-tooth's hands behind his back and marched him over to the toilet pits. The same hole which was just recently dug by the boy became the man's prison.

He was unceremoniously dumped into the pit and a mesh of thick branches, tied tightly together by pieces of rope, was thrown across the opening. Two heavy rocks, almost the size of boulders were rolled onto the edges of the mesh to weigh it down.

The man named Bubba was thoroughly imprisoned in that vile-smelling hole. A hole which was by then filled almost a foot deep in human waste. No guards were needed to keep an eye on him.

CHAPTER 18

Jamba joined the world of the conscious again sometime just after sunrise. His left arm was almost completely numb. It was burning slightly and swollen. He felt light-headed from the loss of blood and the slightest movement threatened to send him back into the darkness again.

The boy was alone in the hut and spent a few moments collecting his thoughts and replaying the events of the previous evening over in his mind.

After some minutes of just lying there and gathering his strength he got up slowly, picked up his rifle and moved towards the door. His head started to spin and he decided to rather just sit by the entrance and observe the activities in the camp.

He noticed Tito who was strolling towards him and holding a small jar. Tito gave him a broad smile and then offered him a crumpled cigarette. Jamba declined politely and wondered when Tito had started smoking.

The other boy sat down next to him and unscrewed the lid of the jar. It contained a yellow-green paste which looked as if it was something which came out the back of a bird that had eaten too much fruit. The odor matched the same image.

"Mganga sent this," Tito said after lighting his cigarette and dragging on it with some satisfaction. "It's to heal your wound and stop the infection."

Jamba sniffed at the disgusting green paste and decided the witch doctor would probably know best. He started unwrapping the bandage around his arm and winced as the last part came off where it was sticking to some clotted blood.

The cut was a few inches long and showed white in some places where the fat under his skin was visible through the gash. There were patches of thick dried blood running the length of the cut.

"You must first clean it," Tito suggested and the two boys ambled over to the shower area where Jamba washed the wound and winced a lot. He needed to dry it with something and for the first time noticed he wasn't wearing his T-shirt any more. The boy would remain barefoot and wearing only his shorts until he somehow managed to find another shirt somewhere. The idea upset him since his clothes and rifle were his only possessions. He spat in disgust as he thought about Bubba.

After carefully applying some of the foul-smelling ointment and replacing the bandages, he asked Tito about Bubba. Puffing away at another cigarette, the boy gestured with his head for Jamba to followed him. He moved off towards the toilets.

Tito pointed at the pit covered by the mesh and Jamba peered down between the bars of branches into the semi-darkness. Bubba was standing ankle-deep in human waste and was peering back up at him. The boy recoiled and anger welled up in him again. "*Puta*," he whispered and with that he stomped off in the direction of the kitchen to find some food.

"Wambuzi said you have to stay in the infirmary until he needs you. DaD and the others will be back soon." Tito flicked the burning cigarette butt into the hole imprisoning the man without teeth. Then he jogged off in the direction of the radio hut.

Jamba entered the kitchen where he encountered the young girl with the swollen cheek whom he had seen the first time on his arrival. It already felt like a lifetime ago. She was busy waiving a large leaf at the drying hog-meat in an attempt to keep the flies at bay. He found it strange that her cheek was still swollen after all this time.

The boy mumbled a halfhearted 'hello' but she completely ignored him. He just shrugged, found himself a slice of bread and sat down on a bench to eat. He watched the girl from underneath his lashes.

It suddenly occurred to him that the girl was quite pretty. A strange feeling washed over the boy which made him feel both excited and uncomfortable. It was an emotion entirely new to him. Even stranger was how it seemed to choke him.

The girl was probably about his age, barefoot and wearing a plain white dress which was almost as dirty as Jamba's lost T-shirt used to be but not quite as filthy - that would take some doing. She just continued waving the big leaf at the meat and ignored the boy.

Jamba suddenly had an urge to speak to her and to be noticed by the pretty girl. He liked her and this unfamiliar new emotion taking hold of him now badly wanted for her to like him also.

"I'm twelve. Look at my cut." The boy proudly presented his wounded arm so she could see his bandages. The girl kept waving the leaf at the meat.

Jamba shifted uncomfortably on the bench. He suddenly felt quite helpless. "I killed that pig. With my AK." He unslung the rifle and lay it on the table where she could properly see it.

The girl rolled her eyes and said in a soft voice, "So what? Everybody has a gun."

Jamba felt offended and reacted with some venom. "Not true! Only some get one. DaD gave it to me." He immediately regretted his outburst and then added in a calmer tone which trailed off into a whisper, "And it's a *rifle*. Not a gun..."

The boy was now staring at his toes, wondering what he could say next or whether he should rather just leave. He was feeling both hurt and embarrassed.

"My name is Annie." Her words took the boy by surprise. A broad smile appeared on his face.

"I'm Jamba," he blurted out. Just to feel embarrassed again the moment he said it because his overly eager reply sounded stupid to him. And she will probably laugh at his name.

The girl nodded and the boy kept staring at his toes again. He was happy that she offered her name at least. He liked it – 'Annie'. But he felt that he made an arse of himself by snapping at her. Suddenly he needed to escape and get out of there before he made things worse. Again that choking feeling crept up on him.

"Bye," he simply said and got up to leave. The boy was halfway to the door of the hut when he heard that sweet voice call out to him.

"Jamba." His heart almost stopped. How weird is this? he thought to himself. He gathered his courage and turned to face her.

"Your gun... rifle." She was pointing towards the table.

Jamba sheepishly walked towards the table, collected his rifle and had to force himself not to run from the hut. He kept thinking to himself - Ugh, what an idiot I am. How stupid. She made me forget my rifle. I'm such an arse.

If his skin wasn't so dark, Annie would surely have seen him blush.

Jamba headed back to the infirmary, his emotions in turmoil. He was still clutching the slice of bread in one hand, now completely forgotten. The boy decided that he needed to ask Okot some questions. The clever Okot knew the answers to everything. He would certainly know everything regarding this annoying business involving girls.

Just as he reached the infirmary, he saw Sergeant Wambuzi hobbling towards the parade area in great haste and blowing a long shrill note on the whistle. Within moments the camp became a hive of activity as men and boys appeared from all directions. Some were in the act of carrying wood and others appeared from the darkness of the jungle where they were patrolling the perimeter.

The soldiers who took part in the mission must be returning.

Jamba noticed how few of the boys were actually carrying rifles and felt some pride and a sense of worth overcome him. He checked his beloved rifle and jogged towards where everybody was gathering. Wambuzi immediately sent him back with a shake of the head and a pointing finger.

"It is just a scratch, sergeant. I'm good," the boy complained with a sense of indignity. There was nothing wrong with him. He wanted to be part of the proceedings. He was a part of MoD.

Wambuzi gave him a look which could kill a hundred men and Jamba returned to the infirmary entrance where he sat sulking and picking at his bandages.

It seemed like the entire village had assembled on the parade ground where at least twenty were grouped together and standing at attention. Wambuzi was pacing up and down giving his speech. "DaD and some in our victorious army are on their way. You'll show them the necessary respect for their bravery. They've taken prisoners and have gathered new recruits. You'll all join at the fire tonight for there is a lot to be celebrated and much to be decided on."

Jamba wondered what Wambuzi meant when he said there were things to be decided on. He imagined a lot would change after the battle. Prisoners, new recruits, men lost in the conflict. The radio said many men had died. He still did not know how true that was though. He was certain that DaD would clarify everything that evening.

As if on cue there was a rustling of leaves and three weary-looking soldiers emerged from the undergrowth at the edge of the encampment. Their spirits seemed to lift and their shoulders straightened as they entered the clearing.

They were followed by bearded comrades who emerged one-by-one and patched with bandages in various places on their bodies. One had a bandage wrapped around his head. Another with an arm in a sling and yet another leaning on a stick, his thigh heavily wrapped. They looked exhausted but their determination was clear for all to see.

Jamba later heard that those with more serious injuries were left behind at their main camp across the border. There was no way that they could have made the long march back and still be alive.

Then followed a number of boys and a couple of young girls who looked at best pathetic and miserable. They were carrying boxes and crates on their shoulders or heads. These children had to be the new recruits Wambuzi had spoken about since Jamba had never seen them before.

Then entered a black man with a bewildered expression on his face. He was wearing an unfamiliar uniform and his features were foreign to the boy. Not the usual look of those men from these parts. Maybe this was what a South African looked like, Jamba thought.

The man was blindfolded, his hands tied behind his back and another rope had been tied around his neck. Ahead of him walked an MoD soldier, holding the end of the rope as if leading a dog on a leash. At the sight of this spectacle, the men and boys on the parade ground cheered and some pumped the air with their rifles. The prisoner appeared forlorn and bowed his head towards the ground.

More soldiers emerged, mostly boys he recognized and who were carrying more crates. Jamba recognized Yoweri among them and even though he did not like the boy very much he managed to crack a smile at seeing him back alive. Yoweri must have done well.

The men following behind the toiling boys were only carrying their weapons. The hierarchy was pretty clear. There were a few however who had on them very long and slick rifles which Jamba had never seen before. These were definitely not *Kalashnikovs*.

Finally DaD emerged from the growth, his massive arms carrying that enormous PKMS machine gun of his. Jamba felt some relief, even though it never crossed his mind for a moment that DaD might not return from the mission. It was impossible to imagine the man ever dying in combat. He was surely invincible.

Sergeant Wambuzi barked an order and the men on the parade ground saluted as one.

As was his custom, DaD first stood still for a moment, looked at those gathered before him and then slowly raised the heavy PKMS above his head. He needed only one arm for the gesture.

The entire welcoming party cheered and ululated. There were shouts and howls of pleasure and approval.

DaD was strolling towards them sporting a huge grin on his face, absorbing the atmosphere. He was pumping a fist which made his muscles ripple and nodding his head in approval.

As he passed Jamba, who was standing all by his own at the entrance to the infirmary, a quizzical look momentarily crossed his brow and his eyes flicked towards the bandage around the boy's arm.

Sergeant Wambuzi had made a subtle statement to their master.

Jamba stood at attention and saluted his leader with what he hoped to be perfection. The monstrous man kept on walking but flicked a brief salute back at the boy. Jamba's heart skipped a beat. His Commander had returned his salute before even saluting anybody else. The boy felt immense pride and something which resembled joy.

Sergeant Wambuzi dismissed those on the parade ground and they scattered to assist with the crates and boxes which had arrived. The sergeant then shouted some instructions at the new boys who had returned with the soldiers and they gathered in a huddle looking sorry for themselves. With more barks and shouts the huddle was quickly organized into a disciplined line of boys standing abreast.

Feeling left out and completely excluded, Jamba jogged off towards the radio hut to see if he could at least seem useful somehow. There was already somebody manning the radio but the boy remained anyhow. He watched the activities in the camp from the entrance of the hut.

He looked on as some of the new boys gathered spades from the back of a pick-up and then started walking toward the toilet area. Jamba smiled to himself. Then he noticed a guard undoing the prisoner's hands and handing him a spade. The intentions seemed pretty clear. They were going to dig his new prison. His blindfold had been removed but the rope around the man's neck remained and his guard gave him a shove between the shoulder blades.

The gathering at the fire was going to be interesting.

CHAPTER 19

Evening finally arrived. Jamba did not see DaD or any of his officers again during the day. He passed the infirmary a couple of times where he saw some of the wounded men being tended to by a woman and a girl. For a brief moment he caught himself hoping it was Annie and then felt disappointed when he saw it was somebody else.

More of the jars containing the nasty yellow-green contents could be seen standing around. He noticed that the man with the head wound was wearing the red ribbon of a captain around his arm. Jamba barely ever saw any of the captains. It was as if they were permanently holed up in a hut with DaD.

Everybody from the camp, save for those on guard duty, was arriving in disconnected groups at the clearing in the jungle's bowels. Even the injured were there. A large bonfire was burning ever higher and brighter, licking at the sky with its furnace-like flames. Jamba was only too grateful that he wasn't consigned to patrol duties that evening.

Chunks of dried meat from the forest hog were being passed around and men were cutting off big slices with their knives. There was a rusty tin plate on a stone slab near the fire which contained something resembling an organ of some kind. The boy studied it for a while and decided that it looked like the heart of an animal. It was all shriveled up and dry.

The scent of smoke and stale beer filled the air. Some of the men were passing a jug among themselves. Those who took a swig would eventually just sit there dead still staring at the ground or into the sky with eyes seemingly not quite seeing what they were looking at.

Jamba was sitting next to Yoweri and both boys were clasping their rifles to their chests. There hadn't been enough opportunity to question Yoweri on his adventures yet. He asked the other boy about the stuff the men were drinking and Yoweri explained to him that it was something called a hallucinogenic. Apparently it made you see things which weren't really there. The boy seemed much more quiet than usual, as if he had changed somehow.

They were sitting on the outer edge of the fire just as they had the last time, but after some minutes Yoweri got up and joined the older men sitting nearer to the fire. Jamba realized that until he had joined the other men in battle, that he would remain a relative outsider to them, even now that he had his own rifle. Yoweri had earned his place by the fire.

The witch doctor Mganga was his usual self, dancing around the flames and foaming from the mouth. He scattered white powder in all directions and every now and then he would take deep swigs from a transparent glass bottle in one hand. There was a thick pink liquid sloshing around inside.

DaD joined the men without ceremony. He simply entered the circle and took up position on a log. Two of his captains flanked him. The third was absent this time around.

The ceremonial entry was reserved for their prisoner. The witch doctor was in a wild frenzy and led the man into the circle by the leash tied around his neck. Mganga screamed with a voice which sounded as if it was coming from a demon trapped in some distant spirit world rather than that of his own. A chill ran down Jamba's spine.

Mganga tugged at the rope with great force and the man stumbled to the ground. He pushed himself back up onto his knees with hands tied tightly in front of his body. The foreign soldier was observing his surroundings with obvious fear in his eyes. More like terror. No matter how one looked at it, the man seemed somehow doomed.

Jamba wondered what was going to happen to the man. Maybe DaD would sell him back to his own people for a lot of money or maybe he will work in the diamond mines for him. But the foreigner now knew where their camps were located and he surely cannot join the MoD. Maybe he was purely there to motivate the soldiers and remind them of their victory.

DaD got up and slowly circled the man. Silence fell over the gathering. Just moments before the men were almost out of control. Some were dancing and some were jumping wildly. One man was rocking forwards and backwards, clasping himself where he was sitting in a drug-induced daze. The scene was chaotic when the prisoner was paraded before his captors.

But as DaD circled his captive like an animal sniffing at his prey, all was deathly quiet and a tense atmosphere of expectancy impregnated the air.

Then DaD stood anchored to a spot behind the hapless man and said with in air of dignity, "A few days ago our glorious Merchants attacked the comrades of this man you see here before you. We killed at least twenty of them and took possession of some lovely toys of theirs." He grinned and motioned towards one of his captains.

The captain handed him one of the sleek rifles Jamba had seen earlier that day. It was almost as long as his own body, had a long glistening rifle stock and an enormous telescope mounted on the barrel just in front of its chamber.

"This is the latest in sniper technology. Apparently you can hit a target over two miles away. It has night vision and all kinds of fancy extras." DaD smiled and handed the rifle back to his captain.

"Our guerrilla tactics had just been given a major injection. With these weapons we're going to create havoc among the enemy before they even know we existed. A silent death from the darkness awaits them." He pointed towards the jungle surrounding them and smiled broadly. The men cheered.

"Our mission was a success. The pigs claim they had killed as many as six hundred of us. Now I ask you how they could have killed six hundred of our best fighters when we only attacked them with a hundred men?" He paused and the soldiers murmured among themselves. Heads were nodding in agreement.

DaD started pacing up and down in front of the captured man and said, "We don't listen to the propaganda of liars and imbeciles. We know the truth... and the truth reigns supreme. We returned with weapons. We took prisoners. It's clear who the victors are." He stopped pacing and gestured towards the prisoner. "Here before you, kneeling in the dust, is more evidence of that ultimate proof."

Some of the soldiers spat at the man whose lips were now quivering. Others kicked dead leaves in his direction. A chunk of meat struck the side of his head. He just continued to stare down at the ground beneath him.

"Ah... and before I forget. We also reinforced our glorious army with new recruits. Boys we rescued from villages completely destroyed by the pigs and their agents." With these words DaD gestured towards a group of boys ranging in ages from between eight and fourteen years old. They were peering wide-eyed from the darkness behind a group of bearded men, only the whites of their eyes visible in the light of the flames.

"Now, during our various discussions on the way back here, this man told me he knew a great secret. Something which will make us *invincible* in battle. He'll share this secret with us if we let him go. A brave man indeed. Why don't you tell my men about this secret of yours?"

DaD stood in front the man and tapped him under the chin so that he would face him. He continued to wait patiently. The prisoner looked up at the colossus in front of him and started blurting out words at a rate resembling an AK-47 firing at full automatic. He had a thick foreign accent.

"I've told you. I know how to make a drug which will make you invincible. It's called *nyaope*, *whoonga*, whatever. I'll show you how to make it. Just let me go. I was blindfolded. I don't know where we are. I can't tell anybody." The more the man rambled on the more the terror and desperation grew in his eyes and voice.

DaD nodded. "Of course we'll let you go." He looked at the men gathered around the fire and smirked. "Of course. Now tell me exactly how you make this *nyaope* or *whoonga* of yours. Look, you don't have even one mark on your body. We've treated you very well, right? Just tell us this recipe of yours and there will be no need for other measures to help you remember."

Jamba could see the man's mind racing. His wild eyes betrayed him. Just how clear his thinking was at that moment was another matter. A sea of wild faces were staring at him and obviously unnerving him and the atmosphere was distinctly hostile. The witch doctor with the painted white face and bones around his neck clearly had an effect on him too.

He glanced up at Mganga who was busy licking away at his strange necklace with its macabre collection of bones. And there was a giant of a man looking down at him which had the effect of acid burning through his insides.

In one smooth movement DaD took a rifle from the nearest soldier, loaded it, flicked the safety leaver and jammed the muzzle against the terrified man's forehead. "The recipe fucker," he commanded with a voice which even gave Jamba goose bumps.

"Efavirenz! It's an antiretroviral drug used for treating HIV and AIDS. Five parts with one part of heroin or cocaine. Smoke it mixed with cannabis or tobacco. Or inject it. Eat it. In a few minutes you'll be angry and aggressive. It will make you invincible..." The last sentence was almost a whimper.

DaD looked at him sidelong down the barrel of the *Kalashnikov*. "Well, considering your current situation my friend, you don't look too invincible to me. I believe this magic drug of yours must be a load of shit."

"Invincible..." the man whispered again. And DaD pulled the trigger.

The head exploded at the back and the ex-prisoner simply slumped backwards, half-sitting and half-lying on his heels. Blood soaked the leaves below his head in torrents. There was no need to confirm that he was dead.

DaD threw the rifle in a general direction without looking and produced a small pocket knife from his camouflage pants. He unfolded the blade and then bent over the dead man. He found a nearby stone and placed the man's tied hands over it. Slowly and deliberately DaD removed the tip of one of his little fingers. The man's body gave a final spasm as if he could still feel the pain of his finger being removed.

Examining the fingertip for a while, DaD allowed most of the blood to drain from the digit before he casually opened the small sack around his neck and dropped the object inside.

Jamba's eyes grew as the realization dawned on him regarding the contents of that sack around DaD's neck. Trophies - the scrotum of an enemy containing bits and pieces of other enemies. Watching the man having his head blown to pieces and then losing his finger was unsettling. It was pretty obvious who was in command here and Jamba's respect for DaD grew tenfold. Or was it pure fear?

The witch doctor was dancing in circles around DaD whilst chanting incoherent words. He was flicking something at the monstrous man which looked like the bushy tail of some kind of animal. DaD fully extended his arms to the sides, closed his eyes and tilted his head back, accepting whatever spell or ritual Mganga was casting.

When the witch doctor concluded his ceremony in a flutter of hands piercing the air, DaD returned to his log. The silence around the huge bonfire was perfect. Only the crackling of burning logs dared to interrupt the quiet.

DaD took a deep breath and after pointing at the corpse with a gesture of contempt and dismissal, four men almost fell over themselves to do his bidding. They realized that not all of them were needed and the two closest to the body continued to drag it away by the arms as if though it was merely some dead tree obstructing their path.

DaD called for Sergeant Oboto, the man who was in charge of their combat readiness exercises. Oboto had been part of the assault team and the boys had no combat exercises recently.

"Take a few men tomorrow and find me these antiretroviral drugs. Efavi-whatever. Some of the village clinics should stock it. No confrontations. Pay them if you must but use some imagination to negotiate the price. You know what I mean." Sergeant Oboto nodded his understanding and DaD handed him some banknotes.

The gathering was still silent. There was a time to be serious and a time to party. The party had to wait for the moment.

"And now for the second issue on the agenda." DaD was

stroking the sack around his neck as he spoke. It was as if this gave him great satisfaction. "Where's the boy Jamba?"

Jamba's stomach turned and his heart was stuck in his throat. He had just witnessed a man practically having his head removed and then literally losing a finger - and now he is being summoned. This cannot be good. Fear gripped his body and kept him rooted to the spot where he was sitting.

Somebody nudged him and he snapped out of his stupor. Before he could even think clearly again he found himself standing before the big man. Jamba did not want to look DaD in the eyes. What if the man could read the fear hiding there? He was certain he would be able to notice it. This was DaD. He was all-knowing. You cannot hide anything from the man.

If DaD had noticed the boy's discomfort, he did not acknowledge it. Jamba was certain though that he knew. He looked down very briefly as something sticky oozed between his toes. The boy was standing in the dead man's blood.

"I was told that our Jamba here survived the tunnels with great courage".

Oh no! His punishment for being disarmed was finally upon him. Death or the diamond mines. He gripped the rifle hanging over his shoulder just to make completely certain that it was there and had not been taken from him again like that last time.

"I also hear that he had been killing big black hairy pig enemies just like we did. Except that this one had huge tusks and snorted like a real pig." The men all laughed, but more out of duty than any understanding regarding as to where this was heading.

"Our boy here killed us a giant bush hog and supplied us with our party snacks tonight." DaD roared laughter at his own comment and the men followed suit. Jamba just smiled nervously. He didn't really know what was so funny about it.

"Sometimes..." and their commander paused. "Sometimes a man must eat the heart of his enemy to gain his strength and ensure that enemy will not return from the spirit world to do him harm." Many of the soldiers nodded their agreement and sipped at their beer.

Mganga was standing next to Jamba now. The boy did not know how he managed to transport himself so quickly without being noticed. In his hands the witch doctor held a cup with some of that pink liquid floating in it.

"Drink," his leader instructed.

The boy took the cup and sipped at the contents. It was bitter and tasted absolutely vile. He decided to rather just gulp the entire lot down in one swig than having to actually taste the horrible liquid.

The boy waited in anticipation but nothing was happening to him. Again Mganga suddenly appeared next to him, this time holding the plate with the shriveled heart. The witch doctor pointed towards it and then to his mouth. It was pretty obvious that Jamba had to eat it. The heart of the giant bush hog.

The boy did not care much for what it would taste like. In Kampala he had eaten things he had found in the garbage which made the heart look like a gourmet meal. What was important was that he had to concentrate on absorbing the strength of the pig. That is what DaD had explained and that is what the boy now thoroughly believed.

He tore at the tough muscle with his teeth. It tasted good. Like the dried meat he had tried before. The boy continued ripping into the heart and with each bite he imagined draining the energy and strength from the forest hog and absorbing it into every fiber of his body.

The soldiers watched patiently as he consumed the entire organ. Mganga was dancing again, flicking the tail he held in his hand and blowing his mysterious powder over the boy.

Suddenly Jamba convulsed and vomited violently. DaD and a few other men took a few steps backward. The boy at once felt like both an embarrassment and a failure. Before he could say something he was lying flat on his back. His world started to spin and the trees above him twisted into shapes resembling faces. It was not scary at all. In fact, it was strangely comforting.

He heard DaD's voice although he had not a clue where it was coming from. "*Ayahuasca*, my boy. You've got no idea what I had to go through to get hold of that magic vine. All the way from Brazil." He could hear DaD laughing.

Jamba could now see small white men crawling around the leaves of the trees. They were all hanging upside-down and were giggling at him. One of the trees morphed into the face of a woman and called out to him. It looked as if she was telling him to 'come, come.' A branch shaped like a finger was moving in the breeze and motioning him to follow.

The boy felt himself floating into the tree and then being absorbed by it. He was flowing inside the veins, pumping through the branches as if being a part of the sap, water and juices giving it life.

Then he heard the sound of a multitude of insects buzzing around his ears, swarms and swarms of them. So many he could not possibly guess at their numbers. The swarm formed a dark cloud from which suddenly emerged the shape of an enormous bush pig. It was *his* bush pig - and it was charging.

He could do nothing but to watch on as the giant hog leaped through the air and disappeared into his chest. There was no pain. The hog had simply become a part of him. Of every fiber in his body and merging with his soul. The tree-mother spat him out and he floated gently to the ground like a leaf.

Jamba opened his eyes and was greeted by a horde of faces staring down at him. Things were fading in and out of reality. Mganga helped him to his feet and he stood there swaying for a moment, occasionally reaching out a hand towards emptiness in an attempt to grab onto something and steady himself.

Instinctively he felt around for his *Kalashnikov* and found it lying near his feet. The boy reached out and picked it up, steadying himself once again. He was feeling nauseous and wanted to be dismissed.

"You now have all the powers of the giant bush hog, boy. You'll be brave and you'll be strong. You will charge at the enemy without any fear," DaD declared triumphantly. Jamba was certain he detected some pride in his voice and believed the imposing man.

DaD leaned forward from where he was still sitting on the log and placed a giant hand on Jamba's shoulder. He plucked the boy towards him as if though he was just a feather floating in the wind. Then he positioned the child to stand between his enormous knees so that they both faced toward the small army gathered around the fire.

"Before we continue our celebrations, there is one last matter to attend to. It's a small lesson in respect and ownership. Let me explain. Sergeant Wambuzi?"

The sergeant appeared from the shadows and oscillated towards DaD where he handed him a large oblong object. The blade of the knife sparkled in the light of the fire and it reminded Jamba of the diamond he saw in Tito's picture. Except that this was not a pretty sight. He recognized Bubba's knife instantly. He knew it all too well by now.

"Bring me that piece of shit," DaD instructed and two guards pulled No-tooth into the circle within moments. His feet were dragging behind him on the ground and he made no attempt to walk. Just like the prisoner before him, his hands were tied, but this time behind his back. And just like the prisoner before him, he was left standing on his knees facing DaD. But now he was also facing Jamba who was still held tight by one of the commander's enormous hands.

"So let me get this straight..." DaD sighed and again his eyes searched the canopy of the jungle above them. "While I was away risking my life for the benefit of our glorious army and so that we may all one day prosper," he said with a voice rapidly increasing in intensity and rage, "this piece of human waste tried to fuck my boy here. Look," and he pointed towards Jamba. "This boy has no shirt. And look, he's got a cut so deep that he almost lost an arm."

DaD grabbed hold of Jamba's arm and ripped the bandages away. He held the oozing wound towards all those present so that they could clearly observe the long incision and the clotted blood. There was a trickle of blood where some of the scabs had been torn away when the bandages were so violently removed.

"As you all well know, we have a very simple law regarding property. This boy here is my property. I found him. I named him. And nobody fucks with my property!" He screamed his last words and was shaking with mounting rage. DaD's eyes were bulging and large veins were throbbing at his temples.

The colossal man was gripping Jamba's arm so tightly that he felt pins and needles as it interrupted the circulation to his fingers.

Bubba's face was expressionless. He had already given up all hope and knew his fate. The only remaining question was how he was going to die. He had hours to prepare himself whilst standing in the hole. It may have been bravery or simply the signs of a 'fried brain,' as Wambuzi had put it. But Bubba was clearly already detached.

DaD lifted the enormous blade and carefully studied it. He twisted the knife and inspected the sharp edge. Their commander had made his decision.

He shoved the knife into Jamba's hand and said, "Stand behind him boy."

Jamba hesitantly moved towards Babba, feeling unsure of himself and fearing what may follow. He obediently stood behind the doomed man who was looking bored. Even complacent.

"Grab hold of his hair and pull his head back." The boy did as he was ordered. He was breathing heavily.

"Put the knife to his throat." Again the boy complied, looking DaD straight in the eye.

"Now you slice, boy. Cut this pig from ear to ear just as you would slit the throat of an animal."

Jamba's hands were trembling. Somewhere inside him there raged a battle between what is right and what is wrong. But the lines were blurred and the outcome of the battle was deadlocked. He knew he had to obey DaD at all cost.

The choice was simple. He had no choice.

The boy closed his eyes involuntarily and pulled the blade across the man's throat. There was a sigh and then a gurgle. Jamba was still holding on to Bubba's hair and looked down. Small fountains of blood were spurting from his throat. The man's arms were trying to reach something but being tied behind his back they only managed to flail against the insides of Jamba's legs. The boy had failed.

"Again!" shouted DaD at him. His fury was still growing, as if that was even possible.

This time the boy looked at the blade and concentrated on the job at hand. He pulled Bubba's head back further and could see the man's eyes frantically staring up into his own. This time the boy used all his might and cut again, a long, continuous slicing motion. He succeeded to such an extent that the man's head was flapping and almost came clean off.

Blood was spurting in all directions. Some of it covered the boy's chest, arm and legs. The leaves around him was covered in the deep dark liquid. He let go of the gurgling head and Bubba's body lay thrashing on the ground before him. Everybody just stared until the last kicks faded into a shudder. Jamba wanted to vomit again.

He stared at his bloody hands and the blade still quivering there. Without a word he dropped the knife onto the dead man's back and without asking permission he turned and walked away. As he exited the circle he saw a man staring at him intently. It was Castro, Bubba's friend.

DaD allowed the boy to leave.

CHAPTER 20

Jamba needed sleep, but slumber just would not come to him. He lay on his back in relative darkness staring at the roof of the hut. Still feeling sick from a combination of the hallucinogenic *ayahuasca* juice and the dehydrated heart, Jamba had to bolt for the exit on a couple of occasions to retch or vomit.

He refused to admit that the real reason for his nausea was the near-decapitation of his tormentor. Jamba hated Bubba. He planned his death and torture in detail many times over in the past but he never actually thought that it would be realized and he never included decapitation in any of his fantasies.

He had taken another life before but that murder seemed almost justified - almost clean and innocent compared to what had transpired this evening. The boy he had killed in Kampala had a fair fighting chance and an opportunity to defend himself.

In one master stroke DaD had both carried out a punishment for a crime, whilst giving the victim an opportunity to exact revenge at the same time. The boy did not feel satisfaction. He felt repulsed.

Something within him was empty. Something was removed that evening and he could not put his finger on it. If it was his innocence, there was no way of the boy ever knowing or understanding this.

Innocence: *"The state, quality, or virtue of being innocent - Freedom from sin, moral wrong, or guilt through lack of knowledge of evil."*

His wound was throbbing and a clear liquid was oozing from the open cut. He knew he needed some of that lotion Mganga had concocted and he needed new bandages, but he had no desire to move and just kept staring at the roof.

The nightmares came swiftly. The onslaught was brutal. Dark flapping wings scratched at his young mind as the demons came in to land. Worms and maggots were wriggling from rotting intestines spilled on the ground. Flies and cockroaches were crawling from dark mouths devoid of teeth. The mouths would grow bigger and bigger until they consumed him whole, inhaling him as he tried to escape.

He woke up kicking, a hand clasped over his mouth. For a brief moment he thought it was Bubba, but Bubba was not with them any more. The boy tried to bite the hand pushing down on his mouth when he heard Tito's voice whisper urgently, "Jamba! Quiet!"

When his kicking stopped and his breathing had slowed down, Tito said softly, "You're screaming in your sleep. You can't do that Jamba! They'll think you're possessed by spirits. You've got to be quiet!"

"I was having nightmares," the boy replied. His body was drenched in sweat and his wound was throbbing more painfully than ever.

"Yes. *You* know that and *I* know that. But others believe it's the demons. You simply *must* be quiet or there might be bad things happening to you." It was clear that Tito was having great difficulty to keep his voice down. He was almost frantic.

"Okay. Okay," was all Jamba could manage and lay back on his blanket again. He was now suddenly very cold and had to cover himself with the blanket. Moments later he was boiling hot again.

For many minutes he kept repeating to himself that he should not scream. You must not scream. Then, out of the blue, the image of the girl Annie entered his thoughts. The boy was surprised at how the vision of the pretty, barefoot girl with her white dress and swollen cheek comforted him and calmed his mind. Thinking about her, he eventually drifted into a deep slumber.

It was Castro who woke Jamba for guard duty. The boy thought it to be another bad joke by Wambuzi. The workings of the officers' minds were always a mystery to him.

He picked up his rifle and suddenly felt quite naked. Still wearing only his grimy shorts, he just shrugged at the absence of his T-shirt and left for the door. In a hut which doubled as an armory, he got hold of a water bottle which fitted into a pouch attached to a belt. He strapped it around his waste. The boy then grabbed some extra cartridges for his *Kalashnikov* which he shoved into an ammunition pouch and clipped that to the belt too.

Jamba's fever had subsided, but his arm oozed and he needed new bandages. Castro was waiting for him patiently near the kitchen. The boy gestured towards the infirmary and the man quietly followed.

His spirits lifted considerably when he entered the hut and saw Annie and an older woman tending to a wounded soldier. The sight of the girl made him smile and he showed her the open wound without speaking to her.

The older woman nodded at the girl and she left the side of the wounded soldier to scratch around in a metal chest for fresh bandages. Then she very tenderly cleaned Jamba's wound with a cloth and water. The boy enjoyed every moment of it, even when it stung at times. He liked her cool touch on his skin.

The yellow-green bird-poo ointment was applied abundantly. He mumbled his appreciation and then, as he left the hut, he glanced back and saw the girl staring after him. She looked away quickly when he turned. Jamba smiled to himself.

"Which route?" the boy asked Castro.

"Waterfall," the man replied and Jamba took the lead.

They walked for hours without exchanging a word. Jamba did not know what to say to Castro nor whether he should say anything at all. Eventually the events of the previous evening just would not let go of him and he decided he needed to say something to Castro, even if only for his own benefit.

"I killed your friend," he ventured.

"He had it coming," the man replied succinctly. And with that the matter was settled.

They arrived at a narrow waterfall cascading from the rocks above them. All kinds of plants were growing around the tumbling water and colorful birds swept low over a small pool at its base. More beautiful birds sat perched higher up on some branches. Jamba watched a troop of monkeys as they raised the alarm and then fleeing up a tall tree, where they cowered and suspiciously eyed the humans below them.

He filled his water bottle while Castro went to urinate in the nearby shrubs. The boy wondered whether Castro hated him. It was possible, but the man did not seem like he would try to get even.

When they started back towards camp, the skies opened up and the rain came pouring down in gallons. It was an unpleasant two-hour march to the encampment and Jamba kept wishing he had a T-shirt.

The rain had dissipated by the time they arrived at the camp and they both went to the kitchen to scavenge some food. Hog again. Jamba now almost regretted ever shooting the animal. Every meal contained a part of the wild hog these days and it was becoming an overkill. Yet, in a strange way he felt grateful towards the beast and even proud about his own role in feeding DaD's army.

The previous night at the fire, the giant forest hog had become his totem, his spirit guide and helper. He would only know to what exact extent once his first battle comes around one day.

Since Sergeant Oboto was away on his mission to procure antiretroviral drugs for DaD, Wambuzi took charge of the combat readiness exercises with the new boys. Jamba was sitting at the entrance to the infirmary and replacing his soaked bandages while watching the new recruits who had gathered on the parade ground. Annie was not around anymore.

Jamba was going through bandages at some rate and hoped that Sergeant Oboto would return with fresh medical supplies also. While applying more of the nasty ointment, he kept one eye on Wambuzi and his students.

Some of the new boys were still looking uneasy but most showed real interest and excitement as Wambuzi started explaining the workings of the AK-47 to them. One of the boys had already received a cuff behind the ear for picking at his nose. Jamba thought this to be hilarious.

Sergeant Wambuzi was getting to the part regarding the various settings for the lever. He explained the safety, rapid fire and full automatic settings in detail. Then, as if on a whim, he waved Jamba over. The boy pointed at himself questioningly and Wambuzi nodded irately.

He quickly tucked in one end of the bandage and jogged over to where the sergeant was standing.

"Jamba. Demonstrate to our new recruits here as to why we *never* fire a weapon on the fully automatic setting."

This must be one of Wambuzi's bizarre jokes again, the boy thought to himself. The sergeant surely knew exactly what happened on the day Oboto had ordered Jamba to pull the trigger of the *Kalashnikov* when set at full-auto.

He took a moment to consider his options. Then with an air of authority he addressed the boy who had just earlier been cuffed behind the ear. The boy was maybe only around nine or ten years old and had a nose which was permanently in the act of dripping snot all over himself.

"Come here, boy," Jamba said to him. The child approached nervously. Jamba shoved the *Kalashnikov* into his tiny hands. "Now aim at that barrel over there," he instructed and then continued to correct the boy's stance and posture.

When he was satisfied he said, "Okay. Now squeeze the trigger."

Dust flew, leaves shredded, chickens panicked and men came running. The weapon was lying on the ground and the small boy was sitting on his arse picking at his nose.

"And that, ladies, is why small boys will *never* fire their rifles set on fully automatic," he mimicked Sergeant Oboto as best he could. Then Jamba saluted Wambuzi and before he turned to leave he could swear he detected a smile in the one-legged man's eyes.

CHAPTER 21

It was almost dark and Jamba was sitting cross-legged on the floor of his hut, busy taking his rifle apart. Near his feet was a small can of oil and a stained cloth. He carefully rubbed at each part with the cloth and applied a few drops of oil to the spring mechanism.

The boy had just finished reassembling the weapon when he heard footsteps entering the hut at a run. There stood Tito with a fat grin on his face. His white bulging eyes seemed even whiter than usual. In his hands he was holding an *Avtomat Kalashnikova* model 47.

Jamba jumped up immediately and patted the boy on the back.

"Wambuzi just gave it to me," the boy smiled proudly.

"What about the tunnels?" Jamba asked with a hint of concern.

"Nah, nothing yet," said Tito and the boys continued admiring his new rifle. Even though their rifles looked almost exactly the same, they exchanged some compliments involving how nice this part looked or how smooth that part was. This continued for a few minutes until their conversation was interrupted by the sound of a vehicle arriving.

Sergeant Oboto and his men had returned. Two men unloaded a steel chest and was carrying it over to the infirmary. Jamba noticed Yoweri to be one of them. There also other supplies being unloaded and the boys joined the group to see where they could help. A man gave them a crate with some fresh vegetables and pointed towards the kitchen.

Oboto was holding a small white bag with a red cross stitched onto it and walked off towards DaD's hut. It seemed that they had found what DaD was looking for.

The two boys dumped the vegetables in the kitchen and went off to find Yoweri. They wanted to hear all about the adventure. The boy was exiting the infirmary and they intercepted him, overflowing with curiosity and questions.

Yoweri replied in a tired tone that they simply drove from clinic to clinic and bought some supplies. That was it. Nothing exciting happened at all. Jamba was a bit disappointed and decided to prod Yoweri about their battle in the DRC against the South African troops.

"Look, I'm really tired. Some other time," he said in a weary voice. No matter how many times Jamba tried to extract information about the battle from Yoweri later on, the boy always made excuses and nothing ever came of it. Jamba eventually gave up and decided to save up some courage and ask one of the other soldiers one day.

For almost an entire week it was business as usual for Jamba. Patrols, radio duty, collecting wood, changing water for the showers and the kitchen. Fairly regular shooting practice brought along some excitement. The boys who were fortunate enough to have their own rifles would practice their skills by shooting at empty oil drums or marks painted on trees. Jamba was surprised at how accurate he was and how natural it felt to him.

At least there was no more digging. That task became the domain of the new boys. Jamba noticed that Okot was mostly in charge of them and that the boy still wasn't carrying a rifle. This puzzled him. He also made a mental note to himself to ask Okot about girls.

The most exciting events were a radio call which came in one evening while he was on duty and the other was a snakebite. When Jamba heard their call-sign on the military radio, he excitedly went running to call Wambuzi, but it turned out to be nothing more than a radio-check. Then a boy was bitten by a snake while collecting wood, but the snake was only slightly venomous and that was the end of that. Some of the boys hunted the snake down and killed it. They then cooked the serpent in the hope that eating it will give them some powers, even without the help of Mganga.

One evening after returning from another patrol together, Castro walked over to Jamba and offered him a cigarette. Feeling as if he owed the man something, he accepted and then coughed his lungs out. He just puffed at the cigarette while they smoked in silence and looked up into the night sky at the few stars twinkling through the trees. The boy wasn't quite sure whether the man was being sincere or not. After seeing how DaD treated the boy, Castro was maybe simply afraid of going the same route as his friend and now only tried to stay in DaD's good books. Jamba didn't know and didn't really care.

The boy still had occasional nightmares, but his mantras before going to bed seemed to be working and he didn't wake up screaming again. The thoughts of Annie also occasionally helped. Not a night would go by without him repeating to himself not to scream, not to scream. At least his wound had almost completely healed and all that remained were a long pinkish-white scar and a few scabs.

Then one morning he was summoned. He was sitting on one of the toilets doing his personal business when one of the captains personally called on him. The man ordered him to find Yoweri, Tito and another boy and then to meet in front of DaD's hut. Jamba was so surprised at a captain addressing him in person, especially while he was busy emptying his bowels, that he could only sit there at attention and salute.

It took Jamba what felt like an eternity to find the boys. Yoweri was easy. He was sleeping in his hut. The other boy was already at DaD's hut but Jamba only realized this after searching for what must have been fifteen minutes. Tito was the biggest problem since he was on perimeter guard duty. Jamba ran around in circles on the outskirts of the thick growth until he finally spotted two guards making their rounds.

The boys arrived at the hut out of breath where the captain and Sergeant Oboto were already waiting. There were twelve of them gathered there and the captain motioned them into the hut.

Jamba didn't know what to expect. He had always pictured the inside of DaD's hut to be full of large weapons and maybe some women. He probably had a real bed and tables and even chairs.

DaD was relaxing in a hammock, his hands clasped behind his head as he watched them enter. It looked very comfortable.

The hut was spacious. A folded mosquito net hung above DaD's head from a hook in the roof. On the floor next to him were stacks and stacks of books. Evidently their leader was fond of reading. His beloved PKMS gun was propped up against the wall next to him. A wooden pipe and silver lighter lay on the ground within his reach.

In one corner was a table with a small television set resting on it. There were two antennas sticking out the back of it and the TV was hooked up to a car battery. Jamba had seen televisions before, but had never actually watched anything on it. Next to the TV stood a small FM/AM radio, much like the one with the lever in the radio room.

A black board was hanging against one wall with scribbles and diagrams drawn on it in white chalk.

That was it. Nothing more and nothing less.

The captain instructed them all to sit down and then introduced himself as Captain Gut. He was a very serious man and built like ton of bricks himself, yet smaller than DaD still. Just like Dad he was wearing black boots and camouflage pants. Instead of a vest he was sporting a black shirt with a collar and short sleeves. The sleeves looked as if they might tear at any moment under his bulging biceps. The man's clothes were impeccably clean. Studying the captain, Jamba again realized that he was the only one present without a shirt on.

Captain Gut was not his real name. There was a story going around that this man was a bit of a psycho-case. More psycho than most in any case. He thrived on hand-to-hand combat. Getting up close and personal with the enemy and then ripping out their guts with a short blade he carried with him.

It appeared to Jamba that the more brutal the man, the higher and the faster he moved up the MoD ranks.

The captain then started his detailed briefing and was explaining the reason for them all being present. They had recently received reports from the main base in the DRC that increasing government patrols had been spotted near their position there. What was of concern was that these patrols came closer to the border area than ever before.

The enemy also used armored troop transport and even tanks during these patrols.

There were fears that they may discover their camps and those gathered here in the hut were to do a reconnaissance mission to establish patterns and threats. Full-scale confrontation was not the objective as to not draw unnecessary attention to themselves or their positions. However, if the opportunity presented itself to poach some weapons or equipment, it may well be considered.

Captain Gut explained how the MoD used speed and mobility as its main strategy. Almost like a tall, fast boxer who was up against a hard-hitting opponent with a lot of firepower. The objective was to stay on the outside and soften up the opponent with sharp stinging jabs. Then run and circle again, wearing the powerful boxer down. It was classic guerrilla tactics.

Their own army did not employ the use of large weaponry such as heavy artillery or tanks. These weapons impeded mobility, were difficult to conceal and trackers could easily find the deep tracks left by tanks through the jungle terrain.

The largest weapons their army used were small field cannons and anti-tank guns such as the T-12 which could be towed behind a pick-up. These weapons could knock out most of the older tanks or even be used as light artillery support. Speed and mobility were essential, especially since their camp in the DRC had to be relocated constantly.

Their squad was to observe a stretch of road running parallel to the Uganda-DRC border from south to north. Another group from their DRC base would observe the same stretch of road where it turns running east to west. Captain Gut reiterated that the aim of the mission was not to be drawn into a conflict, but purely to gather information as to the extent of the enemy's patrols and their capabilities. Any form of engagement was only to occur in the event of accidental discovery or if the risks were low, the enemy weak and valuable weapons or equipment could be appropriated.

Jamba was almost wriggling where he was sitting, as if being attacked by an army of red ants. He could barely contain his excitement at the prospect of possibly taking part in his first battle. He felt proud of being part of the MoD and of being selected for the mission.

The captain did not inquire whether they had any questions. Those were the orders. DaD would be leading the mission and Captain Gut, together with Sergeant Oboto, would issue them with DaD's orders and control the combat situation in the event of contact with the enemy. Only their assault rifles, spare ammunition, water and limited amounts of food were to be taken with them on the mission.

He dismissed them with orders to get some rest since they would be leaving before daybreak. As the group exited the hut, Jamba heard his name being called. DaD, still relaxing in his hammock, motioned him to approach. The man reached beneath his hammock with a searching hand and it emerged holding what seemed to be a rectangular cloth. The giant chucked it at the boy who caught it expertly.

"Sergeant Oboto found this in a village. We can't have you walking around looking the way you do," he simply said and dismissed the boy with a wave.

The T-shirt was already pulled half-way over the boy's torso by the time he hurriedly exited the hut. It was of a dark green color. An image of the head of a lion with a thick mane was printed on the front.

The shirt was spotless and the material was so new that it made him itch. The boy was ecstatic. He had never owned any brand new clothes before, let alone with such an awesome picture printed on it.

As he entered the armory hut to gather his ammunition belt, a spare magazine and some extra pouches, Jamba reflected on DaD's recent behavior towards him. The huge man had become almost like a father to him in a way. He provided the child with food, shelter and a sense of security. Yet, he had also clearly stated that the boy was his 'property'.

Jamba concluded that he was therefore rather an object than a person to their leader. Just as any weapon, vehicle or piece of equipment was an object which served its purpose in the greater scheme of things. No, DaD was like a father to all of them. Jamba was no exception. Each person in this army served some purpose. There was no preferential treatment. DaD simply needed to keep his war machine running as best he could.

CHAPTER 22

Jamba did not sleep in his new T-shirt that night. He wanted to keep it perfectly clean and new for as long a he could. Sleep came slowly as the prospect of adventure, combined with uncertainty and even an underlying sense of trepidation, toyed with him.

It felt as if he had drifted away only for moments when somebody kicked him in the ribs. It was Yoweri telling him to get ready and to go to the kitchen. He put on his shirt, fastened the ammunition belt around his waist, checked his water bottle and gathered his rifle. The time has arrived.

At the kitchen he was issued with a small, dirty backpack containing some fruit, bread and dried meat. The boy strapped it to his back and joined the small group gathered outside DaD's hut.

To his utter surprise, he saw that Okot and Annie were also present there, even though they were not at the briefing the previous day. Okot still wasn't carrying a rifle and Jamba was again baffled by this. The thin, intelligent boy was only carrying his backpack.

He had mixed emotions regarding Annie. What was she doing here? Was she going to help with carrying food? Maybe assist with cooking or cleaning? While it bothered him to some extent, he also felt excited at the prospect of having her around. Maybe they might even get a chance to talk again. And this time Okot would not escape his questions about girls either.

Captain Gut inspected everybody to make sure they were fully prepared. He was carrying one of the new sniper rifles they had looted from the South Africans. The weapon looked slick, shiny and fearsome, a deadly black mamba ready to strike.

DaD appeared from the hut. Instead of his usual PKMS machine gun he was now carrying a loaded Russian RPG-7 rocket propelled grenade launcher which was casually resting on one shoulder. On his hip hung a holstered pistol. Two extra rockets were visible where they protruded from his backpack like thick, blunt horns on a big antelope.

Without a word DaD took point and set off towards the west. The rest followed in single file and without any specific order.

They marched for the entire day, stopping only once for a short rest. DaD was always in the lead. Jamba was grateful that he carried so little since the pace was relentless. If you needed the toilet you had to do your business quickly and then rush to catch up again before you fell behind or got lost.

There were no conversations and they were moving in complete silence. Great care was taken not to step on dry branches which could break underfoot and betray their presence. Where the growth was so thick that one could hardly see your hands in front of you, DaD simply pushed ahead. Trying to hack a path through the dense jungle would be too noisy and leave too much evidence of their passing. Branches scratched and insects kept biting away at them. The sap from some plants made Jamba's arms itch for hours on end.

They were often climbing up slopes and rocks as if constantly scaling a mountain. With the increase in altitude, the vegetation started to thin out and the jungle opened up. Everybody became more alert out in the open.

The boy's breathing became labored as the oxygen also thinned out with their ascent and the air grew colder. He could see that especially the girl was struggling. But she simply pushed on without any complaints or openly showing her suffering. Jamba felt himself liking her even more.

As they crossed the open terrain and started to descend again, he noticed an enormous mountain peak only a few miles to the north of them. The peak was partly covered in snow and partly covered by clouds. It was a magnificent site. Jamba had never seen snow before and it was Okot who of course explained the phenomenon to him.

With their descent the plants started closing in on them until they were once again completely swallowed by the thick jungle. It was much warmer and humid and the boy's breathing became easier. There was no physical line or fence visible, but they had crossed the border into the DRC.

Suddenly there was a commotion in the foliage ahead of them

and the men instinctively hit the deck or went down on one knee, weapons at the ready. Jamba also immediately went prone and slotted a round into the chamber of his rifle. It all happened within a heartbeat.

Only DaD's raised fist was what stopped the group from opening fire. From the undergrowth an enormous shadow slowly emerged and then came to a dead stop. Jamba would never forget that image for as long as he lived.

The biggest ape he had ever seen stood in front of them, sniffing at the air and peering down at them through beady eyes. Its enormous head was tilted slightly upwards and it was staring at them with immense confidence down a short nose. The beast's arms were the size of logs, dangling all the way to the ground. Huge knuckles supported its massive bulk.

"Shhh!" the boy heard DaD whisper. "Mountain gorilla. It's a male silverback."

The animal snorted at them in contempt, hit its muscled chest once with an enormous hand and promptly disappeared back into the jungle. Plants and small trees could be heard crushing under its stupendous weight.

Jamba was in awe. It was the most beautiful and powerful animal he had ever seen. Now if only that gorilla could have been his spirit beast! Although that would be absolutely awesome to the boy, something within him said that killing such a beast would be a shame. It was just too magnificent.

Not everybody felt the same as he though. Some of the men begged DaD to follow and kill the great ape. DaD would have none of it. They had a job to do.

As night approached, their commander searched for a place to camp for the night. He stopped at the bottom of a cliff with some overhanging rocks and a fairly open carpet of leaves.

DaD produced a small folded hammock from his bag and tied its ends between two trees. The rest of them were left to find a spot somewhere on the ground and make themselves as comfortable as possible under the circumstances. To add insult to injury, a light drizzle came floating down from the heavens above.

Jamba found himself a spot against the wall of the overhang. The rain still penetrated here, but at least it seemed a bit more sheltered. He curled himself into a ball and used his backpack as a pillow. These were tough soldiers, as tough as they could possibly come. They all grew up under miserable conditions and had experienced immeasurable hardships but even to them it was a long, wet and uncomfortable night.

The boy was awakened by the noises from the activity around him as the others prepared to leave. Some were nibbling at bananas or bread to fortify their strength for the coming day and Jamba did the same.

Sergeant Oboto explained that the road was nearby and that they would patrol along it towards the north by following a parallel ridge.

After only a couple of hours marching, the ground beneath them suddenly sloped down steeply and the growth thinned out. About twenty feet below them a gravel road was visible. It was more somewhere between a road and a track. From higher up here where they could spy down onto the road, Jamba could also look across an expanse of endless jungle extending all the way to the western horizon.

The squad veered north, following the edge of the ridge and keeping the road within their view. Their pace had noticeably slowed and even greater care was taken to move quietly. For almost three hours they continued along the ridge until it was abruptly met by a vertical wall of rocks. It was a sheer cliff reaching at least a hundred feet into the sky above.

On the opposite side of the road was an almost vertical drop. The cliff in front of them and the drop across from them were part of the same rock formation. Somewhere in the past somebody, or some government, had actually made the effort to carve a pass through the rocks for the road to continue. It was probably about a hundred and fifty yard stretch before the terrain widened out again. They would have to follow the road on foot and there were risks involved. The group would be exposed and there would be no cover for them whatsoever.

That was not the only danger to them however. Jamba had no

way of knowing this yet, but the roads were often mined by the enemy or their own MoD soldiers alike. Even possibly by other groups who may at some stage have held control over the region in the past.

Captain Gut was studying the surface of the road. Tracks were clearly visible. "Two armored personnel carriers and two tanks," he concluded after returning from the road where he had a closer look. "Cannot tell when exactly. Maybe a day. They were going up north," he said with conviction.

Jamba had no idea how the captain could tell all this just by looking at the tracks, but it was the same direction they were following. DaD nodded and gestured towards Sergeant Oboto who immediately took charge.

"Girl! You and that boy come over here," he ordered firmly. The boy he was referring to was Okot. "Start walking. Five paces apart. Stick to the right-hand side of the road."

Okot and Annie glanced at each other not quite grasping the situation, but they did as they were told. The girl went first, followed by Okot trailing her a few paces back.

The rest of the group waited for almost a minute and then followed in single file, weapons at the ready. This time there was a distinct hierarchy. Sergeant Oboto pointed towards Tito to move next and then another boy Jamba barely knew. He was followed by Yoweri and then the rest of the men trailed in order of seniority or rank. DaD took up the rear and Jamba was instructed to follow behind him with a branch and sweep their tracks.

The girl was walking slowly but at a constant pace and keeping her eyes fixed in front of her on the ground. It was as if she knew to expect something but just didn't know what it was yet. Every now and then Okot would look back over his shoulder towards the group following in the distance behind him. In between his sweeps with the branch, Jamba in turn flicked constant glances in Annie's direction. He was not feeling good about their situation whatsoever.

A mounting feeling of trepidation kept tugging at him.

Not much time had passed before the explosion rocked the world around them. The echo from the blast bounced off the side of the cliff and was ear-shattering. Birds leaped from the trees and hastily flapped off in all directions with loud chirps of alarm.

Jamba instinctively hit the ground beneath him with his finger on the trigger of his rifle. Small rocks and lumps of earth rained down on him from above. With horrified disgust he realized that some of the objects falling into his hair and onto his arms and legs were shreds of flesh. He flapped at it wildly to rid himself of it as he immediately knew what it was.

The girl was half lying on the ground and half propped-up against the cliff. Both her legs and one hand were missing. Blood was gushing from where the limbs once were only moments ago. The dirty white dress was torn and soaked a dark red. Her neck was bent awkwardly and she seemed to be staring at the group. As if calling out to the men, her small mouth flapped up and down like that of a fish out of water. Then the movement stopped and her body went limp. Annie was with them no more.

Jamba was paralyzed. The reality of what had just happened refused to register with him. He was too shocked to think. If that mutilated body lying up the road was anybody else, it would have simply been a bad event. But this was his Annie, what was left of Annie.

The boy's lips started to quiver and he could feel tears coming on. Only the stern voice coming from Sergeant Oboto halted the impending flood of emotions in its tracks.

Like somebody who had been in this exact situation countless times before, Sergeant Oboto instructed Okot to keep moving. The boy stood frozen to the spot with blood running from his left ear and a gash along his right leg. Somehow he had remained on his feet after the explosion.

"Get a move on, boy! They will be coming for us soon!"

Okot was clearly terrified and understandably so. He was next in line and kept looking at the remains of the girl and then again back at the men behind him.

"Move!" This time it was DaD's voice. He had the RPG launcher aimed straight at Okot. It had the necessary motivation and Okot started moving forwards almost at a jogging pace.

When the group reached the girl, Oboto instructed the boys to carefully fill the crater left by the mine and Jamba had to use the branch to level the area to look as natural as possible. He had to force himself with a superhuman effort to cover Annie's spilled blood with soil.

Two of the men dumped the remains of the girl over the edge of the drop-off, nervously watching their every step. Her corpse became a worthless lump of flesh left to be consumed by the insects and wild animals of the jungle. Jamba heard a thud and the crash of branches as the girl's body impacted with the ground far beneath and rolled over a few times before it came to an abrupt stop. Their surroundings were eerily quiet again. The boy quickly wiped away a tear before anybody would notice. He wanted to blame somebody for Annie's death, but wasn't certain who that person would be. DaD, Oboto, Gut... or all of them?

Throughout all this activity Okot had kept on moving and never looked back again. He just continued to stare out ahead of him and walked at a brisk pace, seemingly oblivious to the possible dangers buried below his feet. Maybe his eyes were even closed, but Jamba couldn't tell.

He felt sorry for the boy and had always liked him. Yet, if Okot were to be blown to pieces, it would not affect Jamba even half as much as the death of Annie did. The boy felt ashamed of his private thoughts. But his heart ached. He had really liked the small girl with her dirty white dress and the swollen cheek. Maybe it was even love.

Then Sergeant Oboto took Tito's rifle from him and told him to get moving. Tito just shrugged and did as he was told. If he was scared he did not show it. Maybe it helped to know that Okot had already done most of the work. It dawned on Jamba that if Okot was also to meet his end, that Tito would be the next in line. The logic behind the enforced rule of not being allowed to have close friends became clearer to the boy with each passing second.

At that very moment two of his only friends were busy running a gauntlet for DaD. His beloved Annie was already no more.

CHAPTER 23

When they eventually reached the other side of the pass without further incident, Okot was sitting on his haunches and busy drawing patterns in the sand with a stick. Oboto kicked at the doodles and grunted something about the boy being an idiot and leaving signs for the enemy to see. The sergeant was clearly another breed from the relatively more docile Sergeant Wambuzi back at their camp.

Something in DaD's pocket had started vibrating and he produced a small black cellphone. It was the patrol from their other camp on the east to west route of the road, inquiring about the explosion. After DaD explained the situation he informed them regarding the tracks found on the road. The other men had encountered the same tracks and also came to the conclusion that the convoy was moving north. There was nothing else to report.

The group climbed the steep ridge again and continued on their journey. Okot seemed lackluster and completely disconnected. The boy was just going through the motions. Jamba was more alert than ever after the day's events and with the impending possibility of encountering the convoy with its tanks and armored vehicles. What could they possibly do against tanks? He eyed the rocket launcher which was resting on DaD's shoulder. Prospects still seemed bleak, even with the faith and blind trust he had in DaD.

They trudged along in silence for many hours until darkness finally dropped its veil on them. There were no signs of the convoy and every now and again Captain Gut had gone down to the road to inspect the tracks.

They reached another cliff next to the road but this one was more accessible and they climbed to the top. DaD decided that it made for a good look-out point and that they would make camp under the trees. From there the snaking road could easily be observed for some miles in both directions. DaD produced a pair of binoculars from his bag and stood peering through them for what seemed like hours. It was a pair of military field glasses with the lenses set deep as to minimize any reflection off them.

That evening, with two sentries placed to watch the road, they gathered in a half-circle facing DaD. He had unfolded a rectangular cloth which he spread out on the ground in front of him. On it lay ten small balls of something wrapped in light blue plastic. Each plastic wrapping was tied with a piece of string at the neck.

He explained to them that this was the *whoonga* the South African had told him about that night at the fire. DaD and another soldier had already experimented with the drug and he was happy with the results and had estimated the dosage.

Since the possibility existed that they may have to face some tanks and armored vehicles, they could just as well do so feeling invincible. DaD grinned at this remark. He wanted to see how the others coped with it and who would receive one of the small packages.

Except for Okot and Tito, each of them were handed a plastic ball by Sergeant Oboto. Jamba removed the string and opened it. The wrapping contained five round lumps of a rusty-white colored powder which resembled tiny balls of clay.

DaD then continued to explain that they would ideally smoke it but because of the risk of the enemy maybe picking up the scent, they should simply swallow one lump each. It should also slightly reduce the severity of the effect from the drug.

Jamba would follow DaD's orders without question. He both trusted and feared the man. Choosing what looked like the smallest lump, he placed it on his tongue and swallowed it down with a swig from his water bottle. Then he sat back and waited.

Nothing happened for a long time. The soldiers kept looking at each other in anticipation to see whether somebody was showing signs of intoxication. Then his heart started beating slower and slower. He could hear it pump in his ears, then almost stop and then pump again. Things started looking slightly blurry and his world slowed down.

The boy looked at the other men and they seemed to be smiling at him. Were they smiling only at him or in general? Everybody seemed happy. Jamba also felt happy. Happiness!

The boy experienced happiness. Annie was forgotten - for now.

He was suddenly very hungry and thirsty. His stomach also started to ache but he was feeling gooooood! The boy drank more water and found a slice of bread in his backpack after some difficulty. Everybody continued to smile.

The sensation did not last very long. His heart started racing and he was feeling anxious, even quite paranoid about the enemy being close-by. Originally it was a fantastic and euphoric feeling, but he didn't like the descent very much. The cramps in his stomach grew more intense.

Jamba was becoming agitated and irate. The pain gripping his stomach was uncomfortable and upsetting him. The memory of the dead girl and the vision of Okot paving the way through an unseen minefield was flaming his anger. The smiling faces felt as though they were laughing at him and deliberately provoking or teasing him.

He found himself looking at the unfamiliar boy sitting almost across from him. The boy was laughing at him, no doubt about it. The bastard was laughing at him, right in his face.

"*Puta!*" Jamba exclaimed in a rush of anger. "Don't you laugh at me you *puta!*" He was on top of the boy in a flash and pinned his head to the ground. A knee was thrusting into the boy's diaphragm. The astonished face staring up at him with wide eyes was struggling for breath, hands flailing in an attempt to rid himself of his attacker.

A giant paw had cuffed the side of Jamba's head and he was lying sprawled on the ground several paces away. DaD was standing over him and then said, "Leave your anger for the enemy, boy. You already know what happens to those who fight with our own. Don't you? Would you like to try that shit on me now?"

Jamba was breathing heavily. His rage was slowly subsiding, but there was still an unexplained anger welled up deep within him. Of course he did not want to take on DaD. The thought of possible punishment did not even cross his mind. Anger was still his master and the cramps in his stomach were consuming him.

Others around him were also visibly clutching at their stomachs and he saw one heavily bearded man vomiting. The side of his head where DaD had hit him did not hurt at all. The cramps were overriding all other pain.

They all slept deeply that evening but with occasional grunts and groans disturbing the usually impeccable silence. Jamba tried his best to permanently block the visions of Annie from his mind. He knew he had to protect himself or he might go insane.

The next morning Jamba realized that something was wrong. DaD and the officers were in serious discussion. Without having to be told what was happening, he noticed that Okot was nowhere to be seen. The boy had disappeared during the previous night.

All attempts by the experienced Captain Gut to track him had failed. The carpet of leaves on the jungle floor was too thick for any footprints to be visible and the foliage here wasn't dense enough to force a person to break branches or bend leaves as they passed. The captain had quickly abandoned the search for the boy.

DaD was visibly upset. Sparks were flying from his eyes. He clearly had to make an effort in controlling himself before he perhaps exploded and hurt somebody.

The implications of Okot's disappearance were significant. What if he was caught and gave away their position and strength to the enemy? What if he deliberately searched out the enemy and surrendered to them? Okot also knew where their base across the border in Uganda was situated. After many years it would now have to be moved. DaD looked beyond furious. He couldn't risk any form of discovery.

DaD immediately phoned Wambuzi at the recruitment HQ and gave instructions for them to start destroying all evidence of the huts. All vehicles and equipment had to be moved to a new location known to Wambuzi and which was located many miles to the south. Extra care was to be taken to look out for approaching aircraft and helicopters. Jamba could not help feeling vexed at the thought of the many hours and much sweat he had wasted on digging tunnels which would never even be used.

The group moved on along the ridge with some urgency. A couple of hours up the road they came upon another easily accessible cliff and DaD decided that this was to be their new vantage point and would remain their base until further notice. The previously steep drop on the opposite side of the road had receded and now opened out into a gradually declining hill.

Within only minutes after arriving at their new location, another explosion was heard in the distance. DaD immediately contacted the other reconnaissance team which was patrolling the western road to get a report. They knew nothing of the explosion and had not encountered anybody as yet.

DaD divided his small army into two. One group was to continue patrolling by following the ridge along the road whilst the others got some rest.

It was not until another two hours had passed when a sentry rushed over to DaD where he was busy relaxing in his hammock. The guard had spotted approaching vehicles through the binoculars. DaD went to have a look himself. There were only three vehicles, two troop carriers and one tank. Could Captain Gut have been wrong? Yet, there were tracks on the road clearly belonging to two different tanks.

The group which left on patrol arrived back in a hurry. They had heard the approaching vehicles and rushed to regroup. Orders were for everybody to lay low in the trees. Not a sound or movement was to be made. Only DaD, the captain and the sergeant crawled to the edge of the cliff to observe the approaching vehicles.

The roar from the tank drowned out any sounds coming from the other vehicles. Jamba was lying motionless in the thick foliage, itching with curiosity. He wanted to see a tank close-up and he wanted to see the faces of his enemy for the first time. It was not going to happen just yet. The boy had to wait like everybody else. He checked his weapon for the hundredth time during the past ten minutes. He was burning for some action. Not a single grain of fear was to be found anywhere within him. Jamba was as ready as he could ever be.

The roar intensified as the vehicles slowly approached them. A high-pitch squeal could be heard coming from the unoiled tracks grating over metal wheels. Then the noise gradually faded as the convoy passed their position without incident. The vehicles were traveling at a very slow pace, almost at a crawl. Maybe they were being extra cautious? Was it because of Okot? The explosion which killed the girl? Or maybe because of the other explosion they had heard earlier that morning? Jamba found his mind racing in his excitement.

The boy was imagining DaD aiming his RPG launcher at the vehicles and blowing them to pieces one by one. Then they would mow the occupants down from their position high above.

None of this happened. The men waited until the vehicles completely disappeared into the distance. DaD called the western patrol from his phone and warned them of the approaching convoy. No action was to be taken or he would eat their intestines for breakfast. It would only draw unwanted attention to the location of the main HQ.

The big man gathered them together. There was a huge smile on his face. Jamba found it mystifying how this colossus could so easily go from rage to a broad grin within only moments.

"Peacekeepers," DaD said. "Bunch of glorified boy scouts."

Jamba had no idea what either a peace keeper or a boy scout was. He wondered whether he was also considered to be a boy scout since he was a boy and they were busy doing scouting.

"Two BMP's and an old T-55 tank. Some Indians, Africans and a couple of Whiteys. Those blue helmets are perfect for target practice or to take a piss in," he exclaimed with some disgust.

The boy had never seen Indians or Whiteys before. He badly wanted to see these white men who were so rich that they could afford to buy diamonds for their women. He briefly thought of Annie and how he would have liked to have given her one of those sparkling stones.

Dad was not done yet. "Captain, we need to find that second tank. I've got a feeling that explosion this morning had something to do with its disappearance. Maybe we can salvage some weapons and equipment. Better get a move-on. Their help will arrive soon. Helicopters. More patrols. I seriously doubt that they'll abandon their hardware."

The hunt was on. There might even be some action on the horizon, the boy hoped to himself. A surge of adrenaline rushed trough his body.

Chapter 24

Before moving off they first checked their weapons. Jamba saw Sergeant Oboto slide a round into the chamber of his *Kalashnikov* and the boy followed his example, making sure his rifle was on safety. The group left their temporary camp at a brisk pace, yet still slow enough as to not make any unnecessary noises.

Oboto had taken point. Things were clearly escalating. DaD obviously needed somebody with experience and trained senses to take the lead. Sometimes Oboto would leave them behind and move far ahead of the group as he made a few probing reconnaissance trips.

After another of his solo recce's, Oboto returned in a stooping posture and clenched his fist as a signal to halt the advancing group. With his other hand he was holding an index finger to his mouth. 'Quiet!'

Jamba literally started trembling in anticipation. The entire group went down on one knee and Oboto shuffled over to DaD to brief him. They waited for Captain Gut to join them. The boy could hear the entire conversation from where he was kneeling just behind their commander.

"There's a broken-down T-55 about three hundred yards from here," Oboto whispered. "Seems like an anti-tank mine took out one of their tracks. There's also a man working on the engine."

DaD just nodded and waited patiently for the rest of the information.

"Looks like four men. One sleeping, one on guard, one working on the engine and one on the radio in the turret cupola. All armed. There's an SGMT heavy machine gun mounted on the turret."

DaD smiled at hearing the words 'SGMT heavy machine gun.' He considered the information for a few moments and then gave his orders in a low whisper.

"Oboto, you take six men and circle them from behind. I will take the other six men and move towards them on this side of the road for a frontal assault. Gut, you take a position higher up on the ridge from where you can see both me and the tank. On my signal I want you to use that sniper rifle of yours to take out the man in the turret first." DaD gripped Captain Gut's shoulder tightly. "*None* of them can be allowed to enter that tank. And kill whatever else you can see. My men will then open fire. Should any of the pigs take cover behind the tank, Oboto's men will attack them from behind."

The commander paused to think what else he could add. "And use grenades only if really necessary. I want this to be swift and deadly. Their help will arrive soon. We need to finish this and get out of here. Got it?"

The officers nodded their understanding and Oboto immediately gestured towards three veterans and three younger boys to follow him. They stayed low and quickly ascended the ridge and then crossed the road in a hunched position. This left Jamba and Tito in DaD's group. The captain disappeared between the trees on the ridge, the slick new sniper rifle resting on his back.

DaD waved at his men to gather closer. He repeated the plan to everybody present. "Check your weapons. Safeties off! If you make a noise or fire before Gut fired, I will kill you personally."

Now that things were getting real, some anxiety took hold of Jamba. On an impulse he scratched around in his pockets and produced the blue plastic bag containing the *whoonga*. He swallowed one of the small balls before anybody could notice.

The group cautiously made their way down the ridge until they were near the edge of the road. Staying behind cover they moved almost at a snail's pace with DaD in the lead.

After sneaking their way through the foliage for a few yards, crouching low and as noiseless as leopards, Jamba could hear some distant hammering. Then followed the distinct sound of radio static which was occasionally interrupted by a man's muffled voice.

The *whoonga* was kicking in. Jamba felt good. Jamba felt ready. The assault felt like an exciting excursion to a movie theater or the zoo. None of which he had ever visited.

Everything was just perfect. Surreal!

The outlines of the tank became visible through the shrubs. DaD halted them with a fist raised. Getting any closer would be difficult because there was a man patrolling up and down the road about fifty feet in front of them. They risked being detected and for the others at the tank then possibly taking cover inside the vehicle or getting to that massive machine gun mounted on the copula. To try and take them on from this distance would be folly.

Jamba could see a man lying on his back on the front of the tank seemingly taking a nap. He had a pair of dark glasses over his eyes and a long stem of grass between his lips. An invisible man was at the rear of the tank hammering away at the engine. One of the tank tracks were split in half and partly lying in the road. A small crater could be seen in the road near the back of the vehicle.

A man with a light brown skin and thick mustache was sitting on top of the turret. On his head was a light blue helmet with white letters printed on the front. Jamba couldn't read them. The man was clearly having difficulty with the radio. He would attempt to call somebody on it and then wait patiently, only to be answered by static. To his right, just above the tank's main gun, was mounted the enormous SGMT machine gun.

Even when wounded, the tank looked monstrous and formidable.

But the boy's attention was on the guy patrolling the road. Instead of a blue helmet, this man was wearing a maroon beret with some kind of insignia or shield pinned to one side. Jamba looked at the beret as if it was a new toy in a shop and he knew he wanted to posses it. Everything about the person underneath that maroon beret made the boy desire it.

The man had a pinkish-white skin and was colossal. He was a white version of DaD, down to the clean-shaven face. The only differences other than his skin color and uniform, being the beret on his head and the fact that he was carrying a very short snub-nosed sub-machine gun.

As the man patrolled the road he was flexing the arm holding his machine gun up and down as if though he was lifting weights except that the weights could just as well have been made of feathers. Set against the backdrop of his enormous bulk and bulging muscles, the machine gun rather looked like a small pistol. The man was alert. His eyes did not for a moment leave the trees and shrubs surrounding him and his comrades.

Under the spell of the *whoonga*, the entire scene seemed fantastical too Jamba. Owning that beret would be his personal symbol of might and power. He just *had* to have it. He had to be the one to kill this white man.

DaD was using his binoculars to search the ridge for his captain. From here it was difficult to see anything and trees were obstructing their line of vision up the ridge. The man patrolling the road in front of them had evidently complicated the original battle plan. DaD could not see Gut to be able to signal him yet.

The commander seemed to have made up his mind and grabbed hold of the nearest man's rifle. He checked it and then lay prone, taking aim at the guard. If DaD could take down the white man, Captain Gut would hopefully interpret it as his signal to target the one sitting on the tank's turret.

But by now the big white man was busy walking past the tank and patrolling the area of road behind it already too far away for a certain shot. Jamba was growing impatient and irritated. His small mind, warped by the *whoonga* drug was in conflict with himself. It was a battle between waiting patiently or to somehow get the signal out to Captain Gut to get this party started.

DaD clearly had difficulty finding the captain, so Jamba decided to help his leader out. Without the others noticing, he slipped into the foliage and very quietly made his way closer to the tank.

Undetected, the boy reached a tall tree barely twenty feet from the monstrous armored beast. He checked the road. All was exactly as it had been a few moments earlier. A sleeping man in sunglasses, a blue helmet struggling with his radio and a giant wearing a purple beret patrolling the road. He could now also finally see the one working on the engine. It was a small black man with spectacles resting on his nose. He too had a blue helmet perched on his head at an angle. All the men were armed with the exception of the one working on the engine.

The white guy had turned around and was busy walking back towards the tank and its crew. As he drew level with the boy, Jamba casually strolled into the road and faced him. The *whoonga* had made him fearless, impatient and lacking all judgment. The boy's AK-47 was hanging at his side by its strap around his neck with the barrel facing downwards.

"Hello, mister. I like your hat," he said calmly as if he was merely addressing some of the kids on the parade ground.

Time almost stood still. The man with the sunglasses slowly rolled onto his side and peered at the boy over his rims. The radio man just sat there with his lips frozen in mid-sentence. The one working on the engine was so taken by surprise that he kept hammering for a few more seconds and then continued to tap at the engine subconsciously without registering what he was actually doing. Only the white monster reacted instantly and had raised his sub-machine gun towards Jamba. Then he stood frozen and seemingly torn between decisions.

"Can I see your hat, mister?" the child asked.

"What the hell? No! Put your hands up away from that gun, boy," the Whitey said in a strange, almost lyrical accent.

"It's a rifle, mister. Not a gun," Jamba replied indignantly. He then promptly continued to do a little jig and while grabbing at his crotch he repeated the rhyme Sergeant Oboto had taught them that first day on the parade ground.

"This is my rifle,

This is my gun,

This is for fighting,

And this is for fun..." he sang to the men.

They could only stare in astonished silence. The giant finally found his voice and said, "Well, this is called a *beret* and not a hat."

The *whoonga* was starting to wear off and with it the boy's patience was running out, but his irritation and anger was now growing. The rage was only intensified by sudden painful cramps in his stomach.

Jamba already hated this man for what he perceived to be taunting him on purpose. "*Well, this is called a beret and not a hat,*" the boy repeated mockingly, imitating the man with a voice which was dripping with sarcasm. His face contorted as he said this.

The men were clearly starting to look uneasy. The situation was becoming too weird for them. The white guy again instructed the child to raise his hands. He was now also glancing nervously towards the trees.

"You're going to shoot a little boy, *puta*? I just wanted to see your hat... beret." There was hostility in Jamba's voice now.

The men's eyes darted between each other and the child. Something was clearly out of place here. A small child armed with an AK-47 and dancing in the middle of a road to nowhere was definitely not 'normal'.

And then the Lord of Chaos was summoned. He arrived in the form of flames and smoke which darkened the sky as a deafening explosion ripped into the tank. The rocket did almost no damage to the armor at all. There was only a black, smoking blotch where the turret and body met and a small sheet of metal plating had been curled slightly upwards.

Where the man in the sunglasses was only moments before, there remained nothing but empty space and globs of bloody flesh littering the khaki-colored paint of the tank.

Almost instantaneously a shot rang out and the man in the cupola slumped backwards, arms stretched to the sides and his lifeless eyes staring into the blue sky above.

The engine man frantically took cover underneath the tank. Without a weapon he was at least pretty well protected from most sides for the time being.

Jamba was thrown off his feet by the shock wave, but immediately rolled over a couple of times and started firing at the white man who had also reacted instantly. In three long strides the man had reached the tank and dived underneath it where he joined the black guy with the spectacles.

Bullets were bouncing off the tracked wheels and sparks were flying everywhere. Jamba kept firing as he was trained, squeezing off two shots at a time, but the boy was cursing himself for not taking down the big brute who had been standing within spitting distance of him just moments ago.

He realized that puffs of dust and stones were popping up into the air near him. Too close for comfort. The owner of that awesome beret was actually shooting back at him. Jamba kept rolling and rolling until he reached the tree from which he had emerged earlier. After finding the relative safety of its fat trunk, he unclipped his magazine and counted the remaining cartridges using the small holes punched down the narrow part as a reference.

The boy had spent fourteen rounds. From his ammunition pouch he impatiently fed sixteen more cartridges into the clip, briefly checked that his spare magazine was also fully loaded and then cautiously peered around the tree. Almost immediately a bullet shattered the bark near his face. This is a bad situation, he thought to himself.

Jamba decided that the only option for him was to wait for the other men. He could hear gunfire now coming from the opposite direction of the tank too - must be Sergeant Oboto.

Captain Gut appeared from between some foliage and crawled towards the boy hiding behind the large tree. He immediately started cursing at the boy and slapped him hard through the face. It stung Jamba, but again the cramps emanating from his stomach were so painful by now that he barely felt the blow.

"Idiot! I should kill you right here!" the captain spat. "Now give me some cover fire so I can get a mark on those pigs."

Without exposing himself from behind the tree, Jamba pointed his rifle in the general direction of the tank and pulled the trigger in short bursts. Gut rolled towards the opposite side and quickly tried to line up a target in the powerful telescopic sights. Without looking, Jamba kept pumping bullets in that general direction, two at a time.

"I can see the bastard," the captain breathed, calmly taking aim through the sniper rifle's scope. "Only his legs. But I can see him..." And he pulled the trigger.

A scream pierced the air. It was in fact more of a horrible wailing than a scream.

"Got you pig. But I'm not done yet," the captain continued to whisper to himself. Another shot and the wailing intensified.

Jamba stopped firing and reloaded his *Kalashnikov* with the spare magazine.

Then DaD's voice boomed from somewhere to the south of their position. "If you want to live, come out from under the tank. If you want to die a slow and painful death, then stay there. The choice is very simple."

The wailing had subsided and turned into a whimper.

"Okay! Okay!" replied a timid voice from underneath the beast. "We're coming out. Just don't shoot! I'm unarmed."

The small black man with the spectacles peered from underneath the engine of the tank. His already-large eyes seemed magnified by the lenses. He crawled out completely and stood waiting with his hands raised high in the air. Sweat visibly poured down his face.

"Where is your friend?" DaD inquired from somewhere in the undergrowth.

"He's wounded. He needs help," the engineer stuttered.

"Get him out of there." It was an order. The man had no choice.

He ducked down and seemed to grapple with something. Then he emerged with an arm gripped in each hand and was struggling to pull the enormous weight connected to those arms from underneath the tank.

With each tug there was a loud grunt or a shout of pain. Eventually the huge white man with the maroon beret emerged completely and lay on the ground writhing in agony, gripping at both his legs. The pants around each of his calves were soaked in blood. His left foot was nearly amputated by the massive impact of the sniper bullet.

Jamba and Gut pushed themselves off the ground and cautiously walked towards the two men. DaD and his men emerged from the trees nearby and Sergeant Oboto and his group joined from the dense foliage behind the tank.

DaD completely ignored Jamba. He was going to make the boy sweat. "Take that gun off the turret. Gather their weapons. Look for ammunition and grenades inside. Remove the battery. Report anything else of interest." He turned to his captain. "Nice shooting. Need to save that ammo though. It's scarce."

Jamba ambled towards the injured giant lying on the ground. He bent over and removed the beret still clinging to his head. The insignia was a wing holding onto a dagger. The boy liked it a lot. He placed the beret on top of his own head and shifted it around a bit until he was satisfied with its positioning.

"Mercy..." the man croaked up at him.

"What? What's this *puta* saying?" Jamba was asking nobody in particular.

Tito was the one who answered him. "It's French. He's saying '*merci*'. It means thank you."

"What the hell? We just shot this pig and now he's thanking us? Too much *whoonga, puta*." Jamba looked at the man intently. He noticed a pen protruding from a shirt pocket.

The holes where the bullets from the sniper rifle entered his calves seemed small at first, but the exit wounds were massive and his left foot was now pointing in the opposite direction of what was natural. This man was surely going to bleed to death.

"No... no... English... Mercy," he repeated.

Again Jamba was puzzled. "What is this 'mercy'?" he asked Tito. The boy just shrugged.

"He's asking you to spare him," Sergeant Oboto offered from where he was busy disconnecting the tank's battery. "Mercy. Spare him. Save him. Now stop standing around and come help me with this battery."

The boy looked into the blue eyes of the soldier who could have been the equivalent of a white DaD. He felt a deep hatred for this man.

"Okay. I will save you, *puta*." He put the muzzle of his rifle against the man's forehead and pulled the trigger. As an after-thought he removed the pen and slipped it into his own pocket.

There was a depressed silence and men were staring at Jamba from all directions. Again DaD did not say a word to the boy. Instead he commanded, "Let's get moving people. I want to get out of here."

Jamba went over to Sergeant Oboto and started helping him with the battery. The small engineer with the spectacles had wet his pants.

It took only a few minutes for the men to complete their tasks. They made use of the various tools the mechanic was using earlier on. DaD walked up behind the terrified man, aimed his pistol at the back of his head and without a word pulled the trigger. He did not even know that death was coming.

It was going to be a hard slog back with all the heavy equipment.

"I will contact the others to meet us with a vehicle. But we need to make it through that minefield at the pass first. Let's move!"

DaD stared marching off towards the south, nearly effortlessly carrying both his RPG and the tank's SGMT heavy machine gun.

CHAPTER 25

The squad spent many slow hours toiling with the equipment they had salvaged from the tank. The battery proved most problematic, but luckily it had two handled brackets mounted on the sides to make for easier transportation. The men alternated the task between them.

The spare ammunition they had found was also heavy. Some cartridges were stowed in metal boxes and others were already loaded into rather small, straight magazines. Jamba was carrying the weapons taken from the tank crew. On one side of the stubby guns were printed the letters 'MP-5 H&K'. The boy had no idea what that meant.

Over Captain Gut's shoulders dangled a long belt of heavy cartridges meant for DaD's new toy, the 7.62x54mm SGMT. They were enormous and more like mini-shells than cartridges. Jamba could only imagine the damage one of those bullets would do to a man.

It was hard work. DaD had called their headquarters on this side of the border to arrange for two pick-ups. He instructed them to meet his group near the pass and be on the lookout for convoys or helicopters. Taking out the tank crew was a risk, but a calculated risk. The government forces knew of their presence anyway. They just did not know the exact location of the guerrilla base yet, and venturing this far near the Ugandan border posed significant dangers for themselves as well. It was MoD territory and had been so for a long period of time.

Once they arrived at the pass, Tito was relieved of his AK-47 again and instructed to take the lead. The boy who Jamba had attacked after taking the *whoonga* for the first time, was second in line and followed behind Tito. Both did as they were told and Jamba was impressed by how Tito simply strolled next to the road towards the other side of the pass without so much as blinking. The boy seemed very brave and unconcerned.

Jamba was again left with the task of sweeping the tracks behind the group. They all made it to the other side without incident. An unarmed man carefully appeared from the foliage with his hands slightly raised and motioned them towards two vehicles hidden underneath some nearby trees.

The men loaded the heavy equipment and got onto the backs of the vehicles. They were going to have to drive along the road for some distance and hope not to trigger any mines or run into any convoys. It was a tense few minutes. The pick-up transporting DaD and the ammunition drove at a good distance behind the front vehicle.

They headed west for some time at quite some speed. If they tripped a mine, the pick-up might avoid most of the damage with some luck. Eventually they turned off the road. Two men removed some bushes which had been concealing a track. After getting rid of all evidence that the vehicles were ever there, they entered the thick jungle. Jamba wondered what a convoy would think if they noticed tracks suddenly just stopping in the middle of the main road. The plan was not perfect but some care had to be taken at least.

Both vehicles had large bull-bars mounted at the front. The track was barely visible and they crashed their way through much of the foliage. On the way they encountered several of their own patrols. The MoD seemed to be thick in this area and Jamba realized that the army must be much bigger than he had originally thought it to be.

Eventually they finally arrived at the camp. It was a small town consisting entirely of tents scattered between the dense trees. There were no deliberate clearings visible. The natural surroundings had been preserved as much as possible.

Some tents were just big enough for two men, whilst others could evidently house as many as twelve or fifteen. This was a rough life to lead.

Several vehicles and anti-tank guns with long barrels were visible where they were parked under large green camouflage nets. A towed anti-aircraft gun was hooked up to a vehicle. It had multiple barrels, like teeth ready to bite at any unwelcome intruder.

Jamba could count at least fifty men sitting around or busying themselves with chores. There were probably many more in their tents or out on patrols. He was awestruck by the actual size of the MoD. Previously his entire world had consisted of only the few people he always saw at the recruitment camp. To him that was pretty much the entire army. DaD suddenly seemed wealthier and more powerful than ever before.

After they had parked the vehicles and started unloading, two men with red armbands approached DaD, saluted him and shook hands. Captain Gut and Sergeant Oboto followed as they all entered one of the larger tents.

Jamba handed the MP-5's to a fat man with a bushy beard. The man studied the guns as if they came from outer space and then seemed quite pleased. While carrying them to a nearby tent, he kept fiddling with one of the guns, excited like a child released in a toy shop.

The boy went off to explore. He found a tent serving as a kitchen and another serving as a communications room. There were tents with crates of ammunition such as cartridges, shells, mortars and grenades. Others only contained rolled-up blankets and trinkets lying around. Objects such as torches, photographs and even a few books were visible here and there. Jamba wondered where their tunnels and toilet pits were located.

He found a nearby stream and sat down on a rock. He then took the maroon beret from his head and studied it. He gently ran his fingers across the insignia. Jamba had no idea what the image of a wing holding a dagger meant, but he liked it, just as he liked the picture of the lion on his new T-shirt.

The boy looked down at his shirt and noticed for the first time how dirty it was. There was blood spattered across one shoulder and a large reddish-brown stain covered much of the lion's mane.

He continued to study the beret. Jamba reflected on the hatred he felt for the man whom he had so casually shot in the face earlier that day. His prejudices were not quite clear to him yet, other than knowing he hated the enemy, he hated that man and that the enemy had to be exterminated. In a sense the man represented DaD, but there could only be one DaD. Any symbol of power, competition or authority belonging to their enemies had to be disposed of.

The act of physically killing the man did not bother the boy. Concepts such as empathy, compassion and 'mercy' were foreign and unclear to him. He had killed before and he would kill again. If a person threatened him, the value of that person's life became non-existent. He valued his own life and he valued DaD's life. The lives of others were secondary and the lives of his enemies had no value whatsoever. Maybe Annie's life had value to him also. But Annie was no more. Jamba's own innocence was long dead.

The boy remembered the pen he had taken off the body of the white man and searched for it in his pockets. It was a cheap plastic pen with a blue cap covering the tip. Jamba removed the cap and tested the pen on his hand. It struggled to flow on his humid skin.

The boy had an idea. He once saw a man carrying a rifle with crosses carved into the wooden stock. Yoweri had told him it represented all the enemies the man had killed. Jamba had been impressed.

He turned the beret inside out and thought for a moment. Then slowly and carefully he drew a cross on the gray material covering the inside of the beret. The cross symbolized the killing of the white colossus. He stared at it for a moment and then added another cross next to it. This symbolized the slitting of Bubba's throat. Then another. It was for the boy he had killed next to the shebeen in Kampala.

Jamba wondered whether he should add the giant forest hog as well but decided against it. Three crosses. Three kills. He felt a sense of pride and triumph. The beret will be his diary, his book of records. And he will treasure it and guard it jealously.

The boy decided to return to the encampment. He knew that punishment awaited him at some stage. The thought of this bothered him little. Somewhere along his path through life, he had discarded his sense of fear during the past weeks. Whatever will be will be. Death will come to everybody eventually. They were trading in death and their daily lives were ruled by death. It was their occupation. The only uncertainties were always only when and how. Never 'if' - Jamba had accepted this as the truth.

He found Tito and Yoweri sitting on the ground where they were busy cleaning their weapons. The boys nodded recognition and continued their polishing. Jamba showed them his beret. They passed it around and commented on how nice it looked. Tito inquired about the three blue crosses and Jamba explained their significance. The two other boys exchanged glances and mumbled their admiration.

He decided to move along and find some food to eat. His stomach cramps kept recurring. The boy wasn't sure whether it was still as a result of the *whoonga* or whether he was simply hungry. Before he could reach the kitchen tent, the fat man he saw earlier approached him and informed the boy that he was needed in the officers' tent. Jamba pulled a face and exhaled deeply. There was trouble on the horizon.

Two men were stationed on sentry duty outside the tent and told him to wait. Jamba felt some unease and straightened out his beret in an attempt to make himself look presentable.

It was Sergeant Oboto who eventually stuck his head out the tent and motioned the boy to enter. Inside, several men were leaning over a large map spread open on the ground before them. Some were pointing at spots on the map while others shook their heads or nodded in agreement. Jamba noticed that they all had rank. There were at least three captains and six sergeants. This was the command center, the heart of all MoD operations. DaD was stooping over the map with his back towards the boy.

Jamba waited quietly near the entrance, standing at attention, his beret folded over one eye as he remembered the white man wearing it. Standing at attention seemed to be the right thing to do considering his current environment.

After some considerable time DaD eventually turned and faced the boy. "Ah. I see the hero Jamba has taken the time to honor us with his presence," the man said, sour sarcasm clearly audible in his voice.

The boy just blinked.

"Hand over those drugs, boy," DaD ordered and Jamba scrambled to extract the small ball of blue plastic from a pocket in his shorts. It now appeared flattened as a result of all the crawling and rolling that had occurred earlier on in the day.

DaD looked at the lump and tossed it at one of his captains. "So, our hero decided to ignore all orders and dream up his own battle plan. Then thought he's invincible enough to take on four men and a tank all by himself."

Again Jamba could only blink.

"I'm waiting for you to explain yourself, boy," DaD said, clasping his hands behind his back.

The boy already had his story prepared. "I realized you couldn't see Captain Gut for the signal, sir. I had a plan but we are not allowed to talk to you." He paused before adding, "And the drugs stopped me from thinking right, sir."

DaD did not look angry yet, but the man's moods were unpredictable. Anything could happen. He just stood there with his giant paws clasped behind his back.

"So the whoonga made you do it? Maybe I should take some responsibility for that. Maybe I should have taken it away from you when you attacked that other boy."

He turned and briefly spoke to one of his captains before telling Jamba to follow him outside.

"Leave your rifle and backpack here," he ordered as they left the tent. The sentries guarding the entrance fell in behind them without needing any instructions.

"Let me show you your new home, boy," DaD said as they approached a pick-up. He told Jamba to get in the front with him. The commander took the wheel and the sentries jumped onto the back.

They drove in silence, following a well-used track through the trees. Barely fifteen minutes later they crossed a stream and arrived at a mountain of dirt. There were armed soldiers standing guard and spaced in regular intervals. Some of them saluted when they recognized their visitor. A lonely tent was visible to one side.

As they circled the pile of earth, Jamba could see the outlines of a gigantic hole in the ground. The hole was probably forty feet across in all directions, but as they came closer to it, the boy could see that it was almost a bottomless pit. Ladders made of rope dangled down into its fathomless bowls.

From the ladders emerged children of about his size, all covered in mud and dirt from head to toe. On their heads they carried large buckets of fresh, damp earth. Some may have been girls, but it was impossible to tell.

Other children were dumping the contents of the buckets into long gutters which were running at a downward angle towards grilled sifts. Water from a stream was poured over the gravel using a primitive pulley system. Most of the mud were washed away and the remaining stones and pebbles were scraped onto the sifts. Here two boys were busy searching among the stones and discarding whatever seemed worthless into a large wheelbarrow. Jamba knew what they were searching for.

'Showing him his new home,' DaD had said. As the full meaning of those words hit home, the boy's lower lip protruded in a sulky pout without even realizing it. An atmosphere of brutal suffering and untold misery was choking him like Herculean hands from which there was no escape.

DaD brought the pick-up to a standstill and exited the vehicle to inspect his investment. None of the children bothered to look up as they continued their thankless labor with automated monotony.

"This is your future, Jamba boy," he said while gazing over the scene with hands on hips. "This is one of my many mines and it's experiencing a dire labor shortage."

Jamba felt like he needed to say something and he dared to stutter a few words. "But I'm a soldier, DaD. Not a..." He wanted to say the word 'digger' but realized he was in fact more than qualified in that particular field. He cut his sentence short and continued his pouting instead. Then as an afterthought he added, "It was that *whoonga* shit."

The boy should have anticipated the resulting blow against the side of his head. He had been inviting it. His beret went flying through the air and he instinctively gathered it protectively without waiting for permission.

"Don't you use that language when talking to me, you little turd! You disobeyed orders. You went all gung-ho. If they managed to enter that tank, none of us would have survived that mission... *Puta*."

Jamba was completely caught by surprise at DaD's use of the boy's personal, almost sacred motto. At hearing this he gave the big man a quick sidelong look and then continued to ingest the pathetic misery which was unfolding before him.

DaD spun on his heels and entered the vehicle. The boy just stood there, contemplating the fate which awaited him. His insides rebelled against the notion of spending the rest of his life shoveling dirt. He decided that he would run away at the first opportunity, even take some stones with him.

Then he heard DaD's voice call out from inside the vehicle. "I don't have all day. Get onto the back, moron."

Jamba had never experienced such a tsunami of relief in his entire life. DaD's words were like water to a parched man.

It was nearly dark when they arrived back at the camp. Jamba followed his commander back inside the tent to collect his *Kalashnikov*. Since he wasn't dismissed yet, he stood near one corner waiting patiently.

Scouts have reported seeing a gradual but swift build-up of government troops on a hill barely eight miles to the west of their position. Conveying the information via cellphone, the reconnaissance team had noted artillery, some tanks and the occasional helicopter dropping off an increasing number of troops on the hilltop. According to them there were also convoys of trucks spotted which were carrying more troops and arriving steadily.

As the officers in the tent discussed the situation and pondered possible theories, the boy wondered whether this had anything to do with their attack on the tank with its blue-helmeted occupants earlier in the day. Surely the enemy's response could not be that prompt.

After almost an hour of deliberation, DaD started issuing his orders. They should prepare for the worst. The soldiers present in the camp were to start digging trenches in defensive positions immediately. No torches or fires were to be used during the evening. Tents had to be taken down and loaded onto vehicles.

A perimeter of anti-personnel mines had to be laid in a line to the west of their position and all troops needed to be notified regarding their presence. He wanted no accidents.

The heavy equipment such as anti-tank guns, light artillery and the anti-aircraft gun had to be readied. They were impracticable for use in the dense forest, but needed to be prepared for quick transport and deployment. All soldiers had to be issued with extra ammunition and grenades that same evening still.

At the mention of the ammunition he called Jamba over and instructed him to find the weapons expert. The boy had no idea who that was but bolted out of the tent and asked one of the sentries.

"The Fatman," he had simply replied.

The boy headed for the armory first. As he had hoped he found the fat guy who took the MP-5's from him earlier and explained that he was urgently needed. Together they returned to the tent, with the obese man struggling to keep up. Jamba inadvertently became DaD's personal messenger.

DaD wanted the man to take stock of all spare weapons and ammunition available. He needed numbers on anything from shells to mortars and mines. The man also had to attach a bi-pod to his newly acquired SGMT machine gun and a report on how much ammunition was available for the gun.

The Fatman rushed off as fast as his stubby legs could carry his weight and DaD continued with his briefing. Based on the scout reports they would decide whether to move camp in the morning. The diamond mines were of concern to him and any interruption in their operation had to be delayed for as long as possible. All unearthed diamonds had to be loaded into vehicles overnight.

DaD also wanted to be kept up to date on scout reports at least every hour. He clearly did not intend to sleep very much.

One of the captains and three sergeants left the tent and the familiar sound of a whistle pierced the evening air. It sounded like a stampede as soldiers stormed from all directions. Jamba peered out of the tent and saw a sea of faces gathered in front of the command center. Most of those standing at the back were not even visible in the darkness.

Squad leaders were assigned, instructions were given and the men dispersed to tend to their duties.

Jamba spent most part of the evening fetching food and water for the officers. There was even some lukewarm coffee available. Sometimes he had to run over to the various trenches to get reports from the squad leaders as to their progress. Fate had smiled upon the boy. He could have been digging trenches with them – or even worse – been digging in the pits of hell.

CHAPTER 26

It was to be recorded in the annals of DRC history as 'The Battle of Butembo'. According to later reports over the radio and public television, the DRC government had dispatched an entire battalion of almost one thousand troops to deal with the MoD threat decisively.

Pressure had come from both the U.N. commander in charge of the peacekeeping forces as well as from the French embassy. Unprovoked attacks against the Peacekeepers and French paratroopers who were providing the government with logistical support would not be tolerated.

Jamba had spent the night dozing in the command tent. Cellphones kept ringing at regular intervals throughout the night with reports on the enemy position. The troop build-up was continuous and relentless.

Almost exactly at the stroke of dawn, the sound of distant explosions woke the boy from his slumber. The enemy offensive had begun.

DaD took instant command. Man the trenches! Report on the minefields! Ready the anti-tank guns! He wanted them to be used as short-range support fire in the event of an assault. He doubted any tanks would be used since they would barely be able to move through the dense jungle.

It was seemingly too late to make a full-scale withdrawal. The explosions drew nearer by the minute. There had to be enemy scouts in the area who were feeding back their position and coordinates to the artillery batteries on the distant hill. DaD explained that a French Tr-F1 Howitzer could fire a projectile as far as twenty miles from its position, some artillery guns even further. Add the elevation of the hills they were situated on, and the artillery easily had the range to target the camp.

It was imperative to find the enemy scouts and neutralize them. There was no other way that the camp's position and coordinates could have been known. No aircraft or helicopters had been heard all night.

The booming sounds grew louder and closer. DaD wanted his veterans to man the big guns and to defend the rear and heart of the encampment. The more inexperienced soldiers had to serve as the buffer in the front lines, to absorb or halt any direct attack from the front or flanks. He guessed any assault would come from the west, but they might be flanked as the attackers try to avoid their own artillery fire.

An air attack was another concern and yet another reason to eliminate those range-finders. There was no way for the enemy's outdated aircraft to see their position through the thick foliage.

DaD took two cellphones and two small compasses from a carton box and told Jamba to follow him outside. As they walked past the trenches, their commander picked some of the youngest boys at random. He chose seven boys. Tito and Yoweri were among them.

DaD split them into two squads. Yoweri was to lead the first group of four boys and Jamba was to lead the second. The first would move off to the southwest and the second to the northwest. They were to locate and eliminate the enemy range-finders. DaD did not believe the spotters would have positioned themselves in the path of the oncoming artillery fire which was now steadily creeping closer directly from the west.

Jamba's eyes almost popped out of his skull. He was going to be leading his own squad! In his excitement the threat of the approaching bombardment barely registered with the boy.

DaD handed a compass and cellphone to each of the squad leaders. "When you've eliminated the pigs, press '1' and then the green button. It will speed-dial me directly. And don't shoot any of our own!" With that he summarily dismissed them and told them to get moving.

Jamba immediately took charge. "Check your weapons. No auto-settings. Single file. Move quietly, not a word. Stay alert and check for my signals. If you see or hear something, draw my attention. Only shoot when I shoot. If you run from the fight or break any of these rules, I will kill you myself."

Those who were familiar with Jamba knew that he would act

on his threat. They all checked their rifles and waited for the boy to take the lead. He moved off briskly but quietly. The squad was already in a stooped position before they even left the encampment.

The explosions were now so close that Jamba could feel the earth tremble beneath him. There were even some leaves dropping to the ground as a result of the vibrations.

His eyes intently combed every inch in front of them. The jungle was often so dense that he could barely see more than a couple of paces in any direction. On several occasions he halted the squad with a raised fist and went down on one knee. Each time he was certain that he could see a man through the greenery, just to realize it was only a rock or a dead tree trunk playing tricks on his mind. Better safe than sorry, he thought to himself.

The amount of jungle they had to cover was vast. Jamba frequently checked their general northwesterly bearing on the compass to try and maintain a straight line. He decided to move on a fixed bearing for a certain distance and to then move ninety degrees perpendicular to either the left or right of the main bearing. They would continue this way to try and cover as much area as possible.

There was a high-pitched whistle and the next moment the branches around the boys shattered. They were all thrown off their feet and Jamba's ears were ringing. He could feel his nose bleeding and the right side of his shirt was ripped. There was a shallow cut across his ribs where something had struck him and a pulsating numbness was slowly creeping in. His beret was lying on the ground and he quickly picked it up as if scared of ever being separated from it.

The boy had thought that he was immune to fear by now, but the closeness and sheer force of the explosion were frightening. He could feel most of his confidence return as he restored the maroon beret to its position on top of his scalp.

Jamba checked the condition of the other boys. They were visibly shaken but alive. The phone vibrated in his pocket. It was DaD. The boy's ears were still ringing and he could barely hear the man. They were to return to the camp immediately. Forget the spotters. Shells had struck the camp and the enemy was seen closing in. Jamba could hear some gunfire over the phone and also in the distance.

He took a bearing and they moved towards the camp almost at a jog. As they drew closer to the front-line trenches the boy heard shots and the leaves around them started to shred and pop. They hit the deck with their heads almost buried in the ground. Somebody was firing at them! He wasn't sure whether it was the enemy or whether it was friendly fire.

Because of the direction the gunfire came from, he decided to take a risk and shouted as loudly as he could, "Don't fire! It's Jamba! Don't fire!"

There were muffled voices and somebody called out that they could continue. Having little choice but to trust that the reply came from their own forces, the squad dragged themselves up wearily and almost crawled the last few paces towards the first trenches.

A group of boys were staring at them from a hastily dug trench, wide-eyed and obviously on edge. Before they could reach the trench, another whistling sound came tearing through the air and this time the boys hit the ground before the impact. The earth shook violently as rocks the size of footballs rained down on them. Everywhere Jamba looked, panic-stricken eyes met his gaze.

"Concentrate and calm down!" he shouted at them as he scrambled for the trench. "Get ready!"

He saw Tito taking up position next to him. Shells were exploding everywhere around them now. It was the stuff of nightmares. He could hear both small caliber and heavy caliber gunfire. It was impossible to tell who was firing. From where they were positioned, he could see almost four hundred feet through the tree line ahead of them towards a small ridge before the jungle closed in again.

Then he saw them. First just the tops of unfamiliar brown combat helmets were visible where they were poking out from above the ridge. Then a pair of eyes and then another.

"Fire! Fire!" Jamba screamed. He took aim at one of the helmets and squeezed the trigger of his AK-47 in short bursts. Some of the boys were panicked and confused and wildly fired in all directions. Only once they saw a helmet fly through the air by the ridge, did they realize the direction from which the enemy was coming.

A boy to Jamba's left almost emptied an entire magazine as his bullets tore through a line of empty space up into the sky. Jamba stopped firing and cuffed the child against the ear.

"Rapid fire, *puta*! Concentrate!"

He took aim at another helmet and squeezed the trigger. The owner of the helmet was firing back at them. The enemy was so close that Jamba could look right down the barrel of the rifle the man was aiming at them. The weapon started stuttering and spitting bullets in their direction. Leaves were dancing in front and behind the boys now.

Jamba knew that they had to arrest the attack immediately or they were all going to die. Two of the boys had cowered down in the trench, too terrified to stick their heads out. Ignoring the popping leaves all around him, Jamba took careful aim and squeezed the trigger once. Another helmet went flying and the gunfire stopped.

He shouted at the boys cowering in the trench to get a grip. As he checked the remaining rounds in his magazine he noticed that Tito was not moving. Blood was running down his left temple and his eyes were wide open. Jamba was instantly hit by an image of the boy he had killed behind the shebeen in Kampala that day. Tito had the exact same wide, bulging eyes. Except that part of his head was missing. And then there was Annie. No matter how hard he tried to block it out, the way she had stared at them so helplessly just before she died, would always haunt him.

The sound of fresh gunfire jolted Jamba back to reality. The boys in the trench were firing at the ridge again, this time in a more orderly fashion than before. A grenade landed barely five feet from their trench. It all happened in slow motion. First a metallic clink as it bounced over some stones, then it rolled for a few agonizingly slow seconds towards them, before spinning a couple of times and coming to a dead stop.

"Get down! Get down!" the boy screamed. There was so much angst in his voice that it came out hoarse. The other boys ducked instinctively. Dirt and clay rained down on them from above. Jamba's ears were ringing again.

I'm going to be deaf for life, he thought to himself.

Fearing another grenade, he popped his head out of the trench for just a millisecond and ducked down again. There weren't any more grenades that he could see. Instead, what he saw was a wave of men coming towards them. He had judged there must be at least ten of them.

"You have to start firing", he almost whispered at the boys. "They are coming. Many pigs are coming."

Screaming like a man possessed by demons, Jamba swerved his *Kalashnikov* over the rim of the trench and started firing blindly. He barely stuck his head out to see where he was aiming. There was no time for counting shots. Not even time for fear. His mind was on survival and on killing or be killed. He just squeezed and squeezed the trigger as rapidly as his finger would move.

Two of the advancing men dropped like heavy sacks of coffee beans. No shouts, no screams. They just went limp and were dead before they hit the ground. Another screamed in agony as bullets ripped through his stomach and legs. Others flattened themselves to the ground and returned fire.

The boys followed Jamba's lead and they pinned down the remaining men. He saw another man go limp as a bullet ripped into him. Jamba's face was suddenly covered in a hot sticky liquid as the life of the boy next to him was snuffed out. He just kept on firing.

Yet another boy collapsed next to him. The trench was suddenly littered with the dead bodies of young children. Only Jamba and another boy remained. It was the boy who he had attacked the night he tried out the *whoonga* for the first time. Jamba badly needed the *whoonga* now.

One of the enemy jumped up and started charging their trench. The man was screaming like a pig and Jamba suddenly thought about the giant forest hog... his totem...

The boy took aim at the charging man's torso, but shot him in the throat. The man rolled over on the leaves for a couple of yards and came to rest within inches of Jamba's face. Just like the hog, he thought to himself. Lifeless eyes were staring straight at the boy.

The remaining men took flight and ran for better cover. The two boys fired after them but Jamba ran out of ammunition and the other boy missed completely. If the men had charged them directly, the two boys would have been done for.

"We have to get out of here," Jamba calmly said while replacing the empty magazine with a fresh one. Then he remembered the cellphone and quickly fished it from his pocket. He gestured towards the other boy to keep watching the ridge.

After dialing the '1' on the phone, DaD answered almost immediately. "What?" he barked at Jamba.

"We can't hold them any more," the boy said. "Killed maybe ten pigs but only two of us left. Everybody's dead, boss" he almost whispered.

"Where are you?"

"Front trenches. Southwest. No! Northwest! Northwest!" He had to force himself to think straight.

"Hold your position," the order came and the phone went dead.

Jamba looked over at the other boy and shrugged. "Hold the line," he said with a resigned tone. The boy returned his shrug.

The shelling had completely ceased. It was ominous. There was still some sporadic gunfire to be heard here and there. Jamba looked behind him and could only just barely make out the second row of trenches in the distance. Something there was on fire.

With only the two of them remaining, the boy was extremely concerned about the next attack. Would they come from the same direction or flank them? How many will there be in the next wave? When will it be his turn to die?

He looked down at the bodies littering the trench. Only a few minutes ago these boys were still alive. His bare feet were standing in pools of blood. With the moist clay underfoot, almost none of the blood had managed to seep into the ground. Instead it had seeped between the boy's toes. The stench of blood and death was overwhelming.

Jamba tried to take the positives from the situation. At least they will not be running out of ammunition very soon. There were now more than enough spare rifles and ammunition to go around. A wry smile crossed his lips as he thought about the morbid irony of this. The other boy looked at him quizzically and then continued to watch the foliage ahead of them.

Jamba took a few moments to stare at the bulging eyes of Tito again and felt guilty about his own thoughts. Tito was a good guy. He had liked him from day one. Jamba was going to miss the boy. But friends will distract you in battle, he thought to himself.

The reason for the eerie silence which had descended on the jungle around them soon became apparent. In the distance Jamba could hear a noise which at first sounded like a great wind blowing through the treetops. The noise very rapidly intensified to a screeching wail.

The sound of the jets passed overhead just as rapidly as they had materialized out of nowhere. Jamba guessed that there were maybe two of them. He could not see them through the thick canopy of trees.

As the screeching engines rapidly faded, a deathly silence followed for what seemed like a lifetime. Then the entire jungle behind them burst into flames with a deafening roar. The heat struck Jamba in the face with such force that he could almost feel his skin peel back.

The shock wave pushed him against the wall of the trench with a hot steely grip and pushed the air from his lungs. Where he adjudged the main camp should have been, there were now only red-hot flames and dirty black smoke billowing into the air.

From the flames emerged a silhouette running toward them. The boy had to blink to make sure he wasn't hallucinating. Just as with the grenade attack earlier, everything seemed to be happening in slow motion. DaD's enormous black frame was etched against the backdrop of fire. A dark shadow refusing to be extinguished by the intense glow emitting from the flames.

The man continued to sprint towards them and leaped over the second line of trenches while holding his SGMT machine gun above his head. A large belt of heavy cartridges hung around his bull neck. His entire body shook and muscles rippled as he charged towards them. Jamba thought that the man was truly invincible. He was a god.

As he leaped again and joined them in the trench, Jamba could see blisters on the man's face. DaD's eyebrows were singed, his vest blackened and he smelled like a bonfire.

"A close call," the god said calmly as if this kind of thing happened to him every day. "Welcome to hell, boys."

Jamba just stared. The other boy blinked. DaD started firing his beastly SGMT. The next wave had begun.

CHAPTER 27

DaD's heavy machine gun understood only one language. Fully-automatic. With every burst Jamba's eardrums felt like they were going to pop out of his skull. The spent cartridges ejected by the gun constantly hit him against the side of the head and shoulder where he was himself now firing towards the ridge.

The boy's heart surged with pride. He was fighting alongside his leader and he was feeling invincible.

He could see continuous movement through the trees ahead of them as more and more enemy soldiers arrived to join their comrades who were taking cover against the onslaught of the heavy gun. Leaves and branches could be seen moving in the under-brush at the edge of the ridge. The presence of the enemy was ghost-like. Jamba could not see them. Sometimes he would only briefly see a dark shape moving through the thick leaves or catch a glimpse of a helmet as it duck behind the ridge.

The activity was ceaseless, almost frantic. Soldiers were pouring into the area of the ridge directly in front of their trench and filling it quickly. The torrent of bullets unleashed from DaD's gun forced their heads down and kept them invisible. Big chunks of soil danced on the ridge or thick vegetation was torn to shreds above their heads.

"Keep firing," DaD ordered as he paused to unclip a grenade from his belt. He pulled the pin, stood upright and threw the deadly device with all his might towards the undergrowth where most of the enemy activity was noticeable. It was a massive distance for the grenade to travel, close to four hundred feet at the very least.

First there were shouts, then an explosion, and then there were screams. Men had broken their cover in an attempt to get clear of the grenade and Jamba and the other boy picked some of them off with their *Kalashnikovs*.

"We need to fall back or we're dead meat," Dad said nonchalantly. The enemy soldiers had started to return fire sporadically, still weary of the presence of the enormous gun in the trench in front of them.

The boys took cover. DaD unclipped two more grenades. These ones had cylindrical shapes.

"I'm going to create a smokescreen. On my word, make for the trenches behind us," he said and readied himself. "Stay low. They won't stop firing."

DaD threw one smoke grenade to their left and another to their right. Thick smoke started pouring from the grenades and within seconds the entire area was covered in a wall of white fog.

"Now!"

The boys leaped from their trench and started sprinting towards where they guessed the second row of trenches were situated. DaD sent another burst of gunfire into the smoke and followed close behind them. The sound of enemy gunfire rang out from seemingly all directions.

Jamba could hear popping and shredding noises as bullets hit the ground and branches around him. Then there were muffled thumps, followed by more whistles like the incoming artillery shells earlier, but this time less pronounced. There were some explosions to their right but the shock waves were on a much smaller scale than the enormous impact of the artillery shells.

"Mortars," said the boy running next to Jamba, his voice filled with anxiety. Just then another explosion sent a shock wave through the air behind them. Both boys briefly glanced back. Jamba stopped in his tracks.

Through the thin fog he could see the invincible colossus lying on the ground writhing in agony. The man refused to let go of the heavy SGMT as he tried to crawl his way towards them.

The boy did not think twice. He ran back to his leader, firing blindly into the smoke. A metal shard the size of a small plate was buried in DaD's left upper thigh. There was almost no blood. The intense heat of the mortar fragment had fused the wound shut.

The other boy was now down on one knee giving them cover fire. For a brief moment Jamba reflected on the boy's bravery. Then he tried to help DaD onto his feet again, but the sheer weight of the man made it a futile exercise.

"Let me fire your gun", the boy shouted at DaD. The din of the battle raging around them was deafening and his ears were most probably permanently damaged. He hoped that by relieving DaD of the heavy machine gun and laying down some cover fire, that it would give the man more mobility.

DaD let go of the SGMT and commenced his crawling, with the dead leg trailing limply behind him. Then he managed to hop onto his good leg and started hobbling painfully slowly towards the trenches. He did not seem to be fully conscious of their surroundings anymore.

Jamba lay prone with his body pressed as flat to the ground as he could manage. He positioned the gun on its bi-pod and pulled the trigger. The stock recoiled violently and kicked his cheek and shoulder like a wild mule. The boy stopped firing and backed away slightly. This time he pushed down on the stock with one hand to keep it steady. He fired another burst, knowing it will go high and harmless, but it was the presence of the gun which mattered. The boy checked on DaD's progress. The man was disappearing into the foggy smoke.

Jamba squeezed the trigger a few more times and then picked up the gun and started for the trenches behind him. The gun was so heavy that he had to discard his own rifle to make his task easier. The ammunition belt dragged behind it and made his movement even more cumbersome. The boy only managed a few steps before he had to stop and rest, laying the SGMT down on the ground. He took the gun by the barrel in order to drag it, but it was so hot he instantly let go. He got hold of the stock and leapfrogged a few paces before again needing to rest. It felt as if he was dragging an enormous log made entirely of lead.

Jamba saw the hand grenade too late. It landed only a few yards from him. All he could manage was to hit the ground and cover his head, dirty hands clasping at his beret. The grenade exploded and pain instantly ripped through his right thigh and calve. It stung as if a thousand hornets were attacking him. Overcome by sudden terror the boy looked down at his leg. It was still there. Small red cuts pocked the skin running the entire length of the leg. Some of the wounds were actually smoldering and the smell of burning flesh reached his nostrils.

He got up and tested his leg. It was numb and burning like hell, but fully functional. He continued his run. A rush of adrenaline gave him the strength to carry the gun without dragging it behind him. He badly wanted to get to relative safety fast. His current position was being squeezed by the jaws of Death.

Jamba finally reached the row of trenches near where the camp used to be. He recognized the face of Captain Gut. The captain was inspecting DaD's wound where he was lying against one wall of the trench. Dad's head was nodding like a man falling asleep and who was then instantly snatched back to reality again. He was constantly slipping in and out of consciousness. The god was not untouchable, the boy thought to himself.

The other boy was peering into the smoke, now and again calmly squeezing off a few rounds at nothingness. There was nobody else in the trench with them save for some charred remains. One of the burnt bodies was still moving and Jamba felt sick. Close to him lay a scorched arm which once belonged to somebody.

"I'm going to look for a vehicle," the captain said and disappeared. Jamba only now noticed that the once-impeccable man wasn't wearing a shirt. A large oozing blister ran down the entire length of his back, etched white against the healthy black skin surrounding it.

The boy looked at his surroundings. Nothing was recognizable. Destroyed vehicles, still burning, littered the area. An anti-tank gun lay on its side, a chunk of metal ripped from its long barrel. Bodies lay strewn along the charred ground, some still burning in their own fat and others mere blobs of flesh.

The scene was one of utter devastation. The Merchants of Death had been obliterated in a matter of mere minutes.

The smoke towards the ridge and front trenches had dispersed in a light breeze and Jamba could make out some enemy soldiers zigzagging their way towards them. The boy opened fire with DaD's gun and the men went diving for cover, momentarily halting their advance.

He could hear the whine of an engine as Captain Gut returned with a 4x4 vehicle which was virtually unscathed. The only damage was a flat tire. They will have to change that later. Gut and the other boy struggled with DaD's enormous bulk and eventually rolled him onto the bed of the pick-up. Jamba kept the enemy soldiers at a distance with short bursts from the SGMT. It was running very low on ammunition.

"Let's go! Let's go!" he heard the captain shout. Jamba swung the gun onto the back of the vehicle and then returned to the trench to grab hold of an abandoned AK-47. He also managed to find two more magazines on some of the corpses.

Bullets ripped into the body of the vehicle, making metallic popping sounds and leaving small black holes in places.

The whistling of incoming mortar shells started again. Explosions rocked the earth but the shells had landed quite a distance from them. As the boy jumped onto the back of the pick-up, the captain floored the accelerator and they sped off with wheels spinning on the charred earth. They headed in the direction of the mines, driving over ground covered in ashes. Jamba was still overcome by the utter devastation around him.

A bearded man came rushing towards them, flailing his arms wildly. They only slowed down enough to give him the opportunity to throw himself onto the back. The man's one ear was bleeding but other than that he looked unscathed.

The captain was now speeding through the under-brush and bulldozing his way through plants and bushes alike. At one stage he hit a small tree, almost throwing everybody off the back and he first had to reverse before continuing. He struggled to control the vehicle with the front tire being flat.

They followed a track and passed the desolate mines. It was like a graveyard with not a soul in sight. Jamba wondered whether the children had finally found their freedom. He actually hoped that they had.

DaD was being thrown around in the back where he was lying half propped up against the side of the vehicle. He winced as the pick-up bumped its way over uneven terrain, rocks and logs. But he never groaned or complained.

Jamba's leg was still stinging like crazy. He poured some water over the multiple cuts and scrapes caused by the grenade in an attempt to wash off some of the dirt and grime. He nearly drew blood as he bit his bottom lip when the pain shot through his body at once. While stroking his fingertips over the small wounds, he could feel tiny splinters of metal protruding from some of the cuts.

Jamba knew that the enemy would be following. Their little group of fugitives will be hunted down like wild animals. The only possible escape was probably to cross the border back into Uganda. He had no idea where the captain was going or what the plan was.

The other boy pulled Jamba by the shirt sleeve and pointed towards the sky. He could now make out the faint humming of distant rotor blades chopping through air. Jamba banged his palm on the cab of the vehicle a couple of times and Gut stopped.

"Helicopter," he said.

They parked under a dense tree and the sound grew closer. The helicopter briefly passed overhead and moved off. It seemed to be in more of a hurry rather than conducting a slow and thorough search.

They sped off again. The track led to another main road running parallel to the border. Before exiting the cover of the jungle to join the road, Captain Gut stopped again and called Jamba over to help him change the flat tire.

"We need to get across the border," he said. "They'll be looking for any survivors on the run. Maybe they won't cross into Uganda." He cast a brief look in the direction of the big man lying in the back of the vehicle. "And DaD needs proper medical help."

Within five minutes they were on their way again, speeding at about seventy miles an hour down the gravel road. The captain kept glancing up the slopes to their left, seemingly searching for something, perhaps a landmark.

Eventually they slowed and veered off the road. They did not bother to cover their tracks this time. The vehicle labored its way through the dense leaves of plants growing under the tall trees. Their progress was at a snail's pace and most of the time it was near impossible to see where they were going.

Finally it opened up a little and they were snaking their way through trees with a carpet of leaves and almost no under-brush growing there. It seemed that the captain had found the route he was looking for. After a few miles the jungle closed in on them again and rocks obstructed their passage. The vehicle came to a stop and Captain Gut explained that it was time to continue on foot. The border was now close by.

DaD's condition and size presented them with a significant obstacle. At least he was still conscious but the pain was evident on his face. The chunk of metal protruding from the side of his thigh was a ghastly sight and fresh blood had started flowing from the gash. Removing the shrapnel though would surely cause his death. In an ironic way it was his saving grace.

DaD was addressing the captain. "You and Kato support me in turns. I can manage on one leg."

The man who had waved them down back at the destroyed base, immediately grabbed hold of one of DaD's arms and slung it around his own neck and shoulders. DaD tested his leg and limped a few paces. He pulled a face.

"Hang on." He produced a small blue package containing the *whoonga*. "Painkillers," he grinned.

Jamba reached for the SGMT but DaD shook his head and the big gun was abandoned. Instead the boy slung his salvaged AK-47 over a shoulder and started moving off. The boys were of no use in assisting in any way.

Jamba stopped and turned to the other boy. "What's your name?"

"Benjamin," the boy replied and started walking again.

"You're a brave soldier," Jamba said but received no reply.

They needed to find food and water. More importantly, they needed to find a more practical way of transporting DaD. He was clearly struggling and his strength was slowly being drained by the effort to walk.

Captain Gut and Kato took turns to assist him. After about an hour of this, it eventually took both men to help the struggling commander. The inclines became steeper as they started their ascent of the mountainous surroundings. Their progress now bordered on being stagnant.

The group rested at a stream where they filled the only two water bottles they had between them and Benjamin was instructed to gather some fruit. Jamba had to help the captain find bamboo. Gut told them that they were going to make a stretcher.

They finally found a cluster of bamboo after following the stream for almost a mile. The captain went to work and cut down three tall, thick poles with his knife. He then cut down another two long stems roughly half the thickness of the big ones. To this pile he added a couple of fresh shoots.

They carried the collection of bamboo back to where the others were resting. The pile weighed very little. Benjamin had also returned with some African rock figs in the mean time.

Captain Gut started cutting round holes into each of the three thick bamboo poles, spacing the holes at equal intervals in each pole. Then he cut the thin poles into shorter lengths and threaded them through the holes, linking the thick poles and forming a kind of square mesh. One stem would go through the top holes of each large pole, then one through the holes a bit lower down and so they continued to the last row of holes at the bottom, forming a large rectangular shape.

He then sliced the young shoots into thin strips to serve as rope and tied each joint tightly together. They were left with a lightweight and extremely strong bamboo stretcher. It wasn't going to be very comfortable, but it would at least assist with their progress. All four of them would now be able to help carry and distribute DaD's weight more equally between them.

After eating and gathering their strength, DaD lay down on the makeshift stretcher and the men heaved. The bamboo sagged, creaked and bent, but held firm. Jamba and the captain each took hold of a pole at the front and Kato and Benjamin followed at the back. The difference in their body lengths proved to be a nuisance however. But for the two boys to share the load together at either the front or back would have been too much for them to handle.

They had no choice but to struggle on. DaD was growing weaker and in desperate need of a proper doctor. They simply *had* to push on.

After about an hour the captain judged that they had crossed the border. They would make camp for the night after another three hours of toiling. It was a torturous ascent of the hills at the foot of the mountain peaks. It felt as if a lifetime of pain had been bestowed upon them and Jamba's own injured leg started to badly hurt by now. He put up a brave face and did not want to let the others know about his discomfort.

When they finally started descending, the boy felt grateful. They stopped for one of their numerous breaks and Captain Gut went to study the mountain peaks. He needed them as a reference to guide the group to the location of the new camp which DaD had ordered Sergeant Wambuzi to set up.

Its location had been a contingency plan for a long time beforehand and Captain Gut knew of its exact position. The mountains needed to be visible though and that would be a problem once they had descended back into the thick jungle again.

The group was exhausted as night fell. The strain of battling with DaD's huge weight and the lopsided stretcher had taken its toll. DaD's condition was deteriorating. The man was now using more and more of the *whoonga* in an attempt to fight against the pain. He was often agitated but seemed to make an effort not to take it out on his men. They were going through this ordeal together, not only to save their own hides, but also to get their leader to safety.

The group stopped at another of the many streams cutting its path through the jungle. Captain Gut decided that they would camp there for the night and then he promptly climbed up a tall tree in the hope of getting an indication of their position before darkness closed in completely.

Their supper again consisted of figs and Jamba went to fill the shared water bottles and to thoroughly wash his own wounds with the cold water provided by the brook.

Lying down on the leaf-covered ground before sleep, he contemplated the events of the past two days. The boy found himself struggling internally with his perceptions of DaD and how he viewed the great man.

Some of DaD's previous judgments now seemed somehow flawed to him. Was the decision to attack the crew of the tank a wise move? Was it not the reason for the full-scale attack on the MoD army and its resulting annihilation? Should they not have fallen back the previous evening when they still had the opportunity? DaD made it clear that he needed to protect his diamond mines, but that decision was what may have ultimately ended the lives of a multitude of men and children.

DaD's belief in his own invincibility, his confidence and his personal pride, now seemingly cost the man an entire army and his main source of income. Without the mines, the men and the equipment lost in the battle, it will take an enormous effort to rebuild his empire.

Jamba realized their leader was flawed, but the boy owed him a lot. DaD had provided him with food and shelter and had given him a trade, a vocation - even a name. He gave him a reason to wake up in the morning not feeling utterly despondent or wondering where his next meal would be coming from. DaD had given him a purpose. Before drifting off, the boy decided that in the circumstances he had been treated well. His lips moved ever so slightly as he repeated his customary bed-time mantra to himself.

Do not scream. Do not scream.

He was woken by the loud boom of DaD's agitated and angry voice shouting at the men. The whoonga had taken hold of him and the pain on his face was clear for all to see. The man was delirious and obviously in need of medical help.

Jamba's leg was stiff and a clear liquid had started to ooze from the small cuts on his thigh and calve. He knew that it was going to be a hellish day.

The boy dragged himself towards where the others were already in place to take up the stretcher again.

DaD was grumbling and muttering most of the first few hours before falling into a delirious sleep. Jamba was not sure whether the man had lost consciousness or whether he was sleeping. There was a sense of anxiety hanging in the air. They were racing against time and struggling against an unforgiving jungle which stretched for miles on end. It was terribly hard work and Jamba kept hoping they would stop for a rest and that he would not drop the stretcher. Blisters had developed on his hands and his sweat made them sting and slippery.

At a relative clearing, the captain once again scaled a tree and spent almost ten minutes surveying his surrounds from the upper branches. On his return, he informed them that he would move ahead by himself and try to find the new encampment.

The captain then phoned Sergeant Wambuzi and instructed him to send out patrols to the northwest of the new camp in the hope of crossing each other's paths and thus making up for valuable time and effort in locating the new headquarters.

There was no way for Sergeant Wambuzi to send help directly. They would simply never find each other in these dense surroundings. Captain Gut would have to find them first.

As the captain took a compass bearing and started moving off through the foliage, Jamba watched him as he broke branches at regular intervals to leave markers which could be traced back to the stranded group.

Sweat was pouring from DaD's brow and his head was rolling from side to side. The boy took off his dirty and torn T-shirt and doused it in some water. He put the damp cloth on DaD's forehead. Looking at his shirt, he reflected on how that same shirt was still brand new and impeccably clean only two days before. It already felt like weeks had passed.

Benjamin and Kato went in search of more food while Jamba tended to their ailing commander as best he could. At some stage he doused his shirt again and tried to clean some of the oozing puss around DaD's wound. The big man winced and his anger bubbled to the surface again.

Yet, when his eyes eventually registered the boy's presence, the impending rage subsided.

"You did well, boy. You handled my gun like a veteran," he said with great effort. His voice was just a rasping whisper now.

The boy was filled with a sense of pride at the compliment from this man whom he so admired and he continued cleaning the wound. He took great care not to break the scabs which had formed as a result of the clotted blood around the large chunk of metal protruding from DaD's thigh. The man did not lose a lot of blood, but the metal and growing infection was surely severely poisoning his system. The boy wished they had some of the witch doctor's green ointment with them - maybe soon.

He readied himself psychologically for a long wait. Even possibly for a couple of days. There was not much for them to do other than to sit around and entertain themselves with their own private thoughts.

Help arrived sooner than expected. Within only a couple of hours, Captain Gut returned with Castro, two of the adult women and four older boys. They were evidently much closer to the encampment than they had suspected. Jamba noticed that the captain was wearing a shirt again, impeccably clean as ever.

With the fresh manpower, the group reached the new HQ within under an hour. There was a sense of great urgency and DaD had slipped back into unconsciousness again.

Only two makeshift huts had been completed so far. The camp was set against a cliff covered in large hanging plants and aloes. The jungle here was dense and grew tight against the edge of the cliff. The sound of cascading water was audible nearby.

All the vehicles from the old camp were parked in a huddle underneath the dense trees. There were boys cutting away at bamboo poles and gathering large sheets of leaves. One boy was busy twisting strips of some plant into rope.

They carried the stretcher bearing DaD's bulk to one of the huts and almost immediately the witch doctor Mganga made his appearance. He chased everybody except the captain from the hut and Jamba could hear the man chant inside as he started his healing ritual, calling on the strength and protection of beasts and ancestors long departed.

The boy could not help but notice an air of despondency among those busying themselves with their chores. News of the defeat had spread quickly. Uncertainty tainted the atmosphere. Their pride and sense of invincibility had been completely stripped away by a few brief words exchanged between them. Morale was severely damaged. Whatever equipment and people were gathered in the new camp, was all that remained of the once-formidable Merchants of Death.

Jamba's leg was now so stiff he could barely walk. The wounds were itching and burning all at the same time. He decided to explore the area from which he had heard the falling water coming from. Perhaps on his return he might get hold of some of Mganga's ointment.

The boy discovered the tiny waterfall within only a few yards from the camp. It was a very thin stream of water raining down into a small plunge pool from very high above him, creating a mist of cool spray which hung almost motionless in the still air. The setting was peaceful, almost surreal after the violence and horrors of the battle the boy had so recently experienced.

He sat on a nearby rock for a few moments to take in the tranquility surrounding him. A sense of duty tugged at him and he followed the stream leading from the pool to wash his shirt. It was pretty much a pointless exercise. The amount of blood and filth staining the shirt was enough to make even a hardened street child wince.

After giving also his wounded leg a thorough wash, he returned to the camp where he found the captain and sergeant in deep discussion. Upon noticing the boy, Wambuzi ordered him to go to DaD's hut to get some treatment for his leg.

DaD was lying on his back on a blanket. Mganga was perched on his haunches waving the leg of a chicken over the man's body while muttering to himself. Various bottles, jars and flask were littered near DaD's head. There were other objects Jamba did not recognize and could not even begin to guess at.

He saw a jar of Mganga's ointment standing on the ground nearby and picked it up while gesturing towards the witch doctor for his permission.

The man scowled at him and then slowly shook his head. He motioned towards the boy to approach him and to sit down on the ground next to him. Then he ran his fingertips over the cuts while humming softly to himself.

Mganga reached for a stubby candle and lit it with a match from a dirty yellow matchbox. Then he took a small knife from a pouch around his waist and held the blade to the flame.

The blade was covered in black soot and eventually started to glow white-red. Then the witch doctor finally bent over the boy and slowly, but meticulously and with intense concentration started to pick at the wounds.

Jamba winced and almost cried out as the hot blade poked at the numerous cuts and scrapes. Mganga gave him a look of momentary disgust and while holding the blade over the candle again, offered the boy a flask. He tilted his head as a sign for the boy to drink from it. Jamba took a swig and immediately it felt as though air was violently sucked from his brain and out through his ears.

The liquid tasted sweet and not unpleasant at all. His tongue and stomach was burning as if set on fire. Just moments later a numbing sensation took hold of him and a veil of drowsiness fell over his eyes.

The witch doctor continued his poking. Every now and again the boy could feel a rough scraping sensation, followed by the sound of something metallic dropping into a tin plate. Through a teary-eyed blur the boy could see a small pile of bloodied metal splinters slowly growing in size. There were enough shrapnel pieces to fill the palm of his hand.

After what seemed like an eternity, the witch doctor finally applied some of the ointment. Jamba noticed that DaD was observing them.

"Go find the officers," he said to the boy when Mganga had finished. His voice was still weak.

Jamba staggered off a bit drunkenly and saw the captain and the sergeant still busy with their serious discussion. They looked up and the boy just pointed towards the inside of the hut. Both men followed Jamba inside.

DaD propped himself up onto an elbow and said, "I need a doctor."

The witch doctor had a disapproving expression on his face which suggested that he found the statement to be insulting and hurtful.

The three men discussed their options. There were one or two rudimentary clinics scattered through small villages within a radius of about a hundred miles of them. But to find a doctor or surgeon with the necessary expertise, meant going to one of the larger towns.

Captain Gut was very uncomfortable with the idea of entering any of the towns. The news of the battle and the defeat of the MoD army would have reached the Ugandan media and general population by now. It was too risky according to him.

DaD was growing irate and asked whether they had any other suggestions. Wambuzi in fact did offer a suggestion of his own. He knew of a doctor in the small town of Kyenjojo which was just past Fort Portal on the road towards Kampala. This was the same man who had treated the sergeant's leg when he lost it after stepping on an anti-personnel mine a few years ago.

Wambuzi suggested that they should wait until it was nearly nightfall and then enter the town under the cover of darkness. A man could be sent to inquire at the local clinic regarding the doctor or his whereabouts. He may then be able to treat DaD with some relative anonymity and privacy.

The small town of Kasese was near their current location, but too close to the border to risk and would probably be crawling with government forces. Fort Portal was a large town with a hospital and several clinics, but there were also at least three large military bases located there.

DaD decided on Wambuzi's suggestion of going to Kyenjojo and search for the doctor who had amputated the sergeant's leg, but also saved his life in the process. They would have to avoid Fort Portal and make use of the boom to the south of the town. The guards at the boom were well-paid by the MoD and it should make their movement easier even with some risk involved.

There was no other way of reaching Kyenjojo. They could not simply bash their way through forests or over hills. There was also a wide river and several deep ravines which made for formidable obstacles. DaD thought that they should stick with what they are familiar with and risk the boom.

"The boy's coming with," DaD said. "He needs that leg looked at and I could do with some extra protection."

Sergeant Wambuzi and Captain Gut looked at each other and nodded understandingly. They had to get moving though. It was already past midday and they had a long trip ahead of them. The men left to organize a vehicle and the small party which will join them in the mission.

Jamba inspected the new AK-47 slung across his shoulders. The weapon hadn't once left his person since he had found it in the trenches before their flight and epic trek through the jungles. He briefly wondered who it belonged to before he had discovered it lying abandoned in that trench littered with charred corpses. It was a bit sad to have left his own rifle behind. After all, he had named it after DaD and it had traded in death just as Jamba had expected it to. Perhaps even better.

The new rifle seemed operational and the boy got up to leave. DaD called him back. "Find me a rifle boy. A *Kalashnikov* will do."

Jamba offered his own AK-47 to his commander, but DaD refused it for some reason with a shake of the head.

Weapons were in short supply. He decided to ask Wambuzi for advice. The sergeant promptly commandeered a rifle from one of the younger boys who was crouched nearby, busy tying bamboo poles together with the hand-made rope.

The captain, Kato, Castro and Benjamin were gathered at a vehicle which was loaded with a number of diesel drums. DaD joined them on his own steam and got into the back of the vehicle where he could lie down with his injured leg extended.

With that the group left in their search for modern medicine and hopefully even a qualified surgeon. As the boy looked back towards the encampment, he saw Sergeant Wambuzi anchored to a spot, standing at attention and waving a salute at them.

Nobody knew with any certainty whether their commander was going to make it through this day. Wambuzi's salute only seemed to emphasize that reality.

Chapter 28

It was very slow-going towards the main road. A track had not yet been properly established for the vehicles and they made their way at a snail's pace by mostly following the small stream which was meandering through the jungle towards the east.

By the time they reached the main road, DaD was vomiting violently. Against his better judgment, Captain Gut had decided to stop in the small village of Kisomoro on the way to Fort Portal to look for a clinic with some basic medicines. It was one of the towns where Sergeant Oboto went in search of the antiretrovirals for the *whoonga*.

DaD needed medication or he might not even make it as far as Fort Portal. The captain tried to avoid as many of the locals as possible as he zigzagged the vehicle through the muddy streets of Kisomoro. It did not take long for them to find a small white building with a red cross painted on a sign outside.

Gut briefly disappeared into the small rectangular structure. There was seemingly no doctor on duty. Instead he had returned with an overly-obese nurse who eyed the ragtag party with some suspicion. After having a quick look at DaD and pouting her lips as if to whistle at the sight of his wound, she disappeared back into the building and returned with a syringe. The nurse said that this was unfortunately all she could do for him, a morphine injection for the pain. It knocked DaD out almost immediately.

The emergency stop in Kisomoro had made the captain extremely uneasy and he made it clear to everybody. The jungle drums would start beating and the news of their sighting in the town would travel pretty much the entire length of the local grapevine within just hours, if not minutes. Their position was precarious and they would have to stay on their toes. Fort Portal and the boom was still some distance away.

Once again they sped along the asphalt road. Jamba removed his beret before possibly permanently losing it to the wind rushing over them where they sat in the open back of the pick-up. Before tucking his most prized possession into the front of his dirty shorts, the boy studied the three crosses he had made with the pen. How many other crosses did he have to add to that collection?

He wanted to take meticulous stock of the number of enemies he had killed during the battle, but he simply did not have the energy to relive the entire event just yet. It will have to wait. He rolled up the beret tightly and stuffed it into the front of his shorts. Then he covered it completely with the lower part of his filthy T-shirt.

Dusk had already set in as they approached Fort Portal. The vehicle veered off the main road and followed the gravel track towards the boom which Jamba remembered from his first trip that day coming from Kampala. To him it already felt like years ago, yet it had only been a matter of a couple of months. Everybody checked their weapons and lay them down on the bed of the pick-up, well within their reach.

The captain was driving and was the only person inside the cab. Through the rear window Jamba could see his AK-47 lying on the floor next to him. The mood turned tense and anxious as they approached the vicinity of the boom. There was no way of telling how the soldiers there would react. Most were on DaD's payroll, but the old guards could have changed and the news of the battle would surely have reached them by now.

The vehicle crossed the deep gorge and then stopped before crossing the river towards the boom. Jamba could see the watchtower from here and saw that it was manned by the silhouette of a single soldier. The vicinity of the small guardroom seemed quiet and as if abandoned. A spotlight shone onto the boom from the building and fighting against the dusk. Things looked peaceful enough though.

The captain continued on and drove them across the low bridge spanning the wide river. They reached the boom, and just like the last time, a government soldier once again strolled casually from the small square guardroom.

He exchanged some words with Captain Gut. This time there was no exchange of money. Instead the captain handed him a small dirty white stone, an uncut diamond. The soldier nodded.

Instead of moving to open the boom, he returned to the guardroom. This struck Jamba as odd. Something immediately did not feel right and the boy could not quite put his finger on it. It was just a feeling. An instinct.

The lone guard in the watchtower suddenly shouted something and then all hell broke loose. The Lord of Chaos was upon them once again seemingly never wanting to give them a moment's rest. Always following within their wake, ready to pounce and bite at leisure.

At the exact moment that the man in the tower shouted, Captain Gut threw the vehicle in reverse and tried to turn it around in one continuous movement. They hit a rock behind them and the engine of the vehicle stalled.

Jamba saw dark figures piling from the small building like an army of ants whose nest had been disturbed. They were all wearing black uniforms and their faces were hidden by ominous-looking balaclavas.

The boy reached for his *Kalashnikov* but before he could even touch it, a shock wave rippled through his body. The explosion had stunned him into near-paralyses. Another shock grenade went off and then another. Once again the boy's ears were ringing and once again blood was pouring from his nose. All the air was knocked from his lungs. He could not think. He could not even breathe.

Something struck him behind his head and darkness overwhelmed him. Its claws continued to drag the boy down into a bottomless pit.

Jamba had no idea how long he had been unconscious for. The roar of an engine had pulled him back from the depths of that dark hole. His head was throbbing and the boy tried to rub the pulsating bulge he could detect there. It was futile. His hands were tied behind his back.

He realized that he was lying on a flat metal bed and surrounded by khaki-colored canvass on all sides. A military truck. Men in black balaclavas were staring down at him. All the boy could see were black eyes, set between whites, peering from slits in their black masks through the black darkness of the night.

Then he felt a body lying next to him. It was Benjamin and he too was bound. The boy was still unconscious, his tongue lolling from between his lips and spittle dripping down onto the bed of the truck below his head.

Nothing good can possibly come of this, Jamba thought.

He decided to close his eyes and feign unconsciousness. Maybe the ominous men in their black uniforms would ignore him. Maybe he would wake up and everything would be back to normal again. He would be back in his hut, cleaning his beloved *Kalashnikov*. Drawing new crosses on the inside of his beret.

A thought suddenly struck him like a sledgehammer. His beret! It was missing. There was now only an empty space where it had been tucked into the front of his shorts earlier.

The boy sat up in an instant. The pain in his head forgotten and the promise of impending doom which the sight of the men in the back of the truck had conjured up, evaporated.

"My beret! Who took my beret?" Jamba screamed at them. Blind rage had overpowered every other emotion within him.

Dark masks just continued staring back at him. Not a word was spoken. There was no reaction whatsoever. Only the scent of sweat and exhaust fumes hung in the air and only the roar of the truck's engine replied.

He scowled at them. Through the darkness Jamba noticed one of the men toying with something in his hands. Rolling it and unrolling it while he just stared at the boy - his beret!

"Give it to me, *puta*," the boy said to him in a hiss which could cut through steel. There was venom dripping from his words. Once again he was met by utter silence. No reaction came from any of the men.

"Count the crosses on the inside. They're the men I've killed. Then add another ten. They too I've killed. Just yesterday. Now add one more. That cross is you, *puta*."

The boy readied himself for a blow against the head or across his face. But continuous silence met him once again. It was even more unnerving than when he knew the certainty of violence was coming. He would have preferred a confrontation. Some insults shouted at him or a smack on the ear. The deafening silence emanating from these men were gnawing at his nerves.

The one holding his beret unrolled it and seemed to be staring at the material on the inside. He studied it for a while and then calmly tossed the beret into the boys face. Jamba rolled onto his back and grabbed on to it with his tied hands. He scowled at the man. Still there was no reaction. Nobody even bothered to laugh. Nobody said a word. There was only the sound of the truck humming through the night and the wind tugging at the flapping canvass covering the back.

They drove on for hours. Every now and again Jamba could hear a car passing from the opposite direction. Sometimes he could hear music or the voices from a crowd as they passed through villages. Eventually the noises increased. Traffic noise grew denser and all the familiar sounds of a big city met his ears. The boy realized that his hearing had been severely affected. There was a dullness covering his ears, almost as if somebody had stuffed them with cotton wool.

Sometimes a few beams of light would enter through a slit in the canvass covering the back of the truck. It made little difference to what he could deduct regarding his surroundings. His captors' features remained the same. Pitch black, covered in balaclavas and melting into the shadows. Now and again the whites of dark-set eyes were visible when a streak of light momentarily flashed over some of their faces.

Benjamin was still unconscious and Jamba wondered whether he was actually still alive. But the other boy's drooling tongue would sometimes move ever so slightly or a snort would come from his nostrils.

Jamba's body felt stiff and his leg was hurting again. Cramps ran through his arms and the rope binding his hands together was cutting off the blood circulating to his fingers. He was thirsty also. His mouth was dry and tasted of dust, his tongue swollen thick.

The truck eventually came to a standstill with its engine still running. The boy could hear church bells ringing nearby and the sound of dogs barking in the distance. A door at the font of the truck opened and slammed shut again. He could hear footsteps on gravel moving away from the vehicle.

After many minutes the footsteps returned, joined this time by another pair. There were muted voices. One belonged to a man, the other to a woman.

Jamba could not catch the entire conversation. He could only make out the odd word. He heard 'boys' and 'soldiers' and 'dangerous'. Then the words 'wounded' and 'rehabilitate'. He could not hear what the female was saying, but it sounded as if she was agreeing with whatever the man was telling her.

The flap at the back of the truck abruptly lifted and the hinged tailgate dropped open. Jamba and Benjamin were dumped onto the asphalt road like two sacks of potatoes.

The boy could hear the woman exclaim in protest and repeatedly saying, "Oh my God! Oh my God!"

With that the truck moved off and disappeared around a bend in the road. Jamba found himself looking up at a woman in a white dress and a nun's coif covering her head. The woman herself was also white. She was just standing there making signs across her body with one hand whilst kissing her other hand. And she continuously repeated, "Oh my God!"

A chubby black man, wearing a black frock with a white collar, came rushing from a wooden gate and started to untie Jamba. The boys were still lying on the asphalt road near the gate. A massive white cross was planted next to it in the ground.

Jamba got onto his feet without needing any assistance and pushed his dirty maroon beret firmly on top of his head. Benjamin was still unconscious. Jamba untied Benjamin's hands while the man with the frock disappeared again and returned with another man who was wearing a red shirt and blue pants. Together the two men carried Benjamin inside the compound.

For lack of anything else to do, Jamba followed the men. The woman was walking next to him and kept brushing his shoulders with her hands as if trying to clean the dirt there.

"Are you all right my child?" she was now asking. Jamba just ignored her. This entire situation was all too strange for him and the events of the day were unsettling. Everything which happened since the attack at the boom near Fort Portal was a mystery to the boy, a void which needed filling somehow.

The nun was now walking in front of the boy and was fretting. "Come. You must be hungry," she said and Jamba followed her into a double storey building. Inside he was met by a long brightly-lit hallway with many doors set in its sides. There was another large cross hanging on the wall at the opposite end of the hallway.

The woman entered through a door and Jamba limped after her. They were in another long hall filled with rows of tables. The tables were covered with white cloths and there were all kinds of utensils laid out neatly on them. Knives, forks, spoons and glasses were set in rows in front of neatly lined chairs.

"Sit. I will fetch you some food. Then we'll have a look at that leg of yours." She disappeared through a side door.

Jamba sat at the nearest table. The chair had a pillow and was much more comfortable than the rickety chair he was used to sitting on in their radio room.

The boy looked at the utensils. He could not remember ever using a fork. He had used a spoon every now and again for soup, but only when he wasn't simply slurping it from a tin plate. A knife had many uses of course.

There was a jug of water near him on the table and he gulped it down eagerly, not bothering with a glass. The boy was so thirsty that he drained the entire container.

The woman with the strange headdress reappeared and placed some soup and bread in front of Jamba. It had been days since the boy had a proper meal.

"We've put your friend in a bed," she said to the boy who was eagerly spooning the soup into his mouth. "We have a nurse here who will take care of him." She sat down next to him and watched him eat. "The nurse will take a look at your wounds too."

Jamba finished devouring a piece of bread and then finally spoke a few words. "What's this place?" he asked her.

"Oh, this is Saint Mary's Mission," she said and smiled, clearly pleased. "We have many boys here. Also like you, from the war." Her last words were said hesitantly, almost as if she was embarrassed to utter them.

Jamba had no idea what a mission was.

"You wear funny clothes," the boy said. He dunked another piece of bread in the soup.

"I'm a nun. My name is Sister Catherine. The man you saw is a priest. Father Timoteo. We're Catholics. We have a chapel here and a clinic. This is the dining hall and the kitchen is just through that door. There are other halls where the boys sleep and a room where you can watch television or read books."

The boy was just being confused again. He had never heard of nuns and the man he saw earlier definitely wasn't his father. The thought of sleeping in a bed held some appeal though, and so did her mention of a television. Reading books was of no significance to him.

"I don't read," he finally said.

"Oh, but we can teach you. We can help with your education and help you to gradually fit back into society. Of course you can't stay here forever, but we can assist in preparing you for a normal life again. It seems you've had a very hard time by the look of things." Her eyes wandered over the crumpled beret on Jamba's head. Then she looked at the torn shirt, filthy shorts and the oozing wounds on his leg. There was a great sadness in the woman's eyes.

Jamba was not interested in either education or being helped back into society. He was a soldier and was not interested in scraping out a living in the city again. Never again!

"I'm not staying. I must find DaD."

At hearing the word 'dad' the woman's eyes brightened and she immediately asked, "You have a dad? We can help you find him and reunite you again! Would you like that?"

"The government took him today," said Jamba.

She seemed confused. "Your dad was in the military? Oh my. I will see what I can find out for you." She got up and gathered his empty plates. "Time for a shower," she said.

After returning the plates to the kitchen she led the boy to an enormous bathroom with shower heads and taps lined all the way along one wall. She gave him a towel and gestured towards the taps. "Then we can have your leg looked after." She left and closed the door behind her.

The boy stared at the towel and had no idea what to do with it. He assumed that it must be some kind of washcloth and opened one of the taps. The water was boiling hot. He had never taken a hot shower. Only the cold ones back at the old camp. Even though he almost burned himself, Jamba spent countless minutes standing under the hot fluid spurting from the nozzle. There was even some soap which he ignored, his military instinct reminding him about the rules of remaining undetected.

He then spent some time meticulously washing the wounds on his leg with the towel. Still dripping, he put his filthy clothes back on and nestled the beret back on top of his head.

When he entered the hallway, the nun was waiting for him in a chair outside the bathroom. She had been busy reading a big black book.

They walked toward another door which led into a room with two rows of beds along its walls. There was a small black cross hanging above each of the beds.

In the nearest bed Jamba immediately recognized Benjamin. The boy's eyes were still closed and another white woman was leaning over him, holding his one arm and staring at her wristwatch.

She looked up. "He'll be fine. He came round a few minutes ago but I gave him some pills to sleep. Just a big bruise on the back of his head." The woman smiled at Jamba and motioned him to come and sit on the bed next to that of Benjamin.

She too was wearing all white and a nun's coif. The nurse carefully examined Jamba's injured leg and could only say, "Oh goodness."

From a small cabinet between the boys' beds she produced a small plastic bottle containing some orange liquid. She then fiddled around until she found some bandages.

"Your wounds have been looked after quite well. Some antiseptic and fresh bandages and all should go well. Just keep it clean. Do you have pain?"

Jamba just shrugged his shoulders. Nothing he couldn't handle.

"What caused this?" the nurse asked again.

"Grenade," the boy said matter-of-factly.

The two women exchanged glances. Then the nurse instructed him to remove his shirt. The cut over his ribs where something had tore his skin when the first artillery shells fell during the battle was only superficial. Jamba had almost entirely forgotten about it and still did not quite know what it was which actually nicked him there. It could have been shrapnel, a branch or a stone flying through the air.

"And this?" The nurse was pointing at the cut.

"Artillery," said Jamba.

Again the two women exchanged glances and the one who called herself Sister Catherine shook her head and covered her mouth with her hand. When the nurse had rubbed some antiseptic over Jamba's leg, the nun disappeared for a few minutes and returned with an old, but clean T-shirt.

The shirt was also green like his previous shirt, but it had no prints on it and was a size too big for the boy. He liked having a new shirt, but the old one was given to him by DaD and had sentimental significance for the boy. When Sister Catherine tried to take the old shirt from him, the boy objected vehemently. He wanted to keep it.

While the nurse applied the bandages, Jamba studied his surroundings. Three of the other beds further down the hall were also occupied. Two boys were relaxing on their beds, but a third was sitting at the edge of his bed and looking anxious.

Jamba's jaw dropped. "Okot!" he shouted out loud.

Okot looked like a coiled spring ready to bolt. Jamba smiled at him and waved him over. Okot visibly relaxed a bit.

The two women were almost just as surprised as Jamba was, but decided to let the boys be and allow them some privacy for their reunion.

"We'll wake you for prayer and breakfast tomorrow morning," Sister Catherine said. Realizing she was being ignored she left the room, closing the door behind her.

Okot ambled slowly over towards Jamba and seemed weary of the boy. Jamba gave him a pat on the back and motioned him to join him on the bed.

"What happened to you, man? Tell me the whole story," Jamba said in a friendly tone.

Okot sat down next to his old friend and after a long period of silence during which he seemed to be thinking very hard, finally started to tell his story.

He explained to Jamba that he had been terrified. After seeing the young girl blown to pieces just a few feet from him, something inside him broke. He was filled with terror and simply could not stand it any more.

That evening he had sneaked off when he was sure everybody was asleep and the guards were far away. Then he had barged his way through the jungle towards where he thought Uganda was. He just kept running all through the night and the next morning reached a main road. A truck had given him a lift to Fort Portal. There he tried to steal a bread from a local bakery, but the woman who owned the place had caught him. Fortunately for him she was all religious and had taken Okot to a priest at the local church.

The priest had asked a lot of questions, but Okot lied to him, stating only that he used to live in Kampala and was abducted by a rebel group, not the MoD. He was too scared to mention that to the priest. The man had business in Kampala and had dropped Okot off here at the mission just the day before, saying that they looked after children of war.

Jamba listened intently. He told Okot that they had been worried that he would be captured. But he knew the boy would never give their position away. Okot looked relieved after hearing this.

Then, having a sudden urge to vent all which had happened to him in the past days, Jamba told Okot in detail about their attack on the tank and the resulting battle. The MoD was no more and DaD had gone missing. Perhaps he is even dead. Jamba had no idea what had happened during the ambush at the boom or where everybody else was now. They could be dead or in prison somewhere.

From one of the beds down the hall came a loud, "Shhh! We're trying to sleep!"

Jamba was annoyed at the rudeness of the gesture which interrupted his conversation with Okot. The boy got up and hobbled over to the beds where two boys were lying under the sheets. They were probably around thirteen or fourteen years old.

He did not know which one of the boys was the one trying to hush him, but turned towards the bigger of the two. "Why don't you rather shut up, *puta*? I'm busy talking to my friend over there, see? Maybe I should come later tonight and cut your throat while you sleep. Shut you up permanently," Jamba said in a tone which could freeze the entire sun over.

The boy stared at him with wide eyes. Fear was clearly visible on his face. The boy had made a mistake. He looked up at the beret perched on Jamba's head, then down at the scars on his ribs and arm and then at the bandages covering his entire right leg. This small boy standing in front of him was a child soldier - and clearly already a veteran.

"I'm sorry," was all he could manage. Jamba turned and limped back to his bed. He patted Okot on the back again and told the boy that they would talk again tomorrow. He was exhausted. Okot nodded and returned to his own bed.

Jamba fell asleep immediately. It was his first time sleeping in a real bed and the mattress hugged him and put a spell on him. He drifted into slumber without the slightest thought on his mind.

He was woken in the middle of the night by somebody screaming. It was Benjamin. Remembering his own screaming the night he had cut Bubba's throat and then waking up to find Tito clasping a hand over his mouth, Jamba quickly jumped out of bed and did the same for Benjamin.

"Quiet Benjamin! They will think you have bad spirits inside you!" he said near the boy's ear in a soothing tone.

Benjamin's hand grabbed Jamba's arm wildly and his eyes momentarily opened. Then he seemed to register what was going on around him and Jamba let go of his mouth. Benjamin turned on his side without a word and Jamba returned to his bed.

This time he quietly repeated his mantra to himself before finally drifting off to sleep again. Don't scream...

CHAPTER 29

The next morning and the days to follow were all strange experiences to the boy soldier, Jamba. Before breakfast all the boys were herded into a small room with benches, an altar and stained glass windows. There were candles lit everywhere and yet another cross hanging above the altar. A sculpted man was pinned to the cross and had a thorny crown on his head.

Jamba knew nothing about religion and the entire ceremony was very strange and awkward for him. The man whom Sister Catherine called Father Timoteo, talked a lot and about somebody called 'God' and another person called 'Jesus' and yet another called 'Mary'.

He made many signs with his arms and eventually he said, "Let's pray." Some of the other boys went on their knees, closed their eyes and held their hands clasped near their faces. The boy found it all extremely odd and just stood watching the entire spectacle from the back where he, Benjamin and Okot had positioned themselves.

There were quite a few boys gathered in the chapel and this meant there probably had to be more sleeping quarters somewhere in the building.

The strange ceremony was finally over and they all left to have breakfast in the dining hall. The three boys sat together at a table while the other boys clearly kept a deliberate distance. Jamba and his companions received many stares and every time he looked at the unfamiliar boys sitting at the other tables, they would quickly look down, suddenly very interested in their meals.

Sister Catherine joined the three at their table with some news. She admitted right from the get-go that it was not all good news and that she was not going to lie to Jamba. The sister had asked Father Timoteo regarding the men who had dropped Benjamin and Jamba off at the mission. Apparently they were members of the government's elite anti-terrorism squad. If the boy's dad was indeed captured by these men, then chances are that he is in really big trouble.

Jamba absorbed the information in silence while he consumed his breakfast. Bacon, eggs and beans. It was delicious. But the news was disconcerting and he didn't utter a word. The sister sat with them for a moment as if waiting for some kind of reply or question, but then eventually gave up and left the boys alone so she could go and talk to the others sitting at their separate tables.

"We've gotta get out of here," Jamba said to his two comrades. "This place is weird and we need to find out about DaD."

Benjamin, who had woken up looking rested this morning, immediately agreed. He was with Jamba. This place was odd. Okot was not so enthusiastic. He sat poking at his eggs with a spoon and then scraped the beans around on his plate.

"Come on, Okot. What's wrong with you? Come with us," said Jamba.

"DaD will kill me," was all Okot had to offer.

"No. I will talk to him. He'll understand. I will tell him you didn't give us away and that you were just scared of the mines. He'll listen to me." Jamba ate some of his beans and took a swig of the sweet orange juice from a glass in front of him.

"Look. We can't stay here," he continued. "That woman already said it's not permanent and then they will make us stay or work with strange people. Perhaps even back in the shanty town." He was doing his best to convince Okot to join him and Benjamin. "This place is weird, man," he repeated.

The strange religious ceremonies also took place in the evening before bedtime. There were always a lot of praying and singing. Jamba was clueless as to the meaning of it all. The father mentioned this 'God' a lot and constantly used words such as love, compassion, repent, sin and forgiveness. Strange words, all of which were completely foreign and void of any meaning to the boy.

He did recognize one word though - 'Mercy.' Upon hearing that word Jamba's face lit up and he thought back to the day he had shot the colossal white French soldier in the face. The man was asking for mercy. He mulled the word over in his head.

"Mercy," he whispered to himself.

Jamba actually quite liked the sound of it. The man wanted him to spare him. Or save him, as Sergeant Oboto had said. The boy wondered what had happened to Oboto. He had probably become one of the numerous charred bodies Jamba had seen littering the jungle floor. For the first time he realized he had also completely forgotten about Yoweri.

As if fate herself had read Jamba's thoughts, the priest started telling the boys of a battle between a boy named David and a giant named Goliath. The big soldier had teased the boy for a long time and then the boy had killed the enormous man with a stone from a slingshot and had even cut off his head. The boy became a leader of his entire nation after his victory.

Father Timoteo continued with an explanation of all the lessons to be learned from the story, but Jamba found only the part about the actual battle fascinating. He was like David, he thought. The big white man was Goliath! Jamba was incredibly excited about this discovery and had visions of leading his own army one day.

During the day the boys had to help out in a vegetable garden at the back of the big double storey building. Again the other boys kept their distance. They made no attempt to speak to Jamba or his companions. It did not bother the boy one bit and he preferred it that way.

Eventually he decided to ask Sister Catherine regarding the real meaning of the word 'mercy.' She was energetically walking through the vegetable garden dishing out instructions and encouragement to the boys.

When she approached them for probably the tenth time that morning to see how they were doing, Jamba asked her, "What is 'mercy'?"

She was extremely pleased with the boy's interest in such a sober and positive topic. With a big smile on her face she started explaining to him.

"Well. It means many things. It can mean showing somebody compassion or pity or forgiveness. These are all good things." Again she smiled at the boy.

This did not make things any clearer to Jamba. The words compassion, pity or forgiveness meant nothing to him. He had never encountered, nor used those terms before. But he could tell this sister all about hate, killing and destruction.

The boy shook his head and said that he did not understand any of that. Then he decided to tell her where he had first encountered the word in an attempt to help her with her explanation. As if discussing the day's weather he described in detail how the wounded man asked him for mercy and how he had then shot him. How Sergeant Oboto explained that the man was asking him to save him and that by shooting him, Jamba in fact *did* save the Frenchman from what could have been a terrible and slow death otherwise. Surely that was mercy?

Sister Catherine's jaw almost dropped to the ground. Her mouth was moving as if she was trying to say something but could not quite form the correct words. She eventually gathered her thoughts and tried again.

"But that's not showing mercy. You need to show love. You should take pity on a person. Spare his life. Respect his life and let him live. That's true mercy. Killing is wrong. It shows hatred or contempt. It's a sin."

The woman was stuttering and stumbling over her own words in her eagerness to have the boy understand the true meaning of the word. She had failed again. The only word which Jamba truly understood in her latest explanation was the word 'respect'. DaD had taught him that after he had killed the boy behind the shebeen.

She waited for him to reply as he considered her words. Then the boy repeated the story of David and Goliath to her. He wanted to know how his own story was any different to that of David and Goliath? If this David was considered to be a hero by the priest and all the people, then why was killing the Frenchman such a bad thing? At least he did not remove the Frenchman's head like this hero David did, right?

The sister sighed deeply, threw her hands up in the air in resignation and stomped off with an, "Ugh!" Jamba just shrugged and the boys continued their work in the garden.

During the afternoon they were allowed some free time in the recreation room as it was called. Many of the boys paged through books or watched television. Jamba was fascinated by the TV. At first he could not understand how all the people on the screen were made so small. He even wondered whether they lived inside the box.

The man with the same red shirt and blue pants of their evening of arrival was sitting in a chair paging through a magazine. He was short, sported a thin mustache and had an even darker skin than Jamba's. Evidently it was his job to watch the boys.

Jamba walked over to the man and asked him to explain the workings of the television to him. The man roared with laughter which the boy found slightly insulting. He did not appreciate people laughing at him. Anger boiled up inside him again.

Before he could explode though, the man started talking. He explained that it was a bit like a radio. Instead of just the sound, it also received images. The images again were just like taking photographs except that they were moving pictures. Then somewhere in some big building they would play the pictures and send it to all the people on their televisions.

This made sense to the boy and he decided not to confront the man about laughing at him. The boys watched anything, from people dancing and singing, to stories about men and woman kissing each other and then fighting with each other.

It was on their second day at the mission during one of their afternoon breaks that the news came on the television and interrupted their program about crocodiles and hyenas. There was a woman talking to them and saying that some breaking news had just come in. She also warned that the story contained graphic images which might upset sensitive viewers.

Jamba was upset that their program was cut short so suddenly. He enjoyed watching the hyenas and crocodiles kill their pray. Antelope would try to cross a large river and the crocodiles would catch them in mid-air as the leaped through the water in a desperate attempt to make it to the other side. There the hyenas would be waiting for the survivors.

Then the woman mentioned something which almost knocked Jamba off his feet. According to the story, a man claiming to be the leader of the notorious Merchants of Death rebel army had been captured in Kampala by local citizens. Then an angry mob had apparently set on the man and in their rage had beaten him to death. She did not give the man's name.

Jamba was stunned. The story had to be referring to DaD! But DaD was captured by the government forces. Not the civilians. And how could he be dead?

The woman's face had disappeared and there were images of a hysterical crowd throwing stones at something and kicking out at it in a wild frenzy and rage. As the images became clearer, Jamba could see the body of a man being dragged behind a vehicle. A piece of barbed wire was tied around his neck and his body was twisted and broken in several places. The face was bloated and his broken arms were standing at horrible angles in all directions. The clothes had been ripped from his corpse and his one leg almost entirely torn off from the dragging.

People kept shouting and throwing stones, bricks and other objects at the corpse. Jamba refused to believe it. DaD would never be humiliated like that! He would never allow anybody to kill him in that manner. The man was invincible. He was a fighter. He would rather kill his enemies before that would happen to him. Jamba knew the army had captured him. Not the people of Kampala. This was all wrong.

The camera zoomed in on a figure sitting on the back of the vehicle which was dragging the broken body across the asphalt behind it. It was a man with his hands tied behind his back. His face was a bloody mess and severely swollen and the crowd flung stones and bottles at him also. The man's clothes and physique was unmistakable. It was Captain Gut. This confirmed the boy's worst suspicions. Erased any doubt. The mangled body behind the vehicle belonged to DaD.

Jamba suddenly felt ill. He ran from the room and vomited in the hallway. His feet carried him outside and he gasped for air. It was as if his entire world and everything he had ever believed in had just come crashing down in a single blow.

Destroyed, obliterated - just as the MoD had been destroyed in the final battle. Except that then DaD was still alive.

The boy felt empty. There was nothing left. Everything was gone. All hope. All dreams. All aspirations. His source of security and protection was gone in an instant. His aims in life shattered. All stability wiped away. His hero and mentor destroyed. Everything he had ever believed in had been obliterated. The boy had nothing left. Nothing! The implications were profound. The future lay shattered before him.

Benjamin and Okot found him where he was lying on his back in the dirt and staring up at the sky. There was a single tear running down the child's cheek, a vacant look in his eyes. Jamba was in shock and wanted to die.

For the remainder of the day and that evening, the two boys could not get a word out of Jamba. He moved around as if in a trance. He went through the paces like a robot and as if not registering any of his actions. The boy poked at his food but did not eat. Sister Catherine tried to talk to him and had asked what was bothering him so, but he had flatly ignored her. In the chapel he could only think of how David had slain Goliath.

Jamba wanted revenge. He needed retribution like a bullet needed a gun. Hatred took command. It consumed every other emotion which may still have been left inside the boy. He did not sleep that night. He was seething and he was plotting. DaD's killers are going to pay. He had retrieved a pen from the drawer next to his bed and meticulously started adding crosses next to the other three on the inside of the beret.

For the first time he forced himself to replay the entire battle over in his mind again. The exercise was draining, torturous, but his seething hatred kept him going. Once again he saw helmets flying and men falling. Shells and grenades were exploding all around him. Jamba added only the ones he was certain of.

When he was done he counted the crosses. There were now twelve marks on his beret. He had killed a total of twelve people that he knew of for certain. There may have been more. Again he replayed the battle. Again he counted nine certain kills to add to the other three.

There was more news on the television the following day. The government of the DRC and the Peacekeeper Forces had issued statements regarding the Battle of Butembo in which the MoD had been defeated. The government forces themselves claimed to have lost close to three hundred men of their own.

Just as in the case of the attack on the South Africans, the soldiers were deploring and lamenting the use of child soldiers by the MoD. The United Nations spokesperson strongly condemned the use of children in any conflict anywhere in the world.

With these statements came news which tore Jamba back from the depths of his personal world of darkness. According to reports by surviving soldiers, one child soldier of maybe only around twelve years of age was spotted wearing a beret of the French Paratroopers and had been inflicting heavy casualties on the government troops. Soldiers found themselves with a moral dilemma. They had to kill the child to stop the slaughter.

Jamba immediately realized the implications of this news. The men who had brought him here knew where he was. They will now know that he is not dead and come looking for him. His fate might be the same as that of DaD's. He needed to get out of there. He needed to flee.

As if to emphasize his predicament, Jamba noticed that every single person in the recreation room was staring at him. Their eyes were rather resting on the maroon beret perched on top of his head more than on his face. Even Benjamin and Okot were staring.

The boy got up and left the room. His friends followed him outside and to the sleeping quarters. Together they sat down on Jamba's bed to discuss the situation.

"We've got to leave right now," he said to them. "Those men will be back. They'll now come looking for us."

Benjamin agreed but Okot still seemed torn and indecisive.

"Come on, Okot. They'll look for you too. How will you explain arriving here almost at the same time as us? What will you do here anyway? Those other boys treat us like a disease. You'll just end up digging through the garbage again all by yourself."

Okot was fidgeting with his T-shirt. Jamba shook his head. "Come on, Okot! I will find you a weapon and make you a real soldier."

At the mention of owning his own weapon the other boy's eyes momentarily lit up. He never carried a *Kalashnikov* of his own like the other boys did. His reply was a shrug of the shoulders.

"Gather your stuff. We're leaving right now," Jamba said to them. They just looked at him. There was nothing to gather. All they possessed were the shirts on their backs and the shorts covering their buttocks.

Jamba sighed as he realized the absurdity of his command. He took the beret off his head and rolled it up. Then he stuffed it into the front of his dirty shorts. It was crucial that nobody out there recognized the beret. He got rid of the shirt the nun had given him and pulled his old shirt with the lion print over his head. Now he was ready to leave.

The boys sneaked out of the sleeping hall and down the corridor. The other boys were all still gathered in the room with the television. They did not encounter anybody else on their way to the exit. It was an easy escape.

As they exited the wooden gate and reached the road outside, Jamba hesitated. He had no idea where they were or which direction to take. People in this neighborhood seemed to have money. Big houses with tidy gardens surrounded them. There was a hill covered in banana trees visible to the north.

"We walk up that hill. Then we can see where we are," Jamba said and lead the way in that direction.

Once they reached the top of the hill, the enormous lake became visible to the southeast. Tall buildings reached towards the sky in the same direction as the lake and an expanse of tin shacks was blinking in the sun northwest of them.

That was the destination. The shanty town. There they could blend in and disappear. There they could gather some information.

The shacks seemed very far away and the sun was already dipping towards the horizon. After gathering some bananas for their journey, the boys marched on. There was no way of knowing when they would have a chance to find food again.

Chapter 30

As the barefooted group of boys made their way across gravel, asphalt and open fields, Jamba grappled with trying to plan his next move. For now only three things were certain. They needed more information regarding DaD without raising too much suspicion. They needed to find weapons. And he needed to satisfy his lust for vengeance.

Those who had destroyed all he had ever believed in had to pay. They had murdered his mentor and leader, the man who had given him a name and a purpose in life. The man who had provided him with food and shelter. They had crushed the rock which had given him stability and hope.

Jamba knew it was the government who had murdered DaD. Somehow they had used the civilians as a tool to hide their own atrocities. They are not going to fool him too.

As they approached the shanty town, the boys passed several small guard stations where major roads intersected. The posts were nothing more than small round buildings with an open entrance and a bench which could seat at most two men. Their occupants were regular police, but the boys took great care to avoid them. All the policemen they encountered on their way were carrying AK-47's.

Darkness had just descended on the city when the opportunity to find a weapon presented itself. At one intersection a traffic light was out of order. A police officer was doing his best to keep the traffic flowing. He was standing at the center of the intersection directing the chaos of vehicles around him.

In the guard hut was another man, lying flat on his back and apparently sleeping. Within reach of the man, a *Kalashnikov* was propped against the inside wall by the entrance. The temptation was too big for Jamba to ignore. He instructed Benjamin and Okot to wait for him and then casually made his way over to one of the street corners.

The man in the middle of the road was totally absorbed in his mission to direct the traffic. There were several people walking the side walks. The only light came from the vehicles in the street and a couple of shops which were already closed.

Jamba tried to blend in with the people walking next to the road and slowly made his way in the direction of the guard hut which stood on one corner. He had eyes only for the rifle near the entrance. It was pulling him towards it like a magnet.

When he was within just about three feet of the post, he peered inside and heard the distinct sound of snoring. The policeman was in a deep sleep. Jamba gave the one in the road a final once-over to make sure he was still thoroughly distracted, then reached inside the hut, grabbed the rifle and sped off.

He expected shouts, whistles, gunfire. Nothing happened. Not even the people on the pavement seemed to be interested other than swearing at him as he bumped into some of them in his wild escape.

He knew that the other boys would have been watching and would follow. He just kept running with the rifle clutched in his hands and made a turn into the first side street. There he slowed down and looked behind him to see whether Benjamin and Okot were following. Two dark figures came darting after him. The plan had succeeded. His heart was not even racing. Taking the rifle was a mere triviality compared to the battles he had already been through.

Once the other two had joined him they continued at a jog, keeping to the darker and quieter side streets. Whenever they did encounter people, they were met with hostile and frightened faces.

Eventually Jamba spotted a large sheet of yellow plastic stuck to a wire fence and stopped to wrap the AK-47 in it. They continued their journey towards the shanty town at a walking pace without any incident.

Tidy houses and shops gave way to shacks constructed of scavenged tinplate, cardboard, wood and plastic. Roads gave way to muddy tracks littered with garbage. The smell of vehicle fumes was replaced by the smell of urine and rotting food.

Their journey had come full circle. The boys were back where they all once started from. They felt almost at home here. It was familiar territory. Yet, it held many dangers of its own.

They moved in complete darkness. The few people they encountered either ignored them or just scowled at them. Jamba had only one current goal. The only real reference he had and only possible source of information – the shebeen where he had killed the boy and ran into DaD.

The shanty town was vast and it took them nearly an hour to reach the familiar surroundings of the shebeen. Jamba was thirsty and led the boys to the tap which he had spent stalking for so many hours over so many months. He reached it with a sense of nostalgia.

There was no reconnaissance this time around. He simply walked up to the tap and drank from it with content. As Benjamin and Okot took their turns, Jamba observed the area around him and noticed a group of kids gathering in he shadows between two nearby shacks - the usual street gangs looking after their assets. Nothing had changed. Jamba unconsciously stroked the plastic which was concealing his newly acquired *Kalashnikov* and smirked.

The boys turned in the direction of the shebeen but the pitter-patter of bare feet and occasional whispers followed them through the mud and shadows. Jamba halted in his tracks and slowly turned around. There were eight street children facing them. They also came to a halt and the two groups stood glaring at each other, not sure what was going to transpire next.

Having safety in numbers, one of the boys in the gang started moving towards Jamba and his friends. His gang followed carefully and clearly ready for some action.

Jamba had no time for this. The confrontation had to be ended quickly and decisively. He slowly unwrapped his weapon from its plastic sheath and pointed it at the group.

"Piss off, *putas*," was all that was needed.

The entire gang abruptly turned on their heels and briskly walked off in the direction from which they came. The walk turned into a jog and the jog into a run. The matter was settled.

The boys finally reached the shebeen and Jamba had to make a decision. DaD had frequented this establishment and was probably well-known. Maybe the owner was the best bet for any information regarding what had happened to DaD and who was responsible. It was a risk, but a necessary one to take.

They waited in the bushes near the back of the shebeen and hoped that the owner would appear at some stage to discard some of the left-over food as was his habit. They did not have to wait for long.

A door in the shack opened and a burly man wearing only pants appeared in the doorway. Light from within threw a long streak across the ground which reached all the way to the three boys. The man tossed the food and then froze as he saw the boys emerging from the shrubs.

For a moment he seemed caught between either fleeing or fighting, but Jamba's words stopped him in his tracks.

"I need information on DaD, mister," the boy said as he slowly approached. He had left the rifle in the bushes so as not to seem threatening.

"He's dead. Everybody knows that," the man replied irately.

"I know he's dead. I saw the news. I need to know who killed him. I need to know where he is now."

The man scratched at his chin and at the stubble growing on his dark cheeks. His curiosity got the better of him.

"Why do you need to know this? Who are you?"

Jamba was now standing right in front of the owner and carefully considered his reply. Then he made up his mind. "He took care of us. He gave us food and shelter. We now want to take care of him. Give him a ceremony, a burial."

Jamba guessed that in the circumstances this would make sense and sound pretty harmless. The man scratched at his chin again and then started scratching between his buttocks.

"Hmm. Wait here." He disappeared back into his bar and after a few minutes returned with a young girl wearing a flowered dress and looking permanently angry.

"You must go see Kunguru, The Raven. She knows everything about everything that happens here. The woman talks to the spirits. She's their voice."

He looked at the boys and a wry, sarcastic smile appeared on his lips before he continued. "But you must know she always has a price. Be very certain about what you want before getting involved with that kind of black magic, boys."

He pushed the girl towards Jamba. "This child will take you to her." Then the man addressed the girl. "Salina. Take them and hurry back. You have work to do here!" And with that he disappeared back into his noisy shebeen.

The girl did not say a word. Instead she started walking at a brisk pace. Jamba hurriedly grabbed his AK-47 and the little gang followed her through the maze of shacks and through mud, dirt and garbage.

Eventually they arrived at a shack which was immediately quite distinct from the others. The place stood alone among the other shacks with a clear space of privacy being awarded it. It was as if there was some invisible barrier keeping the rest of the town from encroaching upon it. There was enough vacant space available to build at least ten other shacks, yet only open land was visible.

Sticks were planted in a circle surrounding the shack and the heads of some unrecognizable animals were perched on top of each one of the poles, possibly monkeys, perhaps even cats or dogs. Smoke was pouring from a hole in the roof.

The girl pointed at the place and abruptly disappeared into the darkness, leaving the boys standing there nervous and uncertain as to what to do next.

Jamba felt a distinct feeling of foreboding rushing over him. The shack resonated energy. But it was not a good energy. It felt dark and ominous. In the humid draft of a faint breeze, the movement of the smoke resembled a claw with a long finger motioning towards him.

The animal heads which were impaled on the poles seemed to both warn him and call him. It was eerie and Jamba almost had second thoughts. But he needed to know. He needed information more than anything. He was willing to pay the price if it was so demanded.

Jamba handed the wrapped rifle to Benjamin and motioned at the boys to wait for him as he cautiously approached the entrance to the shack. Benjamin and Okot did not complain and gladly found themselves a place to sit in relative comfort. Nearby but not too close.

Jamba was not sure how to go about drawing the attention of the occupant. The entrance had no door. Instead there was just a piece of cloth covering it. He decided to pick up a stone and then banged it cautiously against the side of one of the corrugated walls next to the entrance. Then he waited.

There was a putrid smell coming from within. There were also some shuffling sounds approaching and the cloth covering the entrance flew aside. An old and ugly face thrust itself through the opening and almost collided with Jamba's own face.

The woman smelled absolutely foul. Her rotten breath was assaulting Jamba's nose and face. The breath was emerging from a slit of a mouth which had all its front teeth missing. A single eye stared at him through long, gray strands of braided hair. Yet, the eye did not seem to see what it was looking at. Instead there was only a pale blue and glassy orb there, devoid of life. Where the other eye should have been there was a gaping black hole.

Jamba could swear he could see the woman's skull at the back of that empty space. The woman was ancient. Jamba could still only barely count past thirty. The exact number of rounds needed to fill the magazine of an AK-47, but he was certain each year in this woman's life was enough to fill at least four magazines to the brim.

The witch wore only a dirty black bra which seemed almost unnecessary since her breasts had long been consumed by old-age and around her waste was tied a black sarong. Silver bangles adorned her skinny ankles.

She did not speak but instead thrust a scrawny hand outwards and started touching the child's face. For once, even after all his horrifying experiences, Jamba felt truly scared again. His instincts were screaming at him that he was dealing with something otherworldly. Something he could not possibly understand and which demanded respect and the utmost care. Complete avoidance if possible.

The woman's bony hand slowly crawled over his face like the whisper of Death itself. Long nails traced every contour. She sniffed at him as saliva drooled from between her cracked lips.

"You dark one," she croaked. "Messenger of Demons."

Jamba stood frozen to the spot. Too terrified to move or speak. He started trembling and could not control it no matter how vehemently he scolded himself within. I'm supposed to be fearless, he thought to himself. But not in the presence of this creature crouched before him.

"Come inside. Bring friends." She shuffled back into her lair.

The boy had no idea how she knew he had company. She was clearly quite blind. Maybe she had smelled the other boys. With her anything seemed possible. He turned and waived at Benjamin and Okot to join him. The boys looked at each other hesitantly and it was clear their feelings were mutual. They were scared and things didn't feel quite right.

Jamba led the way. A single candle struggled to throw some light on the interior. The boy wondered what the purpose of a candle was for a blind person. The floor consisted of hard trampled dirt. From the ceiling hung all kinds of ornaments, ranging from bones to skulls, feathers, dried plants and what looked like a hand. Whether it was human or belonged to some kind of primate was not clear to the boy and he would rather not know.

A multitude of glass jars contained more organs and things Jamba would also rather not guess at. Something resembling a fetus which floated in a brownish liquid caught the boy's eye.

A single blanket lay in one corner. It was stained and dirty with bits of grass and leaves stuck in its fibers. A small fire in one corner was trying its best to burn stronger, but only succeeded in filling the place with smoke and was making breathing almost unbearable. Something was crackling inside the fire, fueling the smoke and probably the source of the putrid smell Jamba had already noted whilst waiting outside.

With great effort the woman planted herself on the filthy blanket and pulled a wooden bowl towards her. The majority of its contents consisted of bones, but there were also strange objects such as marbles and plastic bits and pieces which may have been parts of toys at some stage.

Jamba realized that the marbles were in fact glass eyes. He was suddenly wary of looking at the rest of the contents of the bowl too closely.

"You sit," the woman said. One scrawny hand was churning the bizarre ingredients and mixing them together in slow circular motions. The boys promptly obeyed and sat down wherever they found themselves at that moment, quicker than necessary.

Kunguru, The Raven, put the bowl down and sniffed the air. Then she crawled over to Jamba's friends and started sniffing near each of their faces. She laid a hand on Okot's head.

"Weak one."

Then she sniffed at Benjamin and stroked his face with her long nails. "More demons."

A nod and a hum indicated that she must be satisfied with her conclusions and she crawled back to her blanket. "What you need?" she croaked at them and patiently waited while staring into emptiness with her single blind orb.

Jamba gathered all his nerves and said, "A man was murdered. He was our... father. We want to know who killed him. The news says a mob murdered him. But I'm sure it was not those people." The boy's voice was a mere whisper which only managed to scrape dryly across his larynx as he attempted to speak with some courage.

The witch continued to stare into empty space. She was rocking forwards and backwards slowly as she listened. "Ah. Demon Lord. You his spawn," she hissed at Jamba.

The boy had no idea what spawn was but it certainly sounded quite nasty. And if this old witch decided that DaD was a 'Demon Lord', then so be it. He was not going to argue with her.

"What you do when find killers?" she asked.

"Kill them," the boy blurted out without thinking. Anger was again welling up inside him and becoming his master. He slammed his mouth shut just as quickly as he had opened it when he spat out those words.

The woman cackled in a way which may have resembled laughter. "Yes. Demon spawn," she said through her cackles and continued to mix up the odd contents of her bowl with a bony hand. Then with a sudden lightning fast flick she emptied it onto the ground in front of her.

The witch they called Kunguru, The Raven, studied the bones, pieces of plastic and glass eyes for what seemed an eternity. She did so by closing her blind eye and then stroking her hands across the bits and pieces, touching each part with tenderness and intense concentration.

"Me know Dark Lord for long time. He child of mine. You bring heart. I bring power."

Jamba was confused. Did she mean for him to bring her DaD's heart? What the hell? Where will they even find their leader's remains?

"Where is he?" was all the boy could manage.

She stared into emptiness again and mulled this over. "Go hill of hatred. *Nafasi ya Chuki*. Ask there. Bring heart."

As if by magic the old witch produced a long knife from under her blanket. It reminded Jamba of that cold blade which had slit the throat of Bubba, his tormentor.

He hesitantly accepted the blade and studied its sharp edges. Cut out DaD's heart? Will he be able to do that? What happens after that? The boy had many questions. But the witch had mentioned the bringing of power.

Jamba thought about his spirit guide, the giant forest hog. Maybe that was what she had meant. Power and protection such as the hog had provided him during the battle. It seemed to have worked for him thus far, even without him consciously considering this possibility before.

Did he not fight bravely in battle? Did he not bravely stand his ground while facing the enemy's onslaught? Did he not go back for DaD and kept the soldiers at bay? Yes. The hog totem had protected him and had given him courage.

"Okay. We will go. We'll bring back his heart," the boy said and got up to leave. "Then you tell us who killed him."

The woman cackled again. This time it was louder and more sinister than before.

"Me will have price. Spawn pay price for power."

CHAPTER 31

Once the boys had left the shack, Jamba collected the *Kalashnikov* from Benjamin and handed the boy the long knife. It occurred to him that Okot still did not have a weapon and that they will somehow need to find more rifles. It will be very difficult. The sole AK-47 was purely a stroke of good luck.

Once they were a few paces away from the shack he mentioned this to the other boys and asked for ideas. He was met by a collective shrug of shoulders.

"Think of something. We need weapons if we're going to avenge DaD."

The boys started towards their destination. Everybody who had lived in Kampala knew where the Place of Hatred was. Everybody avoided it and nobody spoke of it. But tonight that unwritten law would be broken.

Jamba had absolutely no clue as to how they would be able to locate DaD's body. He was not even certain that it was in fact buried on the hill. Yet, the old which had instructed them so and a little voice had told the boy that she would know.

They walked for almost an hour. The dark shape of the hill grew closer and larger. Its outlines edged against the night sky like a broken spine spanning the horizon. There was just enough light emanating from the city to cast a faint glow in the horrid place. The night was utterly moonless and pitch black otherwise.

Jamba was surprised to see shacks built all the way up to the foot of the hill. Maybe their inhabitants didn't know any better. Maybe they were just that desperate for a place to call home.

The group trod on for a few more minutes until they reached the foot of the hill, unsure how to go about in their search. Jamba's imagination started playing tricks on him. He saw bodies and spirits behind every bush and every rock. The encounter with the witch had unnerved him somewhat. His nervousness rubbed off on the other boys. Everybody seemed uneasy.

After walking around aimlessly for some time and searching for fresh dirt that may have been dug up recently, Jamba looked back down towards the sprawling shanty town. He noticed a man sitting on a crate, drinking a beer and watching them curiously. His shack was right at the very edge of the shanty village. It gave Jamba an idea.

They started back down the hill and slowly approached the man. He was advancing in years and had a white beard which almost touched his naval. The man just blinked and casually observed them while he took leisurely swigs from his beer bottle.

His eyes scrutinized the approaching boys, drifted over the odd yellow plastic parcel and then over the large blade in Benjamin's hands. A frown creased his forehead and he lost interest in his beer.

At only twelve years of age, the boy Jamba was already well-skilled in the art of intimidation. "I have a question for you," the boy calmly said as he unwrapped his rifle. Benjamin was playing along quite expertly and was testing the sharp edge of the knife with an index finger which he had moistened with the tip of his tongue. Okot just stood around and observed. Always the weak one, Jamba thought in passing. Yet, the boy had become his friend.

"Yes?" the old man said. His eyes were now darting in all directions which included a possible way to escape.

"A man was buried here. Maybe today. Maybe yesterday. Did you see something? Anything?"

Jamba made a spectacle of unclipping the magazine and checking the rounds. It occurred to him that he had never bothered to check whether the rifle was even loaded. He cursed himself for this indiscretion. No time to become lax. To his delight the magazine was fully loaded. Thirty rounds of brand new glistening teeth ready to bite. He clipped the magazine back in place and waited.

"Yes, yes. They came in the early morning. Just yesterday. I heard the Jeep. It woke me. I looked out the window. The troops dug a hole and dumped something into it. They were in a great hurry," said the man.

"Where?" asked Jamba.

The man pointed towards a tree barely a hundred yards up the hill. "Just to the left of that tree there." He blinked and waited for appreciation or condemnation.

"Spades. We need to dig," said the boy.

The old man slowly got up and shuffled towards the other side of his shack.

"Don't be going too far now, grandpa," Jamba said to his back.

He returned with a plastic bucket and handed it to Jamba. The boy examined the bucket and decided it would have to do. Maybe they can use the knife for the digging too.

"I think you should just sit here and drink your beer where we can see you. Yes?" It was not exactly a question. The old man nodded, sat back down on the crate and quietly started sipping at his beer again.

They found the site of the grave almost immediately. Vehicle tracks and freshly disturbed soil were clearly visible and marked its location like a finger pointing straight at it. They had missed it by only a few paces earlier on.

Jamba told the boys to start digging while he stood guard. There were no protestations. The boy slotted a round into the chamber of his AK-47 and slung the weapon over his shoulder.

He was gradually becoming irate. There was no telling whether the army patrolled this area and there were already too many people who could be potential witnesses. Somebody might say the wrong thing to the wrong person and alert the authorities. Jamba did not feel like getting into an unnecessary confrontation. And a lot still needed to be done tonight.

"Hurry up, *putas!*"

Benjamin was loosening up the soil with the knife while Okot used the bucket to feverishly scrape and fling dirt in all directions. It did not take very long for them to discover the body. The grave was very shallow.

"Jamba." Benjamin was pointing at the blade of the knife. There were strips of cloth and what looked like skin stuck to it.

"Well. Dig him up!" Jamba said with a voice now betraying some anxiety. "We have to see if it's DaD."

Benjamin and Okot continued their grisly task of exhuming the corpse. Jamba's eyes kept darting between observing their surroundings and wanting to see what they had uncovered.

The two boys pulled hard and something was dragged from the hole. It could not be described as a body. It was a blob of human flesh, partly covered by the remains of an old sheet. The corpse was nothing more than a mass consisting of broken bones and pulpy matter.

The identity of that mess was unmistakable though. An eye, filled with dirt was staring into emptiness from underneath a bald and bruised scalp. The other eye was swollen shut, perhaps even missing. Cuts covered the clean-shaven cheeks. The nose was contorted at almost a compete ninety degree angle. But it was certain. It was DaD. Or what used to be DaD.

The boys stood in silence, trying to make sense of the horrifying scene before them. For the second time, since Jamba witnessed their leader's body being dragged through the streets behind a pick-up, a tear ran down his cheek. The discovery of DaD's body only emphasized and confirmed the reality of it all. Jamba's initial shock was replaced by disbelief and his disbelief was overpowered by his rage once again.

Just as he had done that day after killing the boy behind the shebeen, Jamba howled like a wild animal. The howl released every drop of anger, fury and hatred bottled up inside of him.

Down by the shanties, the old man hurriedly disappeared behind his shack. Dogs started to bark frantically in the distance.

Benjamin shook the boy. "We must go Jamba! We must go! Get the heart!"

Jamba could not think straight. His entire body was trembling as his blind fury and hatred consumed him. His loss had been confirmed. The evidence lay before him in a filthy and contorted mess. DaD was no more. Jamba's life was no more.

Somebody was going to pay for snatching away all that once mattered to him and which had given him a glimmer of hope in his short, young, miserable life.

He took the knife from Benjamin with a quivering hand and stared at the blob lying in the dirt before him. The heart! How would he even find the location of the organ?

As if possessed he started to hack at the chest. There was no blood. Only chunks of fatty tissue. The blade kept striking hard bone. All that time Jamba felt sick. Disgusted at having to further desecrate the already-mutilated body of his mentor and protector. He was intruding on forbidden territory and violating some unwritten law. Even in death, DaD was still making the rules.

Jamba could not penetrate through the chest. The ribs were obstructing his progress. Eventually he sank his fingers into a cavity which he had cut between two ribs and started to pull at the bones. The boy pushed down on the broad chest with his other hand and heaved with all his might. The rib snapped.

Again he stuck his hand into the cavity and felt a large mass of tissue. At first he thought it was the heart but as he pulled at it, it became clear that it was a lung. Jamba cut it away roughly, almost injuring himself. The task was gory. Sickening! Benjamin could only stand with hands on hips and Okot had turned away, looking at nothing in particular.

Yet again Jamba's fingers groped around the insides of the corpse. He found a ball of muscle and knew it was what he came for. He pulled until it was exposed and hurriedly cut away the large veins which held it anchored to the corpse.

Celebrating his perverse victory, the boy raised the heart above his head and howled again. The macabre instructions of Kunguru, The Raven, had been fulfilled.

"Now we bury him," Jamba said, his breath racing from all the exertion and mental effort.

"We've gotta go!" Benjamin repeated again. Even he was clearly unnerved by the entire horrifying spectacle.

Before Benjamin's last word had left his lips, the tip of the knife was already at his throat.

"We bury him."

Jamba removed his torn shirt and gingerly wrapped DaD's heart in it. Then he carefully lay it down on the ground and the boys started clearing the shallow grave as best they could before rolling DaD's remains back into its final, degrading resting place. While kneeling next the grave, the boys used their bare hands to scoop whatever soil they could find to cover the remains.

Jamba removed his beret from its hiding place in his shorts and placed it on top of his head as neatly as he could manage. Then he ejected the round from his *Kalashnikov's* chamber and laid it down on the soil covering the grave. He stood at attention and the other boys joined him in his solemn ceremony. Together they saluted the once-colossal man for the last time.

"I will kill them all... father."

Still high on adrenaline, the boys started jogging back to the shack of the old witch as fast as their feet could carry them. They did their best to avoid any people, but those who they encountered merely stared at the shirtless boy with the maroon beret and his two companions. Some spat on the ground as was the habit around these parts.

Jamba did not wait for permission to enter the old woman's dwelling this time. He was still overwhelmed by the events of the evening, but at the same time excited at the prospect of what awaits him once DaD's heart exchanged hands with The Raven.

The witch was still sitting on the exact same spot on top of the blanket just as they had left her earlier. She was not moving at all and did not seem to notice them entering. A snorting sound emanated from her nostrils and Jamba wondered whether she was asleep. The boys waited on her impatiently, not quite knowing what to do.

Then, returning from somewhere very distant, she started sniffing the air and something resembling a smile cracked over her lips. "Ah. Success!" She reached out with both her scrawny arms and said, "Give to me."

As if handling a volatile landmine, Jamba cautiously approached and handed her the remains of DaD's heart, still wrapped in the boy's torn and filthy T-shirt.

The old woman buried her nose in the material and inhaled deeply. Then she carefully removed the organ and spent countless minutes running her fingers over the large muscle. A searching tongue emerged from between her cracked lips and she flicked it at the flesh, tasting it with every lick. Her single eye fluttered and then closed as she savored the moment with what was obvious delight.

"Strong power. Dark Lord power I give you." She motioned for the boys to sit. "First you pay price. Can you pay price?"

Jamba was gripped by a weary uncertainty. He had no idea what the price would be and had never really considered this before. The old witch mentioned it when they had left on their mission, but the boy was so blinded by his urge to first find DaD's body and exact his revenge, that he did not give it much thought. Now that a payment was requested, things have suddenly become more real again.

"What's your price?" he asked with a slight trace of concern in his voice. What if he cannot meet the demand? Then all their efforts would have been in vain.

"What finger you shoot gun?" she asked.

The boy slowly raised the index finger of his right hand, not knowing what difference this would make since the woman was as blind as a bat.

"I need other hand finger. You give finger. I give power."

Jamba was dumbfounded. He wondered just exactly what he had gotten himself into. The boy expected her to request another task or even money maybe. But the promise of real power to assist him in avenging DaD's death was overwhelming. He did not fear pain and would probably not miss a single finger of his weaker hand much. So with little hesitation he simply said, "Yes."

"Brave one," she said. "Hungry for power. Hungry for death. I take weak finger. It like opposite. Dark, light. Death, life. Good, evil. Strong, weak."

She got up and started scratching around between the odd collection of bottles containing the strange liquids. Then emerged with a clear flask in which a pinkish substance was visible. It seemed familiar to Jamba.

As the witch removed the lid of the flask, the bitter odor confirmed Jamba's suspicions. It was *ayahuasca*. The same hallucinogenic that DaD's personal witch doctor Mganga had given him that night at the fire when he ate the heart of his totem, the giant forest hog.

The woman asked for her knife and Benjamin hurriedly handed it to her. She then shuffled over to a rickety shelf where she gathered a flat wooden board and a small bongo drum. One long dirty nail tested the surface of the drum with a few rhythmic taps.

Jamba watched her movements and could only guess at the possibilities of the ritual which was about to be performed. He eyed the flat wooden board and the long blade with some trepidation, having little doubt about their purpose.

The witch sat down again and lay the flat board on the ground between her and Jamba. Then she took DaD's heart and placed it on the board. With concentrated precision she cut the organ into six equal pieces, humming inaudible words to herself as she did so.

Once she was done she passed the flask with the *ayahuasca* to Jamba and said, "Drink. Friends also drink."

She took the bongo drum, placed it between her knobby knees and started tapping out a rhythm while continuing her humming. The bitter pink liquid almost instantly took its hold on the boys. The tapping slowed and her humming became softer but then intensified with each passing minute, growing louder and more frenzied.

Jamba felt the familiar nausea and before long he and the other boys were vomiting violently. Each one of them gradually disappeared into his own private world of hallucination and fantasy.

It was not long before Jamba felt himself running through the jungles, snorting like a pig. He looked down and saw his hairy hooves pounding wildly through dried leaves. Peering along the length of his nose he realized that it was a snout he was looking at and great white tusks were almost obscuring his vision.

The boy was not sure why he was running, but it felt to him as if he was rather charging at something than running away from something. Suddenly he saw a figure hidden within the shadows of the trees and focused his wild charge towards it.

With a gasp he realized that the figure was himself and that his boy-self was pointing the barrel of an AK-47 at his hog-self. All this time he was acutely aware of the witch's presence, but not certain where exactly she was.

A shot rang out through the jungle and darkness engulfed him. The boy heard heavy footsteps nearby and opened his eyes. An enormous naked man had entered the shack and was looking down at him. DaD!

The witch shoved a chunk of meat into the boy's hand and ordered him to eat it at once. As he chewed on the rubbery raw flesh, the man transformed into a cloud of gray smoke. Jamba inhaled deeply and the smoke entered his nostrils and his mouth. His mind's eye followed the smoke as it ran through his lungs and searched for his heart. The smoke traveled through his veins, mixed with his blood and pumped throughout his entire body until it found the large muscle.

There it changed back into the image of DaD who abruptly turned into half-man and half-beast. The boy was certain that the creature confined within his heart was smiling at him through giant tusks.

A scream pierced the night and he became aware of the old woman's foul breath on his face. Jamba was watching the scene from above, disconnected from his own body. Everything was happening in slow motion. She grabbed hold of his left hand and forced it down onto the wooden board. With a fluid movement, The Raven expertly removed the tip of his index finger with the large knife.

Jamba felt no pain, but experienced a sensation as if his life-force flowed from the bleeding stump and into the severed finger tip which the woman was clasping between her own fingers. He suddenly felt utterly drained and exhausted.

The old witch grabbed hold of his hair and yanked his head back forcefully. Her strength took him by surprise. From the corners of his eyes he could see Benjamin lying on his back and staring into a void while Okot was rolling around on the ground retching.

The woman was now holding the severed finger above Jamba's mouth and hissed at him, "Drink!"

The boy could see protruding bone and a loose flap of skin hanging from fatty and bloodied tissue. He opened his mouth and drops of blood landed on his tongue and slid down his throat, leaving a salty trail behind.

Again his mind's eye followed the blood traveling down his throat and flowing through his veins towards his heart. There he found the hog-man with arms outstretched, waiting to welcome the rush of blood. DaD opened his mouth and the blood flowed into him and covered his hairy hide.

Jamba could hear the witch howl and this time a sweet liquid flowed into his mouth. Within moments darkness enveloped him and the last thing he could remember was his body hitting the ground like a corpse.

Sometime during the night he thought that he heard the voices of several men moving around the shack, but he was not sure whether they were real or just part of his hallucinations. There was also a lot of activity around his left hand which was throbbing dully. A putrid odor filled his nostrils before he fell back into a deep sleep or unconsciousness.

CHAPTER 32

The boy opened his eyes to find Benjamin and Okot staring down at him. Smiles covered their faces as he joined them in what was reality again. There was a faint light creeping through the entrance to the shack and he could hear some cocks crowing nearby. Jamba felt very rested and strong.

The witch was busy with something at her fire and returned with a tin cup filled with hot tea. Jamba realized how thirsty he was and accepted it graciously. Only once he had taken the cup from her with both his hands was he reminded of the loss of his fingertip.

There was a strange hard crust sealing the wound and which completely numbed the pain. The boy sniffed at it and decided that it must be some kind of ointment which had hardened overnight. It felt as if the ghost of his fingertip still remained, yet it was clearly removed.

While sipping on the hot tea he scrutinized the shack. On the witch's blanket lay a glass jar with a clear fluid, slightly tinted by a pink hue. In it floated the tip of a finger as if suspended in mid-air. The fingertip was accompanied by blobs of flesh which probably were the remains of DaD's heart.

Then Jamba notice with surprise that both Benjamin and Okot had *Kalashnikov's* resting across their laps. A third rifle was leaning against the corrugated tin wall next to him. That explains the voices of the men I had heard during the night, Jamba thought to himself. A duffel bag was lying next to him on the ground. The bag was brown, worn and dirty.

Jamba felt a presence staring at him. The Raven was looking in his direction with her blind eye and cackling to herself.

"You give spawn. I give Dark Lord power. Men you seek at Palace. Now you go." With that she dismissed them with a wave of a claw.

Jamba did not want to overstay his welcome and the boys left the shack without a word, carrying the rifles and duffel bag with them. The sun had just started its rise in the east and there were no people visible as yet. Jamba stood outside the shack pondering their next move. He heard the witch call after them and a scrawny arm emerged from the entrance. Only her arm and hand was visible and in it she gripped the long knife.

"You forget," she said and dropped the blade on the ground.

The boys gathered the knife and rifles and stuffed them into the bag. Not wanting to hang around that ominous place, surrounded by its impaled heads, they set off towards nowhere in particular, taking turns to carry their heavy load.

They had stopped to gather some bananas when Jamba asked, "The Palace? What did she mean?"

It was the knowledgeable Okot who replied. "There's only one Palace. In the Nakasero area near the city center. The Presidential Palace or State House."

The full implication of Okot's words struck Jamba like a bullet between the eyes. "So I must kill the President?" He looked at the other boys questioningly but they only blinked and returned his look with blank faces.

"Then we'll go to the Palace and there I will make our plan," Jamba said coolly. With no response forthcoming from the others, he started to stroll towards the city center, struggling under the weight of the bag.

Jamba led his small squad through neighborhoods ranging from slums to posh houses with lush gardens. The houses gradually made way for large business districts, with buildings growing ever higher into the skies.

After a couple of hours they found themselves surrounded by fancy cars and people sporting expensive clothes. The boys looked distinctly out of place and received many disapproving scowls. The bag containing their rifles was becoming a concern for Jamba. If they were caught with that in their possession, there would surely be trouble. There was more visible policing in the area and many buildings had their own private security guarding entrances and gates.

The boys walked past buildings with colorful flags flapping from poles near their entrances. Okot explained that these were called embassies and represented foreign countries in Uganda.

Security was clearly more visible than the usual around here. Jamba's concerns were justified.

A policeman displaying all kinds of decorations on his chest, strolled up to the boys and without so much as a greeting told them to get the hell out of there. This was not a place for street trash like them. It was a respectable area for respectable and important people only.

Jamba snarled at the man but decided not to make a scene which might lead to a premature confrontation. But his disdainful attitude had already drawn the man's attention.

"What's in that bag?" the policeman asked promptly.

"Our clothes," Jamba said without hesitation.

The man looked at the barefooted boys standing in front of him. Then he scrutinized their filthy and torn clothes. Jamba was clearly struggling under the weight of the bag which was slung over one shoulder.

"Something tells me you are talking nonsense, son. Let's have a look."

It may have been DaD's spirit protecting them, or it may have been the Lord of Chaos wanting to ensure the boys succeeded in their mission of revenge, because at that very moment there was a loud screeching of tires, followed by a crash which rang like a gunshot through the morning air. The smell of burning rubber reached Jamba's nostrils as people started shouting incoherently.

A black Mercedes stood crumpled and half buried underneath the back of a garbage truck. The driver of the truck dropped to his knees in the middle of the road and was pulling at his hair while wailing like a trapped soul. Smoke and steam was pouring from the front of the Mercedes and the driver's window was smeared with blood.

The policeman found this development more urgent than a group of dirty boys carrying a duffel bag and ran off towards the scene of destruction.

Jamba did not need an invitation to dart off in the opposite direction, with the other two boys close on his heels. The bag was slowing him down a great deal but he gathered all his strength and pushed on.

As they rounded a street corner, panting and dripping in sweat, they found themselves at the entrance to a large public park. An array of colorful flowers, large lush trees and fountains spouting clear water greeted them. Behind the trees rose the shape of a magnificent white building. It had a bright red roof supported by enormous pillars of marble rising into the sky.

Everything about the building said 'power' and Jamba knew immediately that he had reached his goal - the Presidential Palace!

A very high and very black wrought iron fence surrounded the entire building which stood as an island on its own. A group of four soldiers were stationed at a gate protecting the broad stairs leading up to the front of the building.

Jamba spotted an empty park bench and sat down to rest and survey their surrounds. The other boys joined him on the bench, clearly grateful for the break after their hours of walking and of sharing the heavy bag between them.

Jamba observed an armed soldier at each corner of the fence. The fence itself was close to ten feet high and would be impossible to scale. Electrified wires ran along the top of it. The guards at the gate seemed very alert and not distracted as so many of the police sentries at the various checkpoints around the city usually were.

This is going to be a challenge, the boy thought to himself. He had no idea how they were going to get inside the Palace and even less of a clue what exactly they would do once inside, let alone who they would be targeting.

"Who's in charge of this place?" he asked Okot.

Okot scratched at a knee and took a few seconds to consider his reply. "The President and his ministers. People like the Minister of Defense and Minister of Police and Minister of the Economy," he said with an air of somebody highly experienced in his particular academic field.

Jamba stroked the dirty brown bag resting across his legs and said, "Then they will be our targets."

Benjamin just shrugged but Okot grew visibly concerned. Jamba gave Okot a disapproving look and told him to grow a pair of balls. This was about avenging DaD's murder and avenging the lost futures the people inside that building stole from them.

Jamba wanted to inspect the rear of the building to see if there was any other possibility of somehow getting inside. He left the level-headed Benjamin to look after the bag while he and Okot strolled off trying to look as inconspicuous as possible.

The two boys followed the pavement on the opposite side of the road which encircled the Palace. It soon became clear that there were soldiers guarding the other corners as well.

When they reached the rear, Jamba noticed a second gate. This gate was also guarded and of the same height as the main gate at the front of the building. With a sinking feeling the boy realized that there seemingly remained no other option than a full-frontal assault on the soldiers at one of the gates. This approach would probably not even get them as far as the first door.

Just as he was about to give up and return to the park where Benjamin was waiting with their rifles, a light truck pulled up to the rear entrance. There was something written in bright red letters on the side of the vehicle.

"What does that say?" Jamba asked Okot while pointing towards the truck which was now slowly reversing through the gates. It came to a stop next to the rear entrance to the building.

"Coco's Cakes and Catering," the other boy said, slowly articulating each word as he read it. Jamba was impressed, yet not entirely surprised at Okot's ability to read. What the scared boy lacked in bravery, he made up in knowledge and the occasional useful information.

A broad smile cracked across Jamba's lips as he slapped Okot's shoulder approvingly. That was it. Their way into the enemy's lair.

"We must find out where this truck came from. It will bring us inside," he said to Okot and casually started strolling past the guards at the gate. He needed to get a good look at the driver's face so that he could recognize him in the future.

It was a refrigerated truck and there was a lot of activity going on at its rear. A couple of men were carrying plastic crates into the building while the truck driver sat in his cab reading a newspaper. On his head was a bright red cap and his nose sported a pair of reading glasses. It will be easy enough to identify him again, the boy remarked to himself.

A guard walked over and spat on the ground. "Get moving!" he sneered at the boys and they quickly hurried along as to not draw any further attention.

Then they circled back to the park where Jamba excitedly explained his discovery to Benjamin. The problem now was to find the business premises of those caterers. Surely they will deliver food to the Palace again and when that happens, Jamba wants for them to be part of the delivery.

It would be impossible to follow the truck. They will probably have to ask people if they knew where the business was and just hope for the best. Okot once again surprised him when the boy suggested that he could look up the address in a telephone book. Then all they needed to do was to find the correct address.

Jamba was elated and slapped Okot behind his head approvingly. "See? You are turning out to be a good soldier, my brother," he said in an attempt to lift the boy's questionable spirits.

The squad wondered aimlessly for almost an hour in their search for a public phone or shop with a telephone directory. They managed to stumble upon quite a few public phones, but none of them had a book. Only the chains to which they were once attached remained.

Eventually they came across a man who had a row of telephones lined up on the pavement. The phones were all connected to a box which in turn was connected to a telephone pole behind the man. The informal businessman was sitting on a pile of telephone books while various people were chatting away on some of his instruments.

It took a lot of begging from Okot to finally convince the man to let him use one of his phone books. At first he wanted them to pay for the use of a phone but after considering their appearances he found the lost, good Samaritan within himself and handed Okot a directory after a lot of mumbling and grumbling. If only the man knew the reason for the ragtag group needing that book so badly, he would certainly not have complied with their request.

The catering business 'Coco's Cakes and Catering' which supplied the Presidency with food was situated in Victoria Avenue and Jamba asked the man where they could find the street. To his relief it was a mere three blocks away from the Palace.

The boys made their way towards the business, again struggling with the duffel bag between them. The place was easy to spot since it had a whole fleet of the refrigerated trucks lined up behind a fence which was surrounded by a low hedge.

The hedge immediately became very convenient as a place to hide the weapons and also for them to take cover and observe the comings and goings of the trucks. The fact that the building was in the business of providing food only served to remind Jamba of how hungry he was at this stage. They had not eaten much over a couple of days now, other than for a few bananas. The hunger will have to wait. There were more important things to deal with.

Jamba doubted that the same truck would return to the Palace on that same day and he decided that they would remain there and spend the night. The hedge provided them with good cover and most importantly, the bag was now out of the way of prying eyes.

There was a solitary security guard at the entrance to the business, but the man seemed utterly bored and more interested in getting rid of any trucks leaving the premises as quickly as possible.

Jamba had more than enough free time to come up with a plan. Surviving those many months all alone in the slums had nurtured cunning in the young child. He assumed that the truck would probably service the Palace at around the same time the next day. If not, then he was willing to wait another day, until he saw the man with the red cap and glasses again. He would wait here until the end of life itself if it meant getting him closer to DaD's murderers.

Once they then spot the truck, Jamba would create a diversion to stop it and they would hijack the driver and his cargo. He would accompany the driver in the front while the other boys hid in the back with their weapons. Then he would force the driver to tell those at the Palace that the boys were new and helping him out with the loading and unloading of the cargo.

And if that did not work out, at least they would be inside the premises and would just have to fight their way further inside. With that crude plan as their objective, the boys lay down on the grass behind the hedge, each occupying himself with his private thoughts or fears.

A thunderstorm gathered during the afternoon but the pouring rain was only a slight irritation. Jamba reflected on that torturous time he had spent in the freezing underground tunnels and suddenly laughed as he mockingly shook a fist at the sky which was pouring rain down upon them.

"Bring on your best!" he said to the heavens above.

But his growling stomach did not want to dissipate as easily as the rains and he decided to send Benjamin to gather them some more bananas. He remembered that a soldier should not fight on a hungry stomach and since he was now a leader he also had to make some responsible decisions.

Benjamin returned only after dark because he had to travel all the way to the outskirts of town to find some banana trees. Jamba complimented the boy as though he had just won some major battle and the boys settled down to eat.

Jamba arranged the guard duty for the night and lay down on the grass behind the hedge to get some rest. They changed at four hour intervals according to the digital watch Okot always carried in a pocket.

Before he readied himself for sleep, Jamba removed the maroon beret from where it was stuffed in the front of his shorts and counted the crosses again. For a long time he replayed his entire life and experiences with DaD over in his mind. The boy reflected on each person he had killed and each battle he had fought. He reflected on each act of cruelty against him and also each act of mercy shown towards him. Mercy!

If anything, reliving all the events made him more resolute than ever to exact his revenge. It might mean that he and his comrades would die in the process, but he promised himself that this will not happen without him taking at least three or four of the murdering dogs with him. They owed him something. They dashed his hopes and his future and for that they will pay. Hatred and revenge were now the driving force which kept his spirits alive. Perhaps even fueled the spirits of the giant forest hog and DaD which were now both residing within him.

The boy dozed off and slept peacefully until Benjamin woke him for his turn at guard duty. As he watched the sun rising in the east, he tried to add some details to his crude plan of assault and ran a few possible scenarios through his mind.

By the time the gates of the catering business opened for the first delivery of the day, Jamba was as ready as he would ever be.

Chapter 33

With the first activity inside the premises of the business, Jamba kicked at the other boys to wake them up. He gathered the duffel bag and then walked to within thirty feet of the gates along the road leading in the direction of the Palace.

There the boys stood waiting and watching every truck leaving the entrance. A couple of trucks turned in the opposite direction and a few others passed by them, driven by men Jamba did not recognize

Only after about another hour a truck slowly rolled towards them and he immediately recognized the face of the man with the red cap and glasses resting on his nose. This was it. The operation had begun.

As the vehicle approached them, Jamba took the long blade from the bag, hid it behind his back and promptly threw himself in front of the truck which was still slowly accelerating.

He fell to the ground, writhing as if in pain. The driver stopped just in time before actually almost running over Jamba and exited his cab in a panic. He was shouting and swearing at the boy lying on the ground in front of him and seemed more concerned about possible damage to the truck than any injuries to the dirty street kid rolling around in front of him.

The man's reaction only served to make Jamba's blood boil and in a flash he was on his feet with the knife at the driver's throat. "Get in", he said and spat on the asphalt in an attempt to rid himself of some of his venom.

The man's eyes grew wide and he just repeated, "Okay, okay," as he backpedaled towards the open door of the truck. Jamba climbed over the man and sat on the passenger side, holding the sharp blade against the driver's genitals.

He opened his window and instructed the others to get into the back and hide the rifles in the crates. Once the crates were inside the building, he would give them further instructions. They just had to play along and improvise as things developed. The others nodded and unlatched the door at the back. When he was satisfied that the doors were closed again, Jamba instructed the man to drive on. The boy looked in the side mirror and was relieved to see that the guard at the gate did not bother to inspect the road.

"You're going to the Palace, right?" he asked the frightened man who was constantly peering down at the wicked blade between his legs.

"Yes, yes. But first another delivery," he said with a whimper, again eyeing the knife near his privates. "Please don't kill me. I'm sorry I ran you over," he added with what was almost a sob.

Jamba laughed at hearing this. The poor idiot thought it was all about him almost running him over with his truck.

"We're not going to the other place. We're going to the Palace," Jamba said in a tone which made it pretty obvious that there was no choice in the matter. He stared at the man intently and said, "You'll tell the guards we're new at the job and helping you with the crates."

The man glanced at the boy's torn and filthy shirt. He frowned. "They won't believe me. Look at your clothes," he said desperately.

"Then gimme your cap and tell them we're poor. That's why we got the job. So we can buy new clothes, right? Tell them anything else and I will cut your balls off, mister."

The man nodded and handed Jamba his bright red cap which turned out to be at least three sizes too big for the boy.

They drove the three blocks towards the Palace in silence and Jamba found himself begging DaD's spirit to guide him through the impending battle. It was not fear which gripped him. Only an uneasiness regarding all the unknown and unpredictable obstacles which may come their way.

He also wondered how Okot will behave under his first battle conditions. At the same time he was perfectly certain that the brave Benjamin would take it in his stride. The boy had been an absolute rock during their fight against the DRC forces.

As the truck neared the rear gates of the big stately building, Jamba increased the pressure of the blade between the drivers legs, just to remind him of his previous instructions. Then he slipped the knife behind the man's back so that a guard would not be able to observe it should he happen to look inside the cab of the vehicle.

The gates opened before anybody checked them and the truck reversed into the courtyard towards the back entrance. Only then did a guard approach. He clearly recognized the driver and called him by his first name.

"Isaac," the guard nodded in greeting. "And who's this?"

The driver put up a brave smile and said, "New boys. They're helping me load and unload."

The guard frowned at hearing this. "Boys? There are more?"

"The other two are in the back. No space in the front," he replied. Then added, "They're still training. This is a good start because we've got so many crates today."

The guard moved towards the back and Jamba watched him in the side mirrors as he opened the doors to the refrigerated cargo area. He could only hope that the other two boys would keep their cool through all of this. He heard muffled voices and to his relief the guard reappeared and waved the driver on.

The truck pulled up to almost inside the door of the entrance which led straight into a large kitchen. Benjamin and Okot appeared at the window and Jamba instructed them in a low voice first to carry the crates with the concealed *Kalashnikovs* inside, while he watched the driver and the guards. Then Benjamin should keep an eye on the crates and Okot must come and call him.

As they moved off, Jamba told the driver that a lot of innocent people will die today should he make any attempt at alerting the guards. When Okot returns, they are all going to enter the kitchen calmly and quietly. Any panic and everybody dies. He would not want that on his conscience now would he?

The driver first nodded a 'yes' and then shook his head in a 'no'. He was clearly confused and panicked all at the same time. Just seconds later Okot reappeared and waved at Jamba to join them.

The boy slid the knife under his T-shirt and told the driver to get out and move towards the kitchen. It was a tense moment since he had no control over the man's actions until they rejoined at the back of the truck.

Thankfully, nothing happened. There were two men unloading some of the crates and one was muttering a complaint regarding the lazy boys not helping and just being in the way.

They followed the two workers into the kitchen and Jamba realized that things were becoming complicated. There were just too many people around to control with any degree of comfort. Apart from the men carrying the crates, there were three others inside the kitchen busy with their chores. Then there was the driver and not to forget the four guards at the gate who would soon start asking questions about the truck not moving on. He had to take action while everybody was still inside the kitchen. The guards will have to wait.

Jamba closed the kitchen door behind him and immediately one of the kitchen workers complained. Then the man saw the blade in Jamba's hand and yelped in alarm.

Benjamin was alert just as Jamba had hoped and the boy flicked the lid off the crate containing their weapons. Within a fraction of a second a shiny AK-47 appeared in Benjamin's hands as if by magic and everybody fell silent without the need for any further instructions.

Jamba and Okot also armed themselves and the boys quickly gathered all the workers into a tight huddle. There was a large heavy door leading to an enormous freezer and Jamba motioned them to move inside. One started protesting about freezing to death, but the look Jamba gave him convinced him that he was going to die anyway if he did not do what he was told.

Benjamin latched the door behind the group and they gathered to plan their next move. The guards were now the greatest concern. They will notice that there wasn't any more activity and would become suspicious.

"We put the rifles in an empty crate and carry it back to the truck. Then wait for a guard and take him hostage. We can walk to the other three and take them by surprise," was Jamba's new plan. He was making things up as they were going along but so far things were actually working out just fine.

He did not wait for approval. He was the squad leader and being soldiers, his orders were law and to be obeyed without question. The other boys understood this too well. He just hoped that Okot would remain strong through it all.

They placed their weapons in a crate and returned to the truck carrying it between them. A guard was already standing at the back of the vehicle and inspecting its contents, clearly curious as to the reason for the inactivity. When the boys had opened the kitchen door, the man was just about to open the door himself.

"Lots of crates," is all Jamba could manage and he smiled broadly at the man.

They placed the crate on the back of the truck and Jamba climbed in. The guard looked puzzled and was about to start with his questions when the cold muzzle a *Kalashnikov* almost poked his eye out. With his own rifle slung across one shoulder, there was no time for him to react.

Jamba put a finger over his own lips to indicate to the guard to remain silent. He whispered to the other boys to take the man's rifle and join him in the back of the truck and then ordered the soldier to call his friends over.

"Tell them there's some free food," he told the fidgeting man. "Just that! Wave them over to come and get the food."

With the rifle pointed at his head, the soldier peered around one corner of the truck and called out to one of his friends at the gate. The other two guards were not visible and had perhaps strolled off to patrol the fence.

As the remaining soldier casually approached them, he was summarily disarmed and the boys led the two men towards the freezer where they joined the others. Jamba first removed the spare ammunition from their belts and checked them for other weapons or radios before he closed the door behind them.

The boys returned to the truck and waited for the other guards to return. The two men arrived together but it took them several minutes to realize something was amiss. Those few moments were all the boys needed and the remaining guards found themselves facing three rifles pointed at them. The men slowly raised their hands in submission. They were also paraded off to the freezer after a thorough search.

Jamba hoped that there would still be sufficient time for them to enter the heart of building and find their targets before it was discovered that the guards were missing. He went out one last time to close and lock the gates leading to the street. When he returned to the kitchen, he discarded the truck driver's red cap and replaced it with his beloved beret. A feeling of confidence immediately washed across his entire body.

There was only one other door leading out of the kitchen. It opened into a large dining hall where a sole figure wearing an apron was busy laying out plates and glasses on long tables. They were fortunate that this man did not stumble upon them to raise the alarm.

Jamba did not wait for the man to approach, but simply walked up to him with a raised rifle and pointed towards the kitchen. The man was so terrified that he dropped a glass which shattered on the floor. His eyes were wide and his raised hands were trembling as he was led towards the kitchen.

When they opened the freezer to add the new captive to his cold prison, they were met by a choir of chattering teeth. Some ice crystals were already forming below dripping noses and bushy eyebrows.

That's just the way it is, Jamba thought to himself - casualties of war! He latched the door and led his squad into the dining hall.

CHAPTER 34

The sound of deep rolling thunder was audible outside when the three boys quietly crossed the dining area toward another door on the opposite side of the room.

Dark clouds were gathering outside and extinguished the rays of sunlight which were just moments ago illuminating the room through large curtained windows. It was as if the Lord of Chaos knew of the impending doom and was playing his part in setting the morbid scene.

When he reached the door, Jamba cracked it open quietly, just wide enough to peer through it and see what awaited them on the other side.

The hall looked like the main entrance to the Palace. It was a large, cold foyer with black marble floors and only a flag and a painting of the smiling President of Uganda decorating the walls.

A guard was sitting in the center of the foyer with his back towards them. The man was surrounded by a circular desk covered with screens and monitors. He was immersed in a newspaper and ignoring the images on the screens. Jamba realized that he never gave the possibility of cameras any thought. It was a foreign concept. Luck had been on their side!

Death came quickly and quietly to the guard. Jamba had sneaked up behind him and unceremoniously cut the man's throat with the large blade where he was still busy reading his last ever article. The screens and newspaper were sprayed with streaks of blood as the guard gurgled his last breath through the long incision.

Another guard was sitting on a wooden bench outside the glass doors which led from the foyer to the front gate. Jamba decided to ignore him. The man was facing the street and occasionally studied the ground at his feet for no apparent reason.

The boy signaled the others to follow him toward a flight of stairs which ran upwards in an elegant curve along one wall. A thick blood-red carpet covered the stairs and ensured that their footsteps were completely muted as they ascended it in a crouch.

At the top, Jamba carefully peered over the last step and saw a long hallway stretching out in front of him. It appeared completely empty. Doors were visible at regular intervals on both sides of the hallway. All of them closed.

He decided to check them one by one. There was no real plan. The boy just improvised as they went along. He double-checked his rifle and made sure there was a round in the chamber. Okot and Benjamin followed his example. There was no emotion visible on Benjamin's face, but Okot's eyes were wide and wild, darting anxiously in all directions. Jamba placed an assuring hand on the frightened boy's shoulder and then moved forward.

Benjamin checked the doors on the left whilst Jamba covered those on the right. They tried the knobs and cracked them open just a little. The rooms were all empty. As they approached the end of the hallway, muffled voices could be heard through a door which was larger and more extravagantly decorated than the others.

Without knowing what awaited them on the other side of that door, Jamba could feel in his gut that this was what they had come for. This was their ultimate destination and the heart of the Beast which had destroyed DaD. His instinct was sure.

The boy leveled his *Kalashnikov* and calmly opened the door, not caring what awaited them beyond it. He did not even bother to give his comrades any further instructions.

There was a shocked silence as the three boys strolled in. They were greeted by looks of surprise and disbelief on the faces of the men sitting at the long table running the length of the room. Some were in suits, others in traditional Ugandan attire and one man was in full military uniform, medals dangling from his chest.

Like a magnet to metal, Jamba's attention was immediately drawn towards the military man. He was almost in a trance as he approached him. Nothing else in that room could distract the child soldier at that very moment.

This was it! This was the enemy he had been searching for.

His heart was filled with such deep hatred that it made him nauseous. The hatred for this man and what his uniform represented was as pure as the waters from the mountain streams. As pure as the sparkling diamond in Tito's picture.

Jamba stood next to the officer and slowly ran the muzzle of his rifle across the dark cheek, nearly poking him in his eye. A single droplet of sweat gathered on the man's temple and was crawling towards an earlobe.

A firm voice snapped the boy from his hypnotic trance.

"Who are you? What do you want?" somebody demanded.

Jamba struggled to tear his eyes from the officer and slowly looked towards a man sitting separately from everybody else at the head of the table. He recognized the face from portraits and pictures he had seen and from the painting in the foyer. It was the President of the country and there was now no doubt that they had found what was the Beast's lair.

"I'm the son of Death and Destruction. A Merchant of Death. You've murdered our father. You've murdered our futures. Today you will all pay. And you will all die."

Jamba's voice was as cold as the steel of the AK-47 gripped in his hands and he hissed the words in almost a whisper. Each word was carefully articulated.

No more questions followed. It was as if though the silence only confirmed that these men knew exactly who he was talking about. Fear and anxious looks now darkened their faces. Only the President still appeared calm and confident. Jamba almost felt a hint of respect for the man's courage.

The lack of any further conversation drew his attention back to the man in uniform. The officer was shifting uncomfortably in his chair and by now his entire forehead was covered in perspiration. The special attention he was receiving from the dirty boy with the maroon beret and deadly AK-47, only confirmed to him that things were not looking too bright for his immediate future.

Jamba heard shuffling sounds coming from outside the door. The noises were barely audible but his trained jungle ears easily picked them up. Benjamin and Okot also heard the noises. Benjamin was calmly covering those at the table with his rifle while Okot's eyes were now even wilder and he was fidgeting with the trigger of his weapon.

They must have discovered the dead guard in the foyer or those missing at the back and realized something very bad was about to go down. Jamba could almost picture the men in the hallway, probably armed to the teeth and not quite knowing what to expect or what they would be facing.

The boy continued to stroke the officer's face with the muzzle of his rifle. He was digesting the fear and terror in the man's eyes with immense satisfaction. Drinking it all in with his great thirst for vengeance.

It did not matter to Jamba what was going to happen next. Those he hated were all gathered in this room which had now become their execution chamber. They were going to die and the only question which now remained was 'When?'

The question was answered. A window shattered as a bullet from outside pierced through it. Jamba saw Okot drop to the carpeted floor like a stone. Blood was spurting from a wound in his neck and the wide-eyed boy was still clutching the newly-earned rifle he would never fire. His mouth was flapping as if he was trying to say something. Jamba thought of Annie.

At that moment the gates of hell opened and the hounds of war were released, carrying chaos and destruction with them on their backs. The reaper entered the room, ready to collect the souls of the dead and cast them into the eternal vacuum of the dark unknown.

As Okot lay dying and kicking, Jamba flicked the leaver of his AK-47 to full-automatic and pulled the trigger. The head of the man in uniform disintegrated. The burst released all his hatred and anger upon that man in a split-second. This time Jamba gripped the rifle tight. The adrenaline pumping through his body gave him enormous will and strength.

Benjamin was taking aim and calm as he could, he systematically pumped four bullets into the nearest person to him. Then the next and then the next. There was a flicker of enjoyment on his face and Jamba knew this boy was a true Merchant. Brutal, fearless and brave to the very end!

They were friends. And today they would die together in their final battle. Their eyes briefly met and there was an understanding between them without the need for words.

The door burst open and the deafening explosions of several stun grenades felled the boys to the floor. Smoke grenades followed and Jamba could barely see, hear or breathe. All his senses were numbed at once.

The boys did not stop. They kept firing at any visible targets and into the smoke - Benjamin with his disciplined bursts and Jamba with his rifle still spitting at full-automatic.

Blood was raining down on them in small drops through the smoke and splattered on their faces. Screams of pain and hysteria blended with gunfire and pierced the thick air.

Through burning tear-filled eyes, Jamba saw Benjamin quiver and shake as bullets riddled his torso. He whispered a quiet 'goodbye' to his friend as the boy's body hit the ground.

It was now just a matter of time before he would join him. He kept squeezing the trigger, aiming wildly in any direction. It was impossible to see anything any more and he knew he would not see death coming - there would be only pain and darkness. He would never see the face belonging to his killer.

The end came at the very moment these thoughts were racing through his mind. He felt his body being torn apart as if by invisible claws, yet he felt almost no pain.

When his head hit the soft, bloodstained carpet he stared underneath the long table and met Benjamin's eyes through the haze. The boy was still alive and staring back at Jamba. They both smiled. They knew their final mission was accomplished. DaD's death had been avenged. Their vengeance was total. Annihilation of the enemy was complete and the Merchants had delivered their final and irrevocable message of Death.

The pitch blackness enveloped Jamba as though somebody had simply switched off the lights of a very dark room.

When the smoke finally cleared from that terrible slaughterhouse, only one hostage remained standing unscathed. He was the President of the country. The solitary leader of an extinct cabinet without a single soul left to help him govern.

CHAPTER 35

The icy grip of Death's hand momentarily pulled the boy back from the eternal darkness in which his consciousness had been kept prisoner.

The first thing he felt was pain. Excruciating pain, burning and consuming his entire body like a raging fire. His eyes fluttered briefly and then opened. A fractured beam of light came in through a tiny window above him. Iron bars covered the opening and the light struggled through the gaps to cast a strange pattern on the opposite wall. A tiny black cross was nailed to the wall.

Jamba's eyes traced the outline of the wall and came to rest on yet more iron bars. He was in a prison, lying in a pure white prison bed.

The boy became aware of movement nearby. A face appeared in the beam of light and looked down at him. It was a pink face attached to a black robe and a white collar. The priest was grasping a big black book in one hand as though it was his only possession and as if fearing he might lose it.

The boy could only think of the excruciating pain he was experiencing. He tried to move but it was impossible. Neither his head nor any of his limbs responded. Instead his attempts only served to increase the torment.

It dawned on Jamba that he was dying.

The pain, the lack of strength, the absence of energy, the absence of will, the presence of the priest in his ominous attire told him this - he just knew that he was dying. A single teardrop escaped from one eye and ran down his cheek.

The priest reached out with one finger and wiped the tear away. He bent over until his mouth was almost touching the child's ear.

"Don't be afraid, my son."

The boy tried to say something. There was fear in his eyes and his lips quivered, his tongue trying in vain to moisten them. The priest placed his ear against the boy's lips, struggling to make out the rasping sounds flowing from between them.

"I cannot hear you, my son," he said to the boy.

Jamba gathered every grain of energy he could muster and tried again.

"Mercy..." he whispered.

The priest slowly straightened himself and closed his eyes for a long time. His mouth moved without speech. The boy was certain he could see the man shake his head ever so slightly. The movement was so faint it was almost imperceptible. Was there a 'no' whispered through those lips?

"You will soon be free and in a better place, my child. A place where only peace and love and compassion exist. It's a good place." He gripped Jamba's hand.

The boy heard the priest's words but did not understand. His mouth quivered as he struggled with a last superhuman effort to collect the courage and strength for his greatest and most significant battle.

"What's.. peace.. love.. compassion?"

With those unanswered questions remaining on his lips, the small twelve-year-old boy exhaled the last of his life-force and forever slipped away into the dark abyss.

Epilogue

The death of almost every minister and military adviser in Uganda's cabinet as a result of the attack by a small group of child soldiers, left a huge power vacuum in government. The impact of the events was immediate and far-reaching.

Like phoenixes rising from the ashes, new rebel groups, or some long-forgotten, suddenly emerged out of nowhere. Numerous leaders in the military and police broke away from government and formed their own factions.

One military man entered a smoke-filled shanty hut surrounded by heads impaled on sticks and which was standing as if alone in the middle of the slums of Kampala.

The man hobbled into the hut, his makeshift wooden leg clearly visible where his camouflage pants were rolled up to just below the stumpy knee.

The old witch, better known as Kunguru, The Raven, sniffed at her guest where he stood before her. The man was notably nervous in her presence. Her ability to bestow power on those she regarded as worthy was legendary. The untimely deaths of those who dared to oppose or insult her - even more notorious.

"I'm Sergeant Wambuzi." The man checked himself and started his introduction over again.

"I'm Commander Wambuzi. I seek the power of the one named DaD and of the boy known as Jamba. The one who had died while killing DaD's enemies. My wish is to once again give birth to the Merchants of Death and command them so that the spirits of these great fighters may live on."

Wambuzi wondered whether his carefully prepared speech would be successful. He nervously shifted his weight onto his good leg as the witch ran her claws across his face and continued to sniff at him as an animal would examine its potential prey.

"Ah. You want power of Dark Lord and Spawn?" she cackled and blinked her solitary blind eye. "Dark Lord dead. Spawn dead. You want death also?"

Wambuzi seemed surprised at her approach but replied without hesitation. "Their enemies are all dead too. If their power means my eventual death, then yes, let it be so."

The old woman snorted and then shuffled over to her shelf where she gathered a transparent jar containing some mysterious objects floating within. Then she carefully sat down on her dirty blanket and cast a collection of bones and other trinkets on the ground in front of them. For what seemed like an eternity her long dirty nails examined each object carefully.

"I give power. You pay price," she hissed eventually.

"Name your price," Wambuzi said. Again he did not hesitate for one moment.

The witch searched between the folds of her blanket and a claw emerged holding a very long blade. She cackled again.

"I give power. You give eye. Yes?" the old woman said with evil anticipation in her voice.

Then she removed the lid from the transparent jar and Wambuzi could see the small tip of a finger floating between various blobs of other flesh. He felt acidic bile pushing up in his throat.

He did not need to think about her question for very long. "It's a deal. Their power for my eye," he agreed and thus signed the contract which sold his soul to the Devil.

The witch motioned for the man who once trained so many child soldiers for his late master and commander, to kneel before her.

She handed him a familiar vile pink liquid and ordered him to drink. The Raven tested the tip of the long blade with a finger. With a voice which would make a demon flee in terror she said, "We begin. Man with one leg. One eye! No soul!"

The *ayahuasca* quickly took hold of Wambuzi and he mentally resigned himself to his fate. Like a man pinned to a cross he spread his arms wide, tilted his head back and calmly awaited the impending pain.

"I'm ready," said the new commander of the future Merchants of Death, without as much as a hint of fear in his steady voice.

END

The Muse – A Poem

I watch the waves lap at the shore
Like lovers kiss in deep embrace
The sun's last rays deep red and fading
As if the flames of war closes the door
On yet another day to rest through night
Until born again into blissful light

And so fade my love and hope
Whilst I contemplate as men had done
Over centuries the meaning of how it all begun
And where it all leads to
The hermit on his mountaintop
Philosopher under the olive tree
What is the purpose of it all asks he
Who cannot touch or ever embrace
She - who is that red flame of hope and passion
Without her knowing the emotions stirred in men eternal

Recalling poets of the past
Of rivers flowing together until at last
One torrent reaches the same sea
The drop of rain becoming the stream
And stream converging into river
Which finally spends its energy
Into the oceans for all eternity

And so do love and lust flow together
Confusing its unsuspecting victim
And becoming the master of man
Until despair consumes his heart forever

Forbidden love broke stronger men
The peasant's love for his princess
But a prince he'll never be
While she forever will remain nobility
And he forever nothing be

A muse she is...
Helen of Troy with hair blowing in the breeze
Brave men falling on the battlefield
To die for love which never will be theirs
Yet passion drives them to wield
Their weapons against the enemy
With war-hammer, spear and shield
For a woman
Whose love they could never conquer with their bravery

But passion steels the heart
Against all difficulty
Make overcome the pain in life
Help conquer darkness and give light
In times of sadness and of strife
It strengthens will and purpose
Gives birth to happiness, to love, to art

Show me this muse
So I can capture her sweet essence
And lock it in Pandora's box
To release as I please
When a tempest needs to cleanse my thoughts
Before my mind is there to lose

Slowly slip satin silk from that exquisite body
Deeply inhale that infuriating, intoxicating scent
Make sweet love to her forever
Whilst passion and emotions blend together
Until a climax of bliss unmeasured
Hurls us into time and space
Just like a shooting star cuts through the sky
and Aurora Borealis in its race
Against the coming rising of the day
Fly my soul away
As I dream of being one
Deep inside the one true woman
Embodiment of true perfection
Lost there in her, forever lost, forever gone

Wake up! Wake up!
You were dreaming!
Says the voice of reason
Bringing back reality
To those lost in consummate ecstasy

But keep that thought and embrace it
Hold close to your heart
Like a delicate flower
Not too close as to crush it
But to remember and honor
Appreciate the brief encounter
Whose power will make you a stronger man
And she remains in all her splendor
To break more hearts as the sands of time
Trickle away into the trampled dust of history

Again the goddess raises her head proudly
Looks down at those legions of pathetic men
Who trembled and melted under her gaze
Knelt down in that dust at the sight of that face
And many more will wilt and follow
Their souls forever bend under her sweet scent
Since perfect beauty is the destroyer of men
Leaving judgment and common sense in haze
A fog enveloping the mind
Till all emotion is consumed in sheer apocalyptic blaze

No defense exists against perfection
Verily... enjoy, embrace, accept my friend
Then just let go of all affection
For all eternity....

www.ingramcontent.com/pod-product-compliance
Lightning Source LLC
Chambersburg PA
CBHW070556130626
46556CB00001B/180